NUKEKUBI

Stephen B. Pearl

Also by Stephen B. Pearl

By Draumr Publishing
Tinker's Plague

By Club Lighthouse Publishing
The Hollow Curse
Slaves of Love

NUKEKUBI

Stephen B. Pearl

Dark Dragon Publishing
Toronto, Ontario, Canada

This book is a work of fiction. The characters, incidents, and dialogue are drawn from the author's imagination and are not to be construed as real. Any resemblance to actual events or persons, living or dead, is entirely coincidental.

Nukekubi

Copyright © 2011 by Stephen B. Pearl

ISBN: 978-0-9867633-6-6
eISBN: 978-0-9867633-7-3

Cover Illustration © Kari-Ann Anderson
www.kariannanderson.com

Cover Design and Author Photo
© by Evan Dales
WAV Design Studios
www.wavstudios.ca

All rights reserved. No part of this book may be used or reproduced by any means, graphic, electronic, or mechanical, including photocopying, recording, taping or by any information storage retrieval system without the written permission of Dark Dragon Publishing and Stephen B. Pearl, except in the case of brief quotations embodied in critical articles and reviews.

The cover art of this book may not be used or reproduced by any means, graphic, electronic, or mechanical, including, photocopying, scanning or by any information storage retrieval system without the written permission of Kari-Ann Anderson.

Dark Dragon Publishing
313 Mutual Street
Toronto, Ontario
M4Y 1X6
CANADA
www.darkdragonpublishing.com

Printed in the United States of America.

For more information on the Stephen B. Pearl
www.stephenpearl.com

For Joy...

ACKNOWLEDGEMENTS

This book is dedicated to my beloved wife Joy without whose love and support it would never have come to be. You are my everything, Joy, and I'm actually quite happy that you don't even know how to do a pole dance.

I'd also like to mention Mark and Kim from my face to face writers group who helped in the early development of the piece.

The critters on line writing community have been invaluable and I wish to give a special acknowledgment to Michael Teasdale, Clare Frederick and Rhonda Wright.

I also wish to thank Karen Dales for her aid in polishing the work.

Last but not least I wish to thank my Publisher who aided enormously in making Nukekubi shine.

If I've left anybody out please just pencil your name in. No book worth reading is written in a vacuum so the list of those who aided in this writing could fill pages. I owe a debt of gratitude to you all.

– Chapter 1 –

POLTERGEIST

My heart lurched at the sight of Cathy's robed, slender form, hurtling towards the apartment's balcony and a five-story drop. She was chanting frantically, trying to ground out the thing pushing her.

Helping her out, at that moment, wasn't easy! I was busy keeping the furniture on the floor. Flying chairs can be hazardous to your health.

We were trying to break a poltergeist's link to Elisabeth, a thirteen-year-old disabled girl. The spirit was using her as a power source. It wouldn't have been so bad a job except the girl's mother wouldn't let us get close to her. Religion is great unless it becomes an excuse for hate and fear. So, there we were, in the apartment above said girl's, at the invitation of a friend who was tired of having her furniture attack her.

Just another day in my life.

Gods, I need to get another hobby!

By the way, I'm Ray, wizard, lifeguard and general poor bastard. How do you do?

Splitting my attention, which resulted in a pressboard end-table slamming into the ceiling, I put my hand in the salt dish on the altar in front of me and tossed a handful of salt at Cathy.

"Ground by Hapi's power!" I commanded. The energies carrying Cathy were drawn into the earth. Unfortunately, the momentum didn't dissipate so quickly. Cathy hit the sliding glass doors hard enough to crack them before she crumpled to the floor.

"Ow! *Son of a bitch!*" Cathy has a way with words.

"*Enough!*" My bellow shook the room.

There is power in a wizard's yell, if he knows how to use it. The furniture, which consisted of a love seat, two armchairs, end tables and a coffee table, stopped bouncing and the end table crashed to the floor allowing me to refocus my thoughts.

"Cath, circle now!" I picked up the crook and flail, the main tools of my trade, and started walking around the altar. Cathy tried to stand, gasped in pain, and then crawled across the carpet to sit in front of the altar. Her job had been to keep the poltergeist occupied while I set up for the ritual. She'd done pretty well; I was just about ready to close the circle when Tartarus came calling. Cathy is no slouch in the zap the baddy department, but sometimes life gets interesting.

"By the power of the crook and flail, I do hereby set these wards that none of ill intent may enter here in." I circled the room once focussing my energies through the blue and silver banded wand with its looped end that was my crook and the multi-tailed whip with a gold and blue-banded shaft that was my flail. The couch began to tremble on the floor. The blast of energy my yell had released only dazed Mr. Spook. Shit!

I could see Cathy's brows furrow in concentration as she tried to ground out our foe's energies.

I moved faster, circling the room once more, repeating the charge. A stuffed animal flew at my head. I felt it hit the ward where it stopped and fell to the floor. I circled once again. A plate from the kitchen hurtled down the apartment's hall, corrected course and came straight at me. The mystical energy stopped at the ward but momentum carried it through. I dodged the plate and it fell to the floor breaking in two on the other side of my circle. I walked the ward a fourth and final time, completely closing the circle. Another plate hit it. This time its momentum was stopped as well. One circle for each element. Fire, air, water and earth. Earth deals with physical energy, like momentum.

"Got it." I took a moment to breathe. The room beyond my circle looked like a Disney movie on crack with dancing furniture and household items. A Barbie doll flew into the air and started doing something with a pair of GI Joe action figures I'm sure the toy manufacturers wouldn't have approved of.

"That is sick! Possibly fun, but still." Cathy sat in front of the altar and watched the dolls for a moment unconsciously toying with a lock of her shoulder-length, red hair. "I'm not that flexible." She turned to me. "Ray, can we get on with this. Some things I just don't need to see." Cathy shifted position and grimaced. She was holding her ankle and in obvious pain. That put steel in me. Cath... Cathy is special to me, nuf said! That damn poltergeist hurt her, and by my Gods, it was going down.

"Right." I watched an armchair lift into the air and ram against my wards. "Damn, I wouldn't mind having this guy around the next time you move."

"Ray." Cathy rolled her eyes.

"I'm just saying, that sofa bed of yours is heavy."

"*Incoming!*" Cathy held up her hand, projecting energy out of her palm to reinforce the ward as a kitchen knife flew straight at me. It stopped at the ward, hovered for a moment then fell. It may have stopped anyway, but I wasn't going to gripe about Cathy's reinforcement.

"Gods!" So I'm not as colourful as Cathy, sue me.

"Can we get this done?" Her voice was strained and I could hear the fear in it.

"On it. Can you help?"

"As long as I can sit."

"Good." I focussed on the altar where a poppet, a magic doll for the uninitiated, lay with a lock of Elisabeth's brown hair tied around its neck. Inside it were some of the girl's nail-clippings. Getting the hair and nail clippings had been Sue's, the apartment's tenant, part of the job. A bit of Elisabeth as a focus. How Sue got the hair and clippings, I don't know. I don't want to know. What I did know is with them the poppet could stand in place of Elisabeth. I picked it up.

"By the powers high and the powers low, by the elements four, in the name of Ra, the flaming sun, by Lady Isis, Mistress of Sorcery. I say this is not a thing of rag and stuffing I hold, but the nature and essence of Elisabeth Jane Montgomery. What is done to one is done to both. So mote it be!"

I passed the poppet to Cathy who held it up before the altar.

"This is Elisabeth Jane Montgomery I hold, by Lady Bast, Mistress of the dance eternal, by Lord Thoth, God of wizardry, by the elements four and the powers low and high. So mote it be!"

Cathy is good. I could see the poppet begin to glow in her hands. To one without the sight it wouldn't look like anything, but to me that bit of rag shone, and, more important, it became Elisabeth in our minds. More items slammed into our wards. I could feel the wards trembling with the impacts. Circles are strong, damn strong, but nothing human-made is indestructible. I also feared for Elisabeth. The more energy the poltergeist drew the less she had. I was sure it was at least partially responsible for the severity of her handicap.

In a worst case scenario a poltergeist can drain a person dry, killing them, before it moves on to another vulnerable individual. I have sworn before my Gods that I won't let innocents suffer because of that kind of crap. I — it hurts too much.

I laid the poppet on the altar, focussed my will, and then picking up the salt dish poured a circle of the crystals around the doll.

"By the power of earth and the purified soul of man, I hereby seal Elisabeth Jane Montgomery. No force or power may intrude upon her. I break all ties around her."

"Ray." Cathy pointed to the circle's edge. A glowing face with long, brown hair and a sweet, sad smile appeared. It was Elisabeth's face.

"You're hurting me, you're hurting me," wailed Elisabeth's voice.

You'd have to be a rock not to be affected, but Cathy and I

both knew that the face wasn't Elisabeth. It was the parasite that fed off her, enhancing the girl's suffering for its own ends.

I turned back to the poppet. Picking up a consecrated knife I scribed a circle around the doll with the blade.

"By the power of spirit and the will of the Gods. I hereby seal Elisabeth Jane Montgomery. No force or power may intrude upon her. I break all ties around her."

I felt the wards shudder and a throw cushion broke into the circle to bounce off my head.

"We better speed this up." Cathy knelt in front of the altar at my side.

"Right." I held my hand palm open over the poppet, Cathy laid her hand over mine and we focussed. How to describe working together? Souls join, the boundaries we normally have dissolve, especially if you work together often, especially if you share other intimacies. Especially if you lo— If you're close. At that moment, I knew Cathy as well as I knew myself, and she me.

Our energies combined surrounding the poppet and reaching out from that to surround Elisabeth. We felt the energy ties the poltergeist put on the girl snap like over-stretched elastic. The furniture crashed to the floor and silence filled the room.

"I think we got it." Cathy slumped back then hissed as the movement flexed her ankle.

"Almost." I stood and picked up the crook and flail.

Opening my mind I imagined a glowing, white tunnel piercing the vale between our world and the next. I thrust out with my tools and swept them in a circle pointing to all sections of the room. "By the power of the flail that commands, I order thee to return to thy proper plane and place, never to trouble the world of man again. So mote it be!"

I felt more than saw a wave of energy lash from my flail catching a pulsing ball of light. Bereft of its energy source and tie to the mortal world, the poltergeist was lost. It fought the energies I sent towards it to no avail. It didn't belong here, and the natural flows of the universe carried it through the glowing tunnel I'd called taking it to where it did belong. That done, I sat on the floor next to Cathy with my eyes closed as my breathing steadied. My sweat-soaked, white robe clung to me like a second skin. A cold, wet second-skin. Magic is hard work; anyone who says differently has never done it.

After a time of wondering if I'd ever have the energy to stand up again someone started pounding on the apartment door.

"*Keep it down in there! I've called the police! I won't put up with this! I have a sick child at home!*"

The shrill voice of Elisabeth's mother penetrated the wood. I ignored it. Her seeing "those horrible Pagans," in Sue's apartment wouldn't help the situation any. The quiet returned interrupted only by the sound of retreating footsteps beyond the door.

"Bitch." Cathy shifted so her side pressed into mine.

"She did complicate things." I shifted so my body became a backrest for Cathy. She pressed into me comfortably. She fits; I just wish I could convince her of that.

"Good thing Sue's place was close enough to Elisabeth for the spell to take."

"Close enough to be in the poltergeist's field of effect too."

"Maybe that's why she got it, to guide us here." Cathy grinned at me and looked up.

I cupped the side of her face feeling the dampness in her hair and kissed her. It was an old debate between Cathy and I. She thought the Gods were more involved in our day-to-day lives than I did. I believe in coincidence. I figure Ra is pretty busy keeping the fusion rate of the sun constant, so we don't freeze or fry here on Earth. That's why there are mystics. We're the oversight committee, cleaning up the messes that slip past the big guys. Yeah, my mother would be so proud, I'm a janitor.

I grunted, too tired to debate.

Cathy looked up at me and smiled then, adding a tone like warm honey to her voice, said, "It's over now. You okay?" I could listen to her talk in that tone all day and not have a single thought I'd rate as PG or below.

I smiled back at her. "I'll live, but tell me again why I let you talk me into these things?"

"You live for it, admit it?" Cathy was half right and I damn well knew it.

"How's your leg?" I shuffled over and examined her ankle. One thing about working as a lifeguard, you have first aid up the wazoo.

"Ow! What do you think? Of course it hurts! ... Sorry, I'll be fine."

I shook my head. "Are you hurt anywhere else?"

"Ray, I'm fine. It's just a sprain." She tried to smile at me then hissed as I shifted her ankle.

"Right, Cath, I think your ankle's broken, and, as much as I'd enjoy doing a full-body exam on you, getting you treated should come first. Now tell me if you're hurt anywhere else, so I know whether I can properly close out the ritual, or if I should just rush you to the hospital."

Reaching under the altar, I pulled out the canvas toolbox that held my first aid kit. This wasn't my first time at the dance. I'd learned to come prepared. Using a cushion and triangle bandages I splinted her ankle.

"I don't need—" Cathy pursed her lips and looked petulant.

I locked gazes with her. Gray-blue eyes stared into emerald and for once emerald looked away first. It doesn't happen often, I normally let her win.

Cathy sighed, she knew better than to argue when I was in first aid mode. "I don't hurt anywhere else. You know you are a party poop. You're going to make me go the hospital, and I had plans."

"Oh, what?" I finished securing the splint.

Cathy smirked and it made my heart lurch, as well as other things. "All I'll tell you is it involved you, me, my see-through, red lace nightie and chocolate syrup."

"Oh Gods!" I'm only human and an imagination is a horrible thing to waste.

"Rain check?" She smiled at me then hissed in pain as her ankle shifted.

"Rain check." I kissed her then went to work closing out the ritual.

I didn't bother with the mess in Sue's living room. I'd done my job. The spook was gone. She could clean up as well as I could.

I did take a moment to throw my gear into a duffle bag and pull on my standard uniform of jeans and a T-shirt. A woman can wear a robe in public and pull it off as a long dress, especially when she looks like Cathy. No guy is paying attention to the robe. A guy, unless he's in circle or the Society for Creative Anachronism, looks like an untalented transvestite in denial.

In less than ten minutes I carried Cathy down in the elevator with my duffle dangling off my arm. She's about as heavy as air, and I'm in pretty good shape from swimming literally hundreds of miles every year. A twenty-something woman stood blocking our exit at the elevator door when it opened on the ground floor. I noticed because she noticed us. I'm just under six foot, heavy set, muscular with rugged features. Not model material, but I do all right. A fact that I'm glad to remind Cathy of on occasion. Despite her leg, this was one of those occasions. The girl stared at me like I was a steak. Cathy glanced at her then tightened her grip around my neck and leaned into me. Ah, possessive displays. Cathy insists on an open relationship, or just being casual. I'm working on her.

Exiting the building, I walked to my car. The crisp autumn air helped drive away the last of the fatigue the ritual had left me with. I had to set Cathy down while I fumbled out the keys to my battered, *Hyundai Accent*. I was glad it was a four door. Once Cathy was settled sideways in the back seat I dumped my duffle in the trunk, climbed into the driver's seat and pulled away.

My car may look like something from a wrecking yard, but under the hood it's magic. I do my own work. Actually, I'm pretty good with a wrench. Magic has its place, but it's not auto-mechanics. Not in anything you can do any way else, really. The reason mystics don't use magic to do mundane things is it takes a lot more effort than doing it the mundane way. Sure, I can start a fire with my mind, with an hour's preparation and about twenty minutes focussed effort that will leave me with a blistering headache. That's assuming the tinder is dry. I use matches. We have a physical body to deal with the physical world. We have a soul to deal with the spiritual world. Where the mystic comes in is where the two worlds overlap.

After an uneventful drive, aside from Cathy's obligatory teasing about my "go cart with an attitude," I soon had her at the hospital. I carried her in. Andrea, Cathy's mum, stood in the waiting room talking to what were probably some patient's family members. She went pale and raced up to us.

"Oh my God! What happened?" Ms. Fitzpatric is like an older, brown-haired, blue-eyed version of her daughter. She made her nursing scrubs look good, which is no mean feat. Hell, she could still pull off a bikini. Not bad for late forties. If I hadn't met Cathy first, our relationship could have been more complex. I like big cats.

"Oh crap, Mother, relax. I forgot you were working tonight or I'd have made Ray take me to St. Joes." Cathy twisted in my arms so she could more easily look at her mother.

"The hell you would. Ray, is it serious?" Those blue eyes bored into my own.

"Probably a simple fracture of the ankle."

"I'll get a wheelchair and rush the X-rays. Go to the waiting room so you aren't blocking the hall." Andrea strode past the glassed in reception station and disappeared through a door.

"Great, what am I going to tell her?" Cathy bit her lip.

"You fell, it's kinda the truth." I walked towards the widened section of hall where the walls were lined with attached plastic chairs.

"Like she'd let it go at that. Look, just smile and nod. If she thinks you agree with me, she'll buy anything."

"Why not just tell her the truth? You're out of the broom closet with everyone but your mum."

"Right, you know how scared she is of anything mystical. She'd tell me I was delusional and no such thing existed, and then worry herself sick."

I had time to shrug before Andrea was in the waiting area with a wheelchair. "So how did this happen?"

I lowered Cathy into the chair and stepped back while her mother examined her ankle. Cathy hissed in pain. "Mom, go easy."

"It's a break, good diagnosis, Ray. Now can someone tell me why my daughter is in the emergency room?"

My perspective narrowed to the two women, excluding the dingy hallway and other people around us.

"Fine, if you must know, I was at work. Ray was taking me out after my last set. Good thing too. Some drunk spilled his beer on the stage and I stepped in it. Next thing I know, I'm on the floor with Ray checking me over."

Andrea's lips narrowed in an expression that Cathy had made her own. Looking between them it was like looking through time.

"I don't like you doing what you do. Ray... You poor thing, you put up with so much from her." Andrea patted my hand. I struggled not to laugh at Cathy's disgusted expression.

"Mother, I am right here! We've been through this. The money's good and I can schedule around my classes. Ray doesn't get a say in it. It's my life."

Andrea sighed and rolled her eyes. "You should go home now, Ray. I'll look after Cathy. I'm sure you have work at your real, respectable job tomorrow."

I looked at Cathy who gave me a nod. My work wasn't as provocative or lucrative as Cathy's, but I did have rent to pay and a cat that liked to be fed regularly. Bending down I kissed Cathy then slipped away as her mother warmed up for another futile attempt to get Cathy to quit dancing, move back home and finish her doctorate in a "respectable way." I wasn't sure how long it would take the robe Cathy was wearing to register and had no idea how she would explain it. I did know better than to get between a mother and daughter. I made it to the exit before being called back for an opinion that could only cost me.

– Chapter 2 –

WHAT PASSES FOR LIFE

The next morning I awoke to twelve pounds of feline grace slamming into my abdomen. My cat decided the shortest distance between my window and the kitty kibble involved using me as a landing pad at the halfway point. Having unfolded from a jackknife position, and learning how to breathe again, I looked at the clock and groaned. It was half an hour before the alarm was set to go off, too little time to go back to sleep and not enough time to do anything else.

"Merowo?" Sekmara queried from the floor before leaping onto the bed. She walked up to press her cold, wet nose against mine and purred. What can you do? Cats are the real rulers of the world. I started petting her. She is a pretty little thing, a calico-tabby cross with grey-tabby markings interspaced with splashes of orange. When her majesty deemed that I had given her enough attention, I got up and scanned my kingdom. Well, it's really Sekmara's, but she lets me live there as long as I keep the food bowl filled and the litter box shovelled.

My apartment's one room was in its usual jumble, with unwashed dishes and pots in the sink and my double bed filling nearly half of the floor. The kitchenette, with its bar fridge and mini-stove, looked like something that belonged in a hillbilly's trailer. I had fought back the invasion of blue mould from the week before. I'm not a complete slob. A reclining chair, that was older than I, sat facing a particleboard, entertainment-unit.

The rest of the wall space was filled with bookshelves and, aside from my personal altar with my collection of statues of the Egyptian god forms, they were full of books.

"Meow, meow, meow, meow." Sekmara walked back and forth over the unwashed laundry that protected my carpet from wear. Her tail formed a perfect question mark. With a glance at me she trotted to the cupboard under the sink and pawed it.

"Right. You're right. Breakfast."

Opening the cupboard I extracted a tin of cat food and a box of cereal. Rooting around I managed to clear enough of the sink so I could wash one plate and a bowl. Thus, breakfast was served. I was out of milk, but orange juice isn't half bad with Shreddies. Another few minutes' effort rendered up a clean life guarding uniform. Then I was off to teach little Johnny how to put his face in the water.

I called Cathy at lunch. She wasn't home, so I tried her mother's place. The boyfriend de-jour answered and passed me over to Andrea. The short version was that Cathy did have a simple fracture and would be laid up for a few weeks. She was sleeping off a bad reaction to the pain meds and I was welcome to visit. I placed a bet with myself that Cathy would be back in her own place by Monday.

After an afternoon of watching a hundred and fifty screaming kids do stupid things, I found myself back home. Can anyone tell me why people don't get that diving in shallow water equals life as a talking head? Urrrr!

I turned on the news while I sat in my recliner and enjoyed what in my opinion is China's greatest contribution to human endeavour. I love Chinese food.

I remember the news because of what came later. The anchor was slender and probably Hispanic. It wasn't the station with the cute weathergirl, my loss.

About midway through the program was a piece on the *Suwa Corporation* of Japan. It was opening a branch in Toronto. Mr. Suwa, the company's president, was personally supervising the expansion. They showed Mr. Suwa, a muscular, Asian man with hair cut short at the front and sides that just touched his shoulders at the back. He looked to be in his forties and wore a high-collared shirt with long sleeves. Suwa spoke English with an Oxford accent and perfect diction.

Seeing him I felt something, a tug at my soul. I'm a reincarnationist and I knew this pull. I've felt it strongly when I met Cathy and a few others. I always felt it was telling me I saw an old associate. Old friend or old foe it wasn't that specific. I shrugged it off as being unimportant to my life now.

Next came a story about a new street drug they dubbed *Terror*. Two people had overdosed on it in the last week. I paid attention in case I came across some idiot using it. The details were sketchy. It was a hallucinogen that induced a fear reaction and possibly affected consciousness and memory. The cops were playing it cool.

My food finished, I moved to my apartment's only concession to extravagance, a private bathroom, and brushed my teeth. Aside from the books that covered the back of the toilet, this was the tidiest room in the apartment. I'm a guy! Soap, shampoo, razor, towel, toothbrush, toothpaste, comb, deodorant. Who needs more than that? Cathy's bathroom scares me; it looks like an alchemist's lab exploded in Technicolor.

My tub was bone dry and a spider had taken up residence by the overflow. I shower at work most days. The sink, which didn't match the tub or toilet in colour or style, was cracked but still held water. My apartment had four things to recommend it. It was cheap, I could walk to my city job, I could walk to Cathy's and it was cheap.

Next, I cleared the centre of my main room's floor of clothing and draped my coffee table with a purple cloth. Taking statues of Thoth and Isis from my shelf altar I set them with a candle in front of each, purple for Thoth and dark blue for Isis. The elemental tools followed; the sistra, an ankh shaped rattle, for fire in the east; a chalice for water in the south; the winged disk for air in the west, this looks like a gold circle with blue wings; the mirror of Hathor, a copper mirror where the mirror is the sun-disk headdress the Goddess wears and her face supports it on a handle, for earth in the north. The salt dish and offering bowl followed then the crook and flail in the middle.

Sitting on my bed, I pulled the poppet of Elisabeth out of my duffle bag where I'd stowed it after the ritual. I'd gone to a lot of trouble for Elisabeth. Clearing my mind and making my emotions as blank as possible I placed pins where the worst of her problems seemed to stem from. I let myself believe it was just a rag doll I was sticking. Attitude is everything in magic. Putting the poppet on the altar, I set the circle, summoned the elements and invoked Thoth and Isis. I started chanting and dancing around the circle.

The power built, energy flowed. It was a warm rush on my skin halfway between silk and water caressing me, the euphoria of magic tingling through my body and spirit. Years of study and practice combined to peak the flow. This was how it was supposed to be, proper preparation and a clear goal. The poppet Elisabeth glowed in my mystic sight. The pins were an ugly intrusion in her nature.

Sekmara poked her head out from under the altar luxuriating in the energy, helping to direct it, adding to it.

I picked up the poppet. "If it be the will of the Gods and the desire of Elisabeth Jane Montgomery, let these energies bring healing. By Thoth Lord of healing and Isis Lady of healing, so mote this be!"

I reached for the first pin and yanked it free. Energy rushed through the link tingling and hot. Another pin followed. I pictured healthy nerves and tissue taking the place of the damaged areas. Another pin and then another. The energy was fading. I pulled the rest of the pins having done what I could. The poppet no longer glowed in my mystic sight, and when I picked it up the lock of hair around its throat fell away. I felt exhausted, drained, but peaceful. I'm not the best healer. My mystical medicine tends to be like my mundane efforts, first aid. We all have our talents. That being said, Elisabeth is a sweet kid, I had to try.

15 INUKEKUBI

I'd met her while looking into the poltergeist before her mother asked about my falcon shaped Harakhti pendant. Truth to tell, I think Elisabeth had a little crush on me, which was probably part of why the mother hated me. I represented her eternal child growing up.

I settled in my circle and began meditating, enjoying the clean, empty feeling the spell left behind.

The next afternoon I life-guarded a pool rental by a church group whose only concern was that I was the best qualified person we had on staff. That I respect.

I came home somewhat richer and with a free lasagne from Mrs. DeFranko. I'd pulled her grandson out the week before when he got pushed into the deep end. Of course, her youngest daughter was about my age and single. Take your pick for reasons.

The light on my machine was blinking, so I hit the button.

"Son, just touching base. Your mother worries about you. I guess you're not there. I'll talk to you later." The defeated tone failed to take into account that I visited once a week and that it was only a month since I'd helped my Dad re-shingle his roof. I love my parents, but can we say black hole of need?

The next message played.

"Ray, I just called to thank you. So far things seem normal, nothing flying around, though what's left to fly around is a question. I expected some breakage, not a tornado in my living room. Oh, I saw Elisabeth at church this morning. She seems — I don't know — brighter. I swear I saw her hand move. Maybe being free of whatever that thing was has done her some good. I hope so. Oh yea, do you know where Cathy is? I can't get through at her apartment. Thanks again. Bye."

The next message was one of my clients. I do private swim lessons and backyard-pool, safety critiques as a sideline. She told me how having the shepherd's hook I recommend she buy allowed her to save her daughter's life. The call reminded me. I added, 'get more business cards' to my To Do list.

The microwave heated the lasagne while I, horror of horrors, washed about a dozen plates and set them on the rack to dry. Feeling vindicated in the house keeping department I settled in front of the TV and popped a *Dresden Files* episode in the DVD player. I own the *Dresden Files* disk set, wish fulfilment, plus the actress that plays Murphy is cute. I mentioned it before, I'm a guy, and I'm not going to change.

The next day at work school groups took up most of my day then I stopped at Cathy's. I figured her mum would feed her cat, but I wanted to be sure. Besides, odds were Cathy would be there.

I took the elevator to the seventh floor and got off. The building was well built, had large apartments, nice tenants and was sound proofed. Ah, bliss. Reaching her door, I put in my key, opened it then called in. I'd learned through experience to never walk in on Cathy.

"Cath, you in?"

"Living-room, 'bout time you got here."

I walked the short hallway to the living room and took in the view. Cathy's furniture consists of good hand-me-downs from her mother. Cathy lay on the couch watching the television on the other side of the room. Her coffee table held an empty, plastic pitcher and glass while a book was folded open on the back of the blue velour couch.

Cathy wore short shorts and a halter with her leg encased in a plaster cast. No makeup, hair clean and combed, nothing more; the way I like her best.

"Hey Cath." I kissed her hello and took a seat in the lounging chair.

"Hey yourself. I was expecting you to rescue me from my mother and Burt."

"Burt?"

She rolled her eyes. "The new boyfriend. I give it two weeks. He was trying to lay tracks with me for later. I mean come on! Mom should never have dumped Kenneth. He at least treated her well. If she'd just wise up and be honest with herself that what she wants is an open relationship, she'd be so much better off. But no! She has to live in denial! She keeps telling herself that the right man will change everything. If she'd only listen to me."

I sighed loud enough to be heard. There are only so many times you can listen to a memorized speech.

"Fine, but she really does need to accept herself and stop living by social rules that don't suit her. She just isn't a one-man woman. She makes promises then something shiny catches her eye, and she's bed hopping again. If she'd only be honest with herself and them and give what she expects then..."

I started cleaning out my wallet. Cathy looked at me and nodded.

"I know, I know. She's my Mom, I love her, and well... if she and Dad had been honest maybe they wouldn't have broken up. It was the dishonesty, not the affaires, which killed their marriage. Patricia and I didn't deserve to be turned into weapons by them. Not that either of them will admit that's what they did." Pain and anger entered Cathy's voice. She was from a broken home, I was raised in one. We shared the experience of our parents hating each other and using us as tools in expressing that hate. I couldn't make it right for the twelve-year-old girl that was, but I could hug the twenty-six year old woman in front of me.

It was a long minute before she patted my back and pulled away.

"Thanks." Cathy smiled. I liked that smile. "So why didn't you get me out of there?"

I shrugged. For casual Cathy expected a lot, and I wouldn't agree to open. I was holding out for monogamy. Are we backwards or what? I was betting that in some ways Cathy was different from her mother, and I knew I was different from her father. If I could only convince her of that. "I couldn't just ditch work, and I figured until you were mobile someone would have to be there all the time."

Cathy shook her head. "Yeah, yeah. Makes sense. The pain pills turned me into a zombie. It took forever for me to detox. Mum said I was sensitive. You could have visited though."

"And listen to you and your mother go at it like a pair of

angry badgers? Do I have stupid written on my forehead?" I rolled my eyes then studied the oil painting Cathy had hung over her couch. It was a stylized image of the Egyptian cat Goddess Bast with a cat's body and a human face. The face was Cathy's. There was another one in her bedroom with Cathy's body and a cat's head.

"If she wasn't so unreasonable and stubborn. Everything has to be her way!"

I stood up and began examining the titles on her bookshelves. This had the advantage that my back was to her so she couldn't see my smirk. I waited until I thought I could speak without my voice betraying me before I answered.

"She wants what she thinks is best for you."

"And she always thinks she knows better than anyone. Will she ever wake up and accept that I'm an adult? I can make my own decisions. Be sure to put that back in the right place."

I bit my lip and mastered my expression as I slid the book I had taken out back in the exact spot it had come from. Cathy's library was organized by subject and author. Mine isn't. I turned around with a bland, vaguely-supportive expression I'd practised in front of the mirror. "So you need anything?"

Cathy looked at me. "You know I can tell when you're not saying something. I am not anything like my mother."

"I didn't say anything." I shrugged.

Cathy looked like she'd just eaten something sour. "You didn't have to!"

I gave her my best grinning idiot imitation.

"Fine!" Cathy pursed her lips in that way that made her look like a younger version of Andrea. I couldn't stifle a guffaw.

"What?" Cathy glared at me.

"I lo— You're cute, that's all. I enjoy you." I moved to stroke my hand the length of her arm as I sat back down beside her.

"Close save. You know the rules. No commitment, no saying the words." Cathy smiled sadly.

"Your idea of commitment isn't what I call commitment. Look, let's not fight. Do you need anything?" I didn't try to hide the pain in my face. To have your dream in sight, to touch it, feel it, hold it, and yet be kept from it by one thing. It is a kind of agony.

Cathy smiled and patted my cheek. "Poor, silly man. I need a few things. First, can you refill my water jug? I'm still dizzy from those damn pills, and with the cast, I'm not too mobile."

"Sure." I picked up the pitcher.

"Good. Second, I've made up a shopping list, it's on the table."

I left the living room and went into the efficiency kitchen. It was clean and tidy except for a few dishes in the sink.

"I'll have to do the shopping tomorrow after work, can you last?"

Cathy answered while I put ice in the pitcher and retrieved the shopping list from the table in the small dining room that abutted the kitchen. "No problem, the next one is a biggie though."

I filled the jug with filtered water, refilled the ice cube trays and returned jug in hand to the living room.

"What, like clearing a poltergeist for your old high school friend?" I set the jug down and fell into the chair examining the list. It was all microwave dinners. That told me that Cathy wasn't feeling as well as she was pretending. Normally, she loves to cook.

"You remember Jessy?"

"Asian, short, pretty, bit of an accent, her Dad drives a taxi back home, big family, works the circuit, lapsed Catholic who does the Christmas and Easter thing, beautiful long, black hair, big brown eyes and—"

"That's her. I see she made an impression." Cathy looked like she'd eaten a lemon and her voice was strained. Score one for me.

"She's certainly worth the price of a dance."

"She's pretty, I'll give you that."

I scanned Cathy's aura. It was dull and pulled in tight. She was putting up a good act, but she was still in a bad way. I took pity on her. "Cath, no competition. Maybe casual at most. I like Jessy, but I'd bulldoze her. I'm too opinionated and out spoken, and she's too eager to please. I need a woman who'll growl back when I'm unreasonable."

"Oh, I'm not concerned. Do what you like. I just didn't want you to get invested and then find out she was wrong for you. She has mentioned you a couple of times."

One of the great challenges in dealing with Cathy is trying not to laugh out loud when she shows her true colours. She'd introduce me to most of the women she worked with knowing that they were no goes from the start. The ones I might actually date, she herded me away from like a sheepdog on a coffee bender. That possessive streak gave me hope.

"So what about Jessy?"

"I loaned her airfare when her father got sick, and she still owes me. I called her up. She can pay me back, but she's going to Sarnia the day after tomorrow. She's working the *Twenty-Four Carat* in Toronto. If you could drive up and get the cheque from her it would be great. My rent's due, and I'm a little short because I topped out my Ontario Home Owners Savings Plan for the year this month. I could borrow from Mom, but... well... you know the strings on that."

"Fine, after I drop off the groceries I'll drive to Toronto and get the cheque. I might even take in a couple of acts." I leered.

Cathy chuckled. "You should, Michelle, the tall, willowy brunette with the fake tits; you met her at my last party, the one who dropped out of the computer engineering program, she'll be there."

"I remember, she took off when you told her nothing harder than weed in your place."

"Yup, she's a coke head, but a good dancer. She's got a new stage routine. It's worth seeing. She's working the *Twenty-Four Carat* this week."

"I'll try and catch it if it doesn't run too late."

"Do that. You know she thinks you're kinda cute."

"Come on, Cath. You know 'no druggies' is near the top of my list."

"I know, and thank you." Her smile lit the room for a second then she yawned. "Sorry, it's the pills. I'm so dopey and they are taking forever to get out of my system."

"Maybe you should go to bed." I patted her hand.

"Love to, but I'm kinda tired." She winked at me.

I knelt beside her and picked her up like a child. In a real way Cathy had what she wanted from me. A helper, support, friendship, an on call lover. Why did I stick around when other guys could and did push me aside? I'm a sucker, a fool, and with her snuggled innocently in my arms as I carried her to bed and tucked her in, I was a man in love. I stuck around to do her dishes. The heart trumps the head every time.

– Chapter 3 –

A BAD NIGH+

The next evening found me hurtling along the Queen Elizabeth Way towards Toronto with a mad on. My boss decided to cut my hours. How he thought I was going to live on what was left I don't know? The city will do anything to keep people from getting in the union. I still had my jobs at the YM and YW CAs but I was seriously thinking of telling Malcolm, my city boss, where to put it in precise detail.

Cathy had been sympathetic, but she thinks I can do better than lifeguarding. Thing is, getting a degree with evening classes takes time. And note: I'm a rotten dancer! I needed two more years at my current rate to finish my Bachelors of Recreation. For that I needed my job. I had almost convinced myself that it would be morally acceptable to arrange a situation where they would have to put me in the union. One can do magic for one's own benefit so long as you're careful not to hurt others. There's nothing wrong with that. The tricky part is not hurting others.

I pulled up to the *Twenty-Four Carat's* parking lot. The club was a long, low building that if it wasn't for the sign advertising French table-dancers, could have been a sports bar. I found an empty spot beside a white, stretch limo and pulled in. My car looked like a shaggy pony standing beside an Arabian thoroughbred. I contented myself by thinking that I got better gas mileage.

I entered the club through the large double doors and gave my eyes a chance to adjust to the gloom. Scantily-clad shooter-girls and waitresses walked between the tables. A blonde, who could have been anything from twenty to thirty five, with the worn out quality drugs give a person strutted across the stage wearing a mini skirt and nothing else. Her makeup was way too heavy, and she looked bored and tired.

Jessy sat at the bar across from the entrance, wearing a tight black dress. It was a view! She spoke with another dancer; a short blond with disproportionately large breasts in a red, spandex dress.

"Ray." Jessy spotted me and ran up for a hug. Some of the other patrons eyed me enviously. Eat your hearts out guys.

"Hi Jessy. You doing okay? How's your Dad?"

She pulled away and led me by the hand to the bar. "He's doing better. The operation went well. He doesn't get chest pains anymore."

Jessy bought me a drink and gave me two cheques made out to Cathy, one post dated to the end of next month.

"I'll have the money by the time the second cheque clears. I'm working extra days and there's a new club in Midland that's doing really well." She spoke with her hands as much as her voice. If she stood five foot tall that was it, and she could trigger a man's protective instincts without trying.

She babbled to me about work and family for a while. I listened until a huge, muscular man with harsh features and a sloping forehead in a chauffeur's uniform stomped up behind her.

"My boss wants a private dance." He indicated a powerfully built, tall, Asian man in a three-piece suit. The Asian looked familiar. I got that feeling I knew him from some other life; beyond that, the emotions were vague but carried a hint of menace. He was sitting at a table and saluted Jessy with his glass.

Looking at this guy brought on a slightly nauseous, edgy

feeling. I didn't want Jessy dancing for him. "I was about to ask the lady to dance for me."

"Yeah... well, you didn't." The satirically shaved gorilla snarled at me.

I came to my feet and found myself looking straight into this guy's throat. I contemplated my odds in a fair fight and got ready to nut him and run.

Jessy came to my rescue. "He was here first. One of the other girls can dance for your boss." She took my hand and led me to the private lounge.

"You know, Ray, I like you. I... You... maybe I shouldn't dance for you here. Maybe we should really go out?" Jessy's voice held a world of promise.

"Jessy... I..."

She pushed me down on a love seat in the dimly-lit lounge and plopped into the seat beside me. The lounge was full of love seats positioned facing each other with an open space between them. "I know Cathy sees other men. I think she is very foolish. You are nice, and... I... You don't need to pay to spend time with me."

"I..." I cleared my throat. "Jessy, um... I really like you, but I don't want to lead you on. I know Cathy sees other guys, and I do date other women, but I'm hoping she'll grow out of it. We could have a lot of fun together, but..."

"Your heart is hers." Jessy's beautiful face filled with sadness.

I felt like a heel. Part of me wondered if I was doing to Jessy what Cathy did to me, so close but no cigar. "I'm sorry."

Jessy smiled as she nodded. "You're sweet and honest. I like that. If you ever decide you're tired of waiting for Cathy to give you what you want, remember me." She winked and looked flirty. "I can at least dance for you here. Maybe it will help you change your mind."

I took the liberty of caressing the side of her face. Why was my life so complicated?

A new song started and Jessy danced for me. It was twenty bucks well spent. She had to charge me; she needed to make a living.

She pulled on her dress, as I tried to convince my blood to head north again, when I saw the large Asian man enter the back room with the girl that had been on stage when I came in. The only change appeared to be that a black halter had been added to her clothing.

"Jessy, I know you need to work the room, but do me a favour." I whispered close to her ear.

"What?" Jessy adjusted her dress under her breasts.

"Stay away from that guy. I get a bad vibe from him."

Jessy kissed my cheek. "For you. Maybe someday you'll see what's in front of you." She led me back to the main room and I watched Michelle's new stage act. It was fair, but her addiction showed. The Lurch wannabe was nowhere to be seen.

I left after Michelle's act. All evidence to the contrary, strip joints really aren't my scene. I don't have anything against them, but I can think of better places to spend my money, Cathy notwithstanding.

The night had closed in, and a cold wind rattled the leaves on the trees by the parking lot as I walked to my car. The limo had pulled out and sat by the back exit lane when a blast of psychic energy tore into my skull like a dagger. The blast left me doubled over clutching my head. I said a wizard's scream has power, this was a psychic scream, but it had nothing to do with wizardry. It was a gut wrenching energy blasting across a sensitive's soul composed of pure terror, and strong enough that it would register on untrained senses as an eerie, unpleasant feeling.

Pumping energy into my personal shields I shifted to mystical sight and glanced around. The world came alive with glowing fields of energy. Life creates magic, so every plant and creature glows with its own aura. The source of the 'scream' propelled an ongoing explosion of mustard yellow just past the limo. I ran towards it preparing a banishing spell. The limo pulled away and circled the parking lot to another exit. I ran to where two buildings formed a dark alley open to a busy street at one end and the parking lot at the other. The mustard coloured energy convulsed.

"Arrrrrr!" This time the scream was physical and echoed off the buildings. I reached the alley just as a dark figure sprinted towards the busy street.

"*No! Stop!*" I raced after her, but it was hopeless.

Screaming, the blonde that had danced for the Asian man ran into the street followed by the screech of brakes and a dull thud. Time slowed as she flew through the air and crumpled to the ground. I hit the sidewalk while she was still shuddering. The car that hit her had stopped. Its driver gazed on in horrified shock. Racing to the injured woman I checked that her airway was clear then looked, listened and felt for her breath. Her breath caught and died. I breathed for her and positioned for chest compressions.

A horrific thing emerged from her chest. A glowing spirit head with a distorted, human face and fangs and a pair of glowing energy hands rose beside it. I glanced around. The mundanes couldn't see this purely spiritual manifestation. The few with a trace of mystic sight looked away because the entity before me didn't match their world-view. The disembodied head and hands hissed and flew away. I started compressions. I watched as the girl's spirit rose and hovered above her body. She looked terrified and a sickly, fear energy surrounded her. I could only guess where that energy would take her if she passed over before it dissipated.

"You, I pointed out a middle-aged woman with a cell phone. Call 911; tell them we have a VSA patient, CPR in progress. Don't hang up until they say you can. Let me know when you get through."

Breathe, breathe, position hands, compress, compress, compress... two to thirty.

"You," I pointed to a twenty-something guy. "Direct traffic around us."

Breathe, breathe, position hands, compress, compress, compress... two to thirty.

"You, keep the crowd back."

Breathe, breathe, compress, compress, compress...two to thirty, hard and fast, keep it up.

"The ambulance is coming," announced the bystander.

Breathe, breathe, place hands on sternum compress, compress, compress... hard and fast, keep it up. Check for breathing, look, listen and feel.

I don't fear death; he is a merciful healer who comes when all other healers fail. I actually like him. I saw the peace and relief from pain he brought my grandmother when cancer made her life a living hell. I know him to be the transition between one place and another, but I'd be damned if I let him win without a fight when the person could have a quality life. I couldn't let him win until the fear left the spirit, so it wouldn't be drawn to the lower planes.

No breath. Breathe, breathe, place hands, compress, compress, compress... Two to thirty, hard and fast, keep it up.

The spirit's face changed from terrified to quizzical, the awful mustard yellow around her dissipated allowing the blues and greens of her aura in life to shine through.

Breathe, breathe, compress, compress, compress...two to thirty, hard and fast, keep it up.

The spirit smiled at me, she seemed to sigh and I heard her whisper, "Thank you." Then the shining tunnel of light came.

Breathe, breathe, place hands, compress, compress, compress. Two to thirty. Hard and fast.

The spirit vanished into the tunnel. I felt it like a click in my head. She was gone. I now worked on a broken machine, nothing more.

Breathe, breathe, place hands, compress, compress, compress, two to thirty.

First aiders aren't allowed to declare death, so I kept going to avoid being sued, but it was over. I hoped she'd signed her organ donor card then at least I wasn't wasting my time.

Breathe, breathe, compress, compress, compress...I was less frantic. I could let them think I was getting tired. A white, stretch limo drove by its mirrored windows hiding its occupants. The paramedics arrived and I stepped aside. I leaned against a building and watched as they tried to defibrillate the corpse. Epinephrine, bicarb, calcium chloride. All the tools of modern, field medicine were applied just too late. I gave a history to one of the medics while the other worked on the girl. I'm not use to losing with the stakes so high. Finally, my failure was put on a gurney and the ambulance sped away. I pushed off from the wall and started for my car.

"Sir?" A young cop with dark hair and a slender build walked up to me.

"Yes." I just wanted to make my notes and go home.

"We have a witness saying that you chased the woman onto the street." He looked at me, and I could hear a tremor in his voice. He must have been new.

"I didn't. I heard her scream and ran over to see if I could help. I gave my contact information to the paramedics. I think I have a business card on me." I reached for my wallet and found myself staring down the barrel of a very young and freaked out cop's gun.

"Freeze." The cop's voice shook.

I didn't have the luxury of being in a daze anymore. I woke up. Scanning his aura I saw a dirty, mustard-yellow beam striking it. Following that beam I saw a glowing, spirit head hovering well above us.

I took a deep breath.

"Put your hands where I can see them." The young cop was being manipulated. Whatever the glowing head was, it was enhancing his fear, overriding his reason.

I held my hands out to my sides with my two outer fingers extended and the middle ones folded into my palm, making the symbol of the sacred bull with each hand. With a mental push I rammed the energies of my aura up and over the cop slicing the beam that was flowing into him. It hurt, I heard a psychic screech. My guess is my enemy felt that one more than I did and didn't like it much. Good!

The young cop swallowed and looked confused. "Put your hands on the wall and spread your legs."

With the emotional manipulation broken I wasn't afraid of being shot for no reason, so I complied. Minutes later I was cuffed and put in the back of a cruiser. Have you ever noticed how much your nose itches when you can't scratch it?

Half an hour later I was in a police station's questioning room. They were decent enough to un-cuff me. The central table and hard, wooden chairs were enough to be interesting for a few moments. I'd never been brought in by the cops before. A video camera in the corner looked over the entire room. The only door was quite notably locked. It was pretty clear I wasn't there to receive any good-Samaritan awards. If life is experience, I was living now. Oh shit!

Two hours and a cup of bad coffee later, found Police Detective Brandon James, the bad cop, still asking me the same questions he started with. PD Waite, who sat across from me, played the role of good cop. James, a tall man with a stick-insect-like quality and a large head surmounted by a brown toupee, stood over me crowding my personal space. I had an impressive view up the nostrils of his huge, hooked nose.

"Let's do it one more time, Raymond?" James leaned on the interrogation room's table.

"It's Ray. I don't even let my mother call me Raymond. And for the tenth time, I didn't kill her. I didn't chase her. I was going to my car and heard a scream. I went to investigate and she bolted into the street."

"Our witness says you were running for the alley before the scream." James shifted position and perched on the desk.

"I need to use the head. Can we pick this up in five minutes?" I looked longingly at the door.

"Suppose you start telling us the truth!" snapped James.

I rubbed my face. Truth was the last thing my captors were interested in. From things they'd let slip my guess was that they wanted a lead on the drug Terror. I couldn't help them with that. I wished I could, I hate street drugs. Weed in moderation, okay if you're into it. Everybody needs something once in a while to take the edge off, but the rest, poison!

Fighting to keep my frustration out of my voice I answered James. "There were two screams. It was a little hectic. Maybe your witness missed the first one." Technically there were two screams. I just didn't tell them that the first one was psychic.

Okay, so I also omitted the flying head and hands with nothing attached in the account I gave the cops. Last thing I need is a stay in a room with rubber walls. To people without the Sight my world, well, they don't want to know about my world. Especially cops, they see enough in the mundane world, why add to their burdens?

"What happened after you heard the first scream?" Waite's smooth baritone was at odds with his heavy build and military bearing. He was almost as tall as James but easily had fifty pounds of muscle over the other man. His shirt collar was unbuttoned and his tie loosened. His hair was black, bushy and real. Badly cut, but real.

"Fine. I went to check out the first scream."

"Why?" snapped James.

"Why? Come on, I thought that someone was in trouble."

"How'd you know it wasn't some slut stripper with a john?"

I'd had it and let it come through in my voice. "Those ladies are people, and I have friends, note friends, that strip for a living."

Hearing the temper in my voice Waite stood up and moved casually around the table.

James opened his mouth but I pointed at him and roared, "*Silence*. I am not finished yet." The energy I projected hit him like a slap in the face. Another dumb ass move, so I have problems with authority figures. I also have problems with men who fail to respect women. So shoot me.

James blinked and closed his mouth.

I continued, pissed as hell. "I have friends that strip. Most of them don't turn tricks, and they are taxpayers, so I suggest, sir, you keep a civil tongue in your head. Furthermore, I am a taxpayer, and I do not think it appropriate for anyone paid from those taxes to use the term slut when on the clock. It is a crude and demeaning word!"

Waite was now in position to control 'the suspect' and I felt his heavy hand on my shoulder pushing down as I tried to rise from my seat.

"You—"

"Brandon, maybe you should take a break." Waite left me, ushering his partner to the door. James was left on the other side of the door as Waite closed it before he smiled as he took a seat opposite me.

"I'm sorry for that. So, you're friends with some of the dancers. Do you know them professionally or socially?"

The good cop was in. With a little luck, I might get to go to the bathroom. "Both, I date a woman who's dancing her way through a doctorate in psychology."

"Lucky you." Waite's smile widened. "Is she the Hamilton number you gave us?"

"Yes." I had to be careful. Bad cop is easy to counter, good cop, answer one reasonable question then another, get use to answering and soon you're telling your life story. It's an old wizard's trick. We used it for centuries before the cops picked it up.

"She has a lovely voice."

"The rest of her's no slouch either." We were bonding, two twentieth century guys talking about girls in a more or less respectful way. If I'd been wearing a blue jays cap we'd be deep into the last game by now. He was good.

"So why did you go to that alley. Most people would just keep walking."

"And how sad is that? If we stop looking after each other this world is in bad shape. I didn't learn how to save lives just so I could get a bad-paying job. Also, maybe, well. It was a woman screaming. As a cop you have got to know about the whole hero thing."

"I thought you said you were dating," Waite checked his notebook, "this Cathy woman."

"We're not exclusive." I rubbed my temples and contemplated just how bad the karma would be for will dominating these guys into letting me go.

"So you reached the alley," prompted Brandon.

My head was beginning to throb, and if they didn't let me go to the bathroom soon, I was going to pee on the floor. I doubted that would win me any points. Probably also mess up my shoes. "She ran into traffic, got hit, I did first aid." The memory made me shudder.

"Would you like a glass of water?"

I shook my head. "I'm not use to losing them." Resting my elbows on the table I massaged my temples. "I work pools, mostly. The rescues are pretty much grab and pull. You train like crazy and pray you'll never have to use what you know. It's not like you guys or the ambulance. Lifeguards don't see it enough to get use to it."

Waite nodded with real understanding and compassion. Nice to know I wasn't a complete wimp. "I hear you. It gets better. All you can do is your best then move on."

"Thanks."

James re-entered the room and stood quietly by the door.

"What happened next?" asked Waite.

"Next I was staring down the barrel of a gun held by a very nervous cop. I guess that's what I get for being a good citizen."

"Don't get smart!" James snapped from the door. I read his aura. It was an act; there wasn't any red, the colour I associate with anger, lies and acute physical damage. I got more the sense he was worried about something.

I took a chance. "Look. I've had it with this. Either charge me and get a lawyer in here, or send me home. It's late, I'm tired, and if you don't let me go to the can, I'm going to make a mess on your floor. If you're worried about me making a stink about the young cop pulling his gun, don't be. No harm, no foul. Just tell me that you guys will talk to him about keeping perspective, and we'll call it a lesson learned. Everyone fucks up."

Waite and James exchanged a glance and the tension in the room lessoned.

"That's decent of you. He's been shitting bricks since we brought you in." Wait tapped the one-way glass and the officer in question opened the door. "We'll let you know in a minute about releasing you. Constable Smith will take you to the washroom."

If I'd had a second x chromosome, I would have kissed the

man.

Minutes later I, much relieved, was escorted to James and Waite's desks in an open office space. The two men stood looking far less hostile.

"We believe you. We called around and your story checks out." Waite handed me a brown envelope containing my keys, jackknife - they'd yapped about that, but come on - wallet and the rest.

"Great. How am I supposed to get to my car?"

Waite smiled. "We'll have a patrol car drop you off. No hard feelings."

"No worries." We shook and that little slice of heaven was over.

– Chapter 4 –

RESEARCH

J got home in time to grab a couple of hours sleep before my alarm sounded. Worrying about the thing I'd seen rising from the corpse would have to wait. I have a life. It may suck, but it needs maintenance too. Rising, I downed a pot of coffee, fed Sekmara and got ready for work. The day was about as lovely as you'd expect little sleep and high stress to make it. I managed to get my last two hours of work covered so that I could hit the sheets.

Three hours of blessed oblivion was followed by more caffeine and a forty minute drive, so I could choke down a meal of half-cooked chicken, mashed potatoes and vegetables boiled to mush. My mother thought she was a good cook. I didn't tell my parents about the dead girl or the police. They already thought I should move back home and stay in my old room until they died. Following that I could have a life that they didn't control. Oh yes, join the Air Force and become a Medical Doctor. My father's failed dreams, the only ones I was supposed to have. You ask why I moved out after high school?

Mercifully, I got home early but I had to work my job at the YMCA the next day. I found out that there was a memorial service for the girl that died but my shift ended too late for me to attend. Her name had been Vivian. It means lovely, full of life. Irony can hurt sometimes. I called Cathy but only got her machine, so I focussed on the problem of what I'd seen in the alley. Turning to my library, I skimmed my books of mythology. Searching for a creature the cops would never consider. If Vivian supposedly died of a Terror overdose this thing was killing regularly, and the cops couldn't stop it.

The next morning I awoke from a nightmare. I saw a pair of woman's hands scrubbing something. Blood welled up from the thing and I realized it was skin, and the hands were my own. I was crying and in some kind of a hut. Then I was running through a forest at night. There was a falling sensation and then I woke up.

On the way into work, I bought a paper and read it over lunch. There was another Terror overdose. Another woman killed by that thing. I couldn't sit back and let this go on, to quote Stan Lee, "with great power comes great responsibility." Or as my grandfather would have said, "See the world you want to live in within your mind. Know it, and then do what you can to make this world match that image." My grandfather was a great man.

Somehow on TV the hero is never busy making a living while the bad guy eats innocent people. I worked the rest of my shift.

That evening I found it. A story about a Japanese goblin. I sat in the middle of my unmade bed poring over the tale and trying to keep Sekmara from laying on the page I was reading.

Long ago, on the island of Japan, a samurai named Isogai Heidazaemon Taketsura set aside his sword and took up the robe of a Buddhist priest, naming himself Kwairyo. With the heart of a warrior he walked the land spreading the Buddha's wisdom to places where strange and evil creatures stalked the night.

One day Kwairyo journeyed along a mountain trail between two villages. As evening approached his anxiety grew, for he had been delayed on his way and he knew of no nearby shelter. Adding to his concern, a storm rumbled in the distance, sending gusts of wind that grabbed at his cloak like living things. Even the solid mountains seemed strange and ominous, skeletal fingers grasping at the sky.

Trudging forward in the deepening gloom, Kwairyo happened upon a woodcutter carrying a burden of sticks.

"Greetings stranger, you are abroad late this evening." The woodcutter bowed as Kwairyo drew near.

Kwairyo bowed in return. "I was delayed in my journeys and fear that I may not reach my destination before the sun sets," explained the priest.

"You should be more careful. There are dark creatures in these mountains. It is said they hunt at night."

"I would not spend the night outside by choice."

"Then come. My home is not rich, but it has a roof and four walls against the darkness and storm."

Kwairyo bowed again. "I thank you. Your generosity does you credit."

Setting a brisk pace, the woodcutter led the way along torturous, mountain trails. Finally, they came to a stop at a cottage in a deep valley. A bamboo aqueduct supplied a cistern by the cottage that overflowed to irrigate a vegetable garden.

"Welcome to my home." The woodcutter opened the door.

Kwairyo stepped into the building and was greeted by the woodcutter's wife and daughter. They both displayed manners more in keeping with a noble's court than a woodland hovel. The wife prepared a simple dish of rice and vegetables and Kwairyo was invited to share in the meal.

Once they had eaten and the wooden bowls had been cleaned Kwairyo praised his hosts. "I am indebted to your hospitality and your gracious ways. It has been years since I have seen such adherence to the forms of etiquette as you all display."

"Thank you. It is a feast for us to host one who so adheres to the proper forms as yourself. If my asking is not too forward, were you of a noble family before you took up the priests robe?" replied the Woodcutter.

37 | NUKEKUBI

The women of the house sat silent, watching the priest with glowing eyes and strange expressions.

"I was once a samurai. When my noble house came to ruin I did not wish to take service with another. Nor did I wish to become *ronin*. I choose the way of the spirit so I might still live with honour. Tell me, how does a woodcutter and his worthy family," Kwairyo dipped his head in a sitting bow to the two women, "come to carry themselves like members of a great household?"

"I was not always as I am. You left your service for noble cause and good reason. Once I served a Daimyo, commanding the servants of his household, but I fell victim to my own greed. I gambled and soon owed more than I could pay. To hide my shame, I took a bribe and was caught. My lord was merciful and terrible. My child was a confidante of his daughter. At the pleading of his child he did not sentence us all to death, instead he decreed that I, my wife and our child should live here as penance for my pride and foolishness. This judgment will stand until I can somehow wipe the stain from my honour. Only then may my wife and daughter be forgiven the shame I have brought on us all."

"It is indeed sad that a family should come to this. Often I have noticed that one foolish in youth may grow wise with age. I hear in your words true repentance. Tonight I shall recite the sutras for your sake and pray that you may atone for your past errors."

The wife and daughter gasped to hear this.

"Good priest, you need not concern yourself for our fate. We brought this on ourselves and we should pay the price of our misdeeds." The woodcutter's wife bowed low.

"I will pray for you this night. What kind of man would I be if I did not do at least that much? Now if you will excuse me." Kwairyo rose, bowed and made his way to the cottage's small back room and began to pray.

The night drew on as Kwairyo prayed until his throat was parched and his voice cracking. Rising, he crept into the main room, hoping to quench his thirst at the cistern outside.

Mindful of his sleeping hosts, he moved silently. He could see they were lying about the fire, three still forms. He looked again in the dim glow of the banked flames and gasped in surprise. He blinked to clear his vision but soon could no longer deny his eyes. Each body was missing its head.

Kneeling by the woodcutter's body, Kwairyo felt the dirt of the cottage's floor. No blood dampened the soil. Investigating the wounds, he saw how clean they were. Not even the sharpest blade could cut so fine a line. He knew then he had been taken in by a family of Nukekubi, goblin beings with an insatiable hunger for human flesh.

What am I to do? He thought. Grasping the woodcutter's body he dragged it from the house and hid it in a ditch under a pile of bracken.

"If the stories are true, he must rejoin with his flesh before dawn or perish," Kwairyo whispered to himself using his voice to focus his thoughts.

He heard a hissing sound. Following it, he saw a strange glow in the darkness. Hiding amongst the trees he crept forward until he was staring into a clearing. Three fanged heads, bobbed and wove about the clearing, devouring worms, beetles and whatever else they came across. A macabre light glowed from their eyes, illuminating the night.

"You and your foolish stories. If that priest was not praying for your sorry state this instant, we would be feasting on sweeter meat," hissed the woodcutter's wife's head.

"I was trying to put him at ease," snarled the woodcutter's head.

"I will see if he has fallen asleep," said the daughter's head which flew towards the cottage.

While the one Nukekubi was gone, Kwairyo listened to the others argue over who would eat which sections of their guest.

Moments later the missing head returned, screeching that the priest was gone and the woodcutter's body was missing.

"Kill the priest. If I am to die, I shall take him with me," screeched the woodcutter's disembodied head.

Kwairyo darted deeper into the trees but his feet fell upon

dry twigs that snapped loudly, revealing his position. The beasts chased him. Unable to outrun his flying foes, Kwairyo, with a strength born of his years as a samurai, uprooted a sapling. Using the young tree as a staff, he beat back the Nukekubi until all but one fled. The woodcutter's head remained, dodging and darting, ever at the attack.

"Give up, priest, and I will make it quick," said the woodcutter.

Kwairyo's only response was to club the head once again.

Dropping low, the Nukekubi rushed Kwairyo, who was tiring with the fight. Kwairyo moved to block the attack but the beast swerved and came in from above. Kwairyo threw his arm up to protect his face and the Nukekubi fastened its teeth into the sleeve of his robe. Kwairyo swung his arm slamming the grisly head into a tree trunk. Bone crunched and Kwairyo swung again smashing the head into a boulder. Soon the Nukekubi was a bloody orb of flesh but still it snapped at Kwairyo whenever he tried to strip off the robe. Kwairyo's strength was all but spent when the sun crested the horizon. The Nukekubi screeched and died, locking its jaws to the priest's sleeve in a grip imposable to release.

Wandering lost along the mountain trails, the priest finally made his way to the safety of a town. The gruesome head still clung to his sleeve for his choice had been to walk naked through the mountains or retain the grisly burden. Stepping onto the main street he watched the town's folk cower in fear of his dishevelled appearance and the decapitated head that hung from him.

Soon the elders were called and they brought the village *torite* with them. The elders and constables stopped Kwairyo outside the inn and challenged him.

"Who are you, and how can a murderer be so bold as to show such a gruesome trophy? Many men have killed, but to wear one's victim's head as a sleeve bob is madness."

Kwairyo bowed to the elders and police. "I am Kwairyo, a priest, who was Isogai Heidazaemon Taketsura, a samurai in service to Lord Kikuji, of Kyushu. I killed this thing that clings to my sleeve, but I killed no man in doing so."

"So it was a woman, an ugly one to be sure, but that is still an evil act. As to being Isogai Taketsura you could have heard his name anywhere. He is honoured as a great samurai. All know his name. Come with us. The magistrate can judge your actions tomorrow," spoke the chief *torite*, a huge man with bulging arms and intelligent features.

Smiling Kwairyo bowed. "I will not resist, but I have done no wrong and would ask to be treated fairly until I am judged. If I am who I claim to be, am I not owed that much? And if I am not, will not your magistrate simply add to my punishment for the misrepresentation?"

"You will stay in my house this night, but be warned, you will be watched," said the chief *torite*.

Kwairyo bowed. "This is acceptable."

Kwairyo was given a simple brown *kimono* then spent the night in a comfortable house, after a good meal. The next day he was brought before the magistrate with the village elders in attendance. There he told the tale of his encounter with the Nukekubi.

The magistrate and elders listened to Kwairyo's tale then discussed his case, turning often to stare at the priest, until finally the magistrate spoke to him.

"Your story is like something I would tell my grandson to scare him away from a dangerous mountain pass. You are no priest but a murderer. I have little doubt that head belonged to the priest whose robes you stole. Then you have the gall to further compound your guilt by claiming to be Isogai Heidazaemon Taketsura. You deserve death a hundred times over for these things." The magistrate stroked his grey moustache and his liver spotted hands shook with rage.

Kwairyo bowed before he replied. "I am who I claim to be. We have met before when you came to visit my Lord Kikuji. I was new to his service. You praised me for my use of the bow when I beat your best man in practice. You were most gracious and gifted me with a silver pin."

"How can you know this?" gasped the magistrate. "Your

story is so fantastic."

"I speak only truth." Kwairyo bowed again.

Bowing, the oldest of the elders spoke. "My Lord, we have not yet examined the head. Let us look to it, for is it not written in the *Nan-ho-i-butsu-shi* that Nukekubi bear marks upon them that will reveal their true nature?"

A murmur passed among the elders and the magistrate sent for the head. It arrived and they examined it, finding the separation of the neck to be too smooth to have been made by a blade. More importantly, red runes formed a band around the dead monster's neck.

"The marks are as they are described in the *Nan-ho-i-butsu-shi*," said the oldest elder.

His case proven Kwairyo was received graciously by the magistrate and put greatly at his ease until he left to continue his wanderings.

Having read the story, I kicked myself. I'd read it a couple of years before and should have remembered. It had registered strongly with me at the time. My bias to the western mystic tradition had blinded me to these creatures of the east. I never said I was the sharpest tool in the box. The shift from a physical entity in a story to the spirit beast I saw didn't disturb me. People like their stories simple and gruesome. Creatures of spirit are forever being given physical form as the oral tradition gets twisted over the centuries.

Now I had a name and some garbled information. For a wizard, more than most, knowledge is power. It seemed likely that someplace there was a physical anchor for my prey. Find that and I could make the killings end. It is said that there is a thin line between courage and foolishness. Looking back, I can see which side I was on. My dunce cap is in the mail.

I continued my search with the pendulum and glass system of divination. Holding my crystal pendulum in a water glass, I specified one click for yes and two for no and asked my questions.

"Is a Nukekubi hunting in present day Toronto?"

One click.

"If undisturbed how often will it hunt? Every day?"

Two clicks.

"Two days?"

Two clicks.

"Three days?"

One click.

So, I knew the creature would strike every three nights. Reason told me it must hunger at that interval. How long it could exist without feeding I had no idea.

This left me faced with the question of where. I suck at dousing! Ask me to locate something on a map and you can count on the pendulum going to the farthest point from what you're looking for. I wasted a month looking for gold once. Found lots of black flies, no gold. This limitation wasn't a problem for Cathy.

The next evening I drove to her apartment. Pulling into the building's lot, I ignored the 'No Visitor' parking sign. I didn't bother to buzz. It would have forced Cathy to walk to the wall unit and I didn't want to risk aggravating her injuries. Unlocking her apartment, I opened the door a crack and called in hoping that her 'dance card' was still empty.

"It's Ray. Mind if I join you?"

"Get in here. Honestly, one little scheduling glitch and you've acted like you're entering Caligula's palace ever since! If anyone should be embarrassed about that it's me." Cathy's voice was mildly annoyed.

Stepping into her apartment, I moved to the living-room.

"It wasn't my fault. You asked me to feed your cat and didn't tell me you'd come back early." I could feel the heat of my blush.

"You could have joined us. Neither Don nor I would have minded." Cathy rolled her eyes. "Turns out, Don would have loved it." She grinned then shifted sexily on her couch. "So have you come to restore my wounded femininity?"

How anyone can make a terrycloth housecoat look so good,

especially with her calf in a cast propped up with pillows, I don't know. My eyes traced over her body, a thousand thoughts running through my mind then her words registered.

"You mean that guy...?" I took a seat in the easy chair opposite the couch.

"He's living with some guy named Frank now, and he's behaving even more feminine than me. Major turn off! I think I was his last gasp at bi."

Shaking my head I tried not to laugh but couldn't hide my smile. My jealousy may be what kept Cathy and me from becoming more than friends with benefits, but at least other barriers didn't exist.

Cathy scowled at me. "Oh shut up." There was a long pause. "It's so weird. You, me... I mean, we're acting like nothing's changed and Viv is dead. I know you tried to save her."

I sobered, Cathy had worked with Vivian, probably laughed with her, maybe even considered her a friend. To me she was a battle lost, what was she to Cathy? I ran the events of that night through my mind for the hundredth time. I'd done everything right. I could let myself off the hook, or could I?

Cathy must have sensed my mood because she tried to change the topic. "Since you're here, could you light some incense for me? I burnt the toast this morning and I can still smell it."

I nodded. "Mind if I choose an air correspondence for the incense type? I have something important to tell you about Vivian."

Cathy smiled but it was strained. "You, prince snuffles, resorting to scent magic? It must be important. There are some citron sticks in the kitchen drawer and tissues in the cupboard."

"Great, and hey, I didn't ask to have allergies." Lighting a stick and placing it in its holder, I carried it into the livingroom. "Have you heard about Terror, the new street drug?" I set the incense on the coffee table.

"It was on the news. Oh Gods, was Viv on that. She promised me she'd stopped using. I was her sponsor."

"I don't know if she was using other drugs, but Terror isn't a drug. A Nukekubi is scaring people to death then feeding off their energies."

"A whattida?" Cathy pulled herself into more of a sitting position. The front of her robe gaped, and I felt a hot flush touch my cheeks. Cathy can remind me that I'm a man without even trying. She's had that affect on me since the day I first saw her dance at a friend's stag party. The fact that I'm in love with her doesn't diminish it any, in fact it makes it stronger.

I forced my eyes to focus on her face. "Nukekubi. It's a form of Japanese goblin. In the myth they're corporeal and feed on human flesh, but you know how that goes."

Cathy took a deep breath then blew it out slowly. "Being a twentieth century Priestess of Lady Bast and Horus, speaking to a wizard Priest of Ra and Isis, this may not carry too much weight. Are you crazy? A Nukekubi, some Japanese boogie man? You've read one too many Jim Butcher books."

I looked at the floor. "I saw it, Cath. It came out of Vivian's body when I arrived. It was so, cold and dark, like a magical black hole. It made the poltergeist at Sue's seem like Casper."

I looked up and Cathy's face was serious. "I know you wouldn't kid about something like this. Ray, I don't know anything about this thing, but I know you. You're scared, and if you're scared of something magical, I trust your judgment. Leave it alone. The Gods will find someone else to deal with it. It's already taken one friend away from me. If it... I don't want to lose you."

I saw the shimmer of a tear in Cathy's eyes. I hugged her. A long time later I pulled away, and she looked at my face.

"You're going after this thing, aren't you?"

"I feel like I'm being appointed the job." I started to pace.

"Oh crap, you're pacing!"

I stopped and looked at Cathy. "So?"

"You only pace when you're really worked up about something. Sit with me." Cathy gestured towards the empty spot on the couch.

I sat. "I am worked up. Vivian died in front of me. I

couldn't save her life. Someone has to stop this thing."

"You're good, but you're not the best there is." Cathy rubbed the back of her neck. That was a real compliment. She only rubs her neck like that when she's lying. I'm not the best overall mystic we know, but where I'm strong, I'm strong. For kicking butt, I'm strong.

I smiled at her. "I know, but I may be the only one with enough of a Lancelot complex to accept the job."

"Bast's whiskers!" Cathy looked exasperated. "You don't want me to talk you out of it, so what do you need?"

I grasped her hand. I knew I could count on her, but it's always nice to be proven right. "Help in finding it. It will be hunting again tomorrow night. I'm guessing somewhere in Toronto. If I can get close enough, I know I can sense it. Your pendulum skills can tell me where I should be looking."

Cathy rolled her eyes. "The only cute guy I know that my mother will let me bring to Sunday dinner and he hunts monsters for a hobby."

"I don't think of this as a hobby."

"No. It's more like a guilt complex. Ray, let it go. You were a half-trained kid when that demon."

"No!" I heard my voice and knew what I must look like. Some things make you hard inside and out.

"You're not responsible for your grandfather's death. You—"

"I told you about that in confidence. I trusted you never to use it against me. I don't need your help. I'll find the Nukekubi on my own." I stood up. What Cathy didn't realize is how close to the bone she was cutting. She was leaving me no escape, and when cornered I lash out.

"Ray... fine! I know I'll never change you. A lifetime of therapy couldn't do that. For the record, I wasn't using it against you. I care; I hate to see you hurting."

I nodded and took a couple of deep breaths. My grandfather's death really wasn't my fault. It was my father's. He chose to marry a woman so terrified of her own abilities that she insisted he forsake the art of magic. If he'd been there, if he'd kept studying. It's all in the past, all in the past!

"Ray?" Cathy's voice was soft. She knows when to leave me with my own thoughts and when to draw me out.

"I'm okay, so how do you want to do this."

Cathy shook her head. "Men with issues, sheesh! Spread a map of Toronto on the coffee table and fetch my pendulum."

It took a few moments to set up for the work. I spread the map then set candles at each of its cardinal points. Next I retrieved Cathy's divining pendant from the altar in her bedroom. The pendant consisted of a small, quartz crystal, suspended by a gold clip at the end of a purple, silk cord.

"Pull the curtains." Cathy shuffled to a sitting position.

I hurried to comply.

"I can't promise anything. Personally, I hope you're on a wild goblin hunt." Taking the crystal in hand, she began to meditate.

Following her example, I went into a light trance and prayed to Thoth, God of wizardry, and Nephthys, Goddess of divination, to surrender the information I needed. A few moments later Cathy placed her elbow on the map and let the crystal hang, its cord suspended over her forefinger.

Her crystal moved back and forth in no particular direction then she spoke.

"If a Nukekubi exists in Toronto, where will it strike next?"

The crystal moved randomly then shifted direction indicating one area of the map. Cathy moved her elbow until the crystal centred over the section indicated. The pendant began to describe a circle about St. James Town, one of the seedier sections of Toronto. The circle shrank and became an oval then a circle surrounding about five city blocks.

"That's the best I can do." She lifted the crystal away.

"That's fine; I appreciate it." I marked the area she had indicated.

"So what do you do now?" Her voice was full of concern.

"I go hunting."

"I wish I could watch your back, but my leg says no."

"Not to worry. If anything happens to me, I'd rather you were safe." I smiled at her and caressed her cheek.

Cathy stared at me; the intensity in her emerald eyes spoke volumes. Swallowing hard, I bent to kiss her. She responded with enthusiasm. I lifted her from the couch to carry her to the bedroom.

Where does one draw the line between friend and beloved? Who can say, but can you think of a better way to kill an evening?

– Chapter 5 –

ALLIES

The next evening, I packed my mystical tools into my duffle bag and loaded it into my car. Before leaving I fetched my ritual sword from its place in my closet. I felt almost guilty bringing my sword, I'd hardly used it since I made my flail, the sword's Egyptian equivalent, but it seemed like a blade might be useful. With my weapons beside me I drove to the area Cathy had suggested. This was a run-down part of the city, populated by hookers and homeless, people who wouldn't be missed.

Parking at a donut shop, I took a seat in a pressed plastic chair. The coffee was bad, but after a few polite refusals the working girls, which came in to escape the autumn chill, pretty much left me alone. Through the large windows I watched women climb into beat-up old rust-buckets, sturdy middle-class family-cars, and limos. It was a white stretch-limo that caught my eye. A girl climbed into its back and I felt the same sensation that had led me to the Nukekubi before. I ran to my car and tailed the limo.

The limo turned down one side-street then another. Fearing I'd be seen I tried to keep back. Finally, it stopped. I waited, my hand slipping to my ceremonial sword. The girl stepped out of the car clutching a bill. The limo pulled away.

I didn't know what to do. Had I been wrong? The sense of my quarry was as strong as ever, and it definitely came from the limo. Had my prey spotted me tailing them? I was so sure of the limo. I'd even written down the plate number. Had the scene been exactly what it appeared to be, some rich bastard out for a cheap thrill?

"Damn!" I muttered, as I returned to the donut shop.

I remember parking, opening my door and starting to step out, before everything went black. My next recollection was of a sharp pain in the back of my neck, candlelight and a grubby ceiling.

"What the—" I began, displaying the full breadth of my rapier wit.

"Silence," snapped a heavily accented voice. I'd met my match for snappy comebacks.

Closing my eyes, I focussed my will then sat up, my hand in the symbol of the holy bull pointing towards the voice, and spoke, "By Horus's might, by Ra's great light, by the spells of Thoth, I command thee be off! Be gone oh demon of the pit! By the powers of the Gods and Goddesses of light. I command you be gone!"

A moment passed and as nothing happened I began to sweat. Facing me, with a hostile expression, was a young Asian man wearing a black pull-over top and jeans. The clothes did little to hide the solid muscle beneath.

"Silence!" He threw the sketchpad he held to one side and moved to hit me.

"Kunio. That will be enough. Do not aggravate your lack of thought with rudeness," snapped a voice from my right.

I turned to see an elderly Asian gentleman, with neatly trimmed grey hair and moustache. He sat in a battered easy chair wearing a housecoat.

Scowling, Kunio stepped back, allowing me to stand and look around.

The hotel room contained two double beds, one large

dresser, a pair of battered armchairs, and a mismatched set of night stands and lamps.

"Where the hell am I?" The dull throb at the back of my neck was overriding my manners and common sense.

"It is we who will ask the questions," growled Kunio.

"Enough, Kunio. Go to your meditations. Our guest and I will speak," snapped the older man.

"*Hai.*" Kunio bowed before sitting cross legged on one of the beds.

"I must be dreaming. I watched one too many theatre of thrills, martial arts marathons and I'm dreaming." My head throbbed with each beat of my heart, but I took the opportunity that being upright afforded to edge towards the door.

"You are not dreaming," replied the older man in slightly accented English.

"I was afraid of that." Sighing, I rubbed my neck. I could feel the bruised spot from the blow I assumed knocked me out. I inched closer to the exit. The door appeared to be a cheap internal one so I was pretty sure I could break through it with a running start if and when I decided to bolt.

"You may do what you can to alleviate your discomfort. Neither of us wishes you harm."

"Yeah, right. That's why my head feels like a baseball after a Blue Jays' game."

"Please. If we had meant you harm, why did we not bind you while you were unconscious?"

I thought on this then decided to take the old man at his word. I didn't have much of a choice if I wanted to figure out what was going on, and the closer I got to the door the more solid it looked. Moving to the empty bed I sat and focussed my will inwards, reducing my blood pressure and blocking nerves, slowly bringing the pain to a stop. I opened my eyes, but things still looked bad.

"You are well now?" asked the old man.

"Better than I was." I met his gaze. Even with strangers I can pick up a lot by looking into someone's eyes. They are energy focal points, and the organ of the most refined of the physical senses. The old man gave me nothing, not even a feeling. He did smile at my attempt. That told me enough. He knew some form of mysticism. The old coot blocked me, which meant my bag of tricks became a lot smaller.

The elder raised his bone rack of a frame from the chair and began to pace the floor.

"Why have you kidnapped me?" I demanded.

"We have not kidnapped you. You are free to leave. Your car is parked in front of the hotel, and your bag is in the washroom."

"My implements!" I bolted towards the washroom. The sudden movement brought a bolt of pain that was less than welcome.

"I regret the necessity of opening your bag. It was essential I learn your nature." The old man stood in the bathroom door and watched as I inspected my bag's contents.

"You, sir, have the nerve of Apep at midnight." I glared at the old fart.

Kunio leapt up from where he was pretending to meditate and moved to his Master's side. "Do not speak to the Master like that!"

I was getting mad. "Shut up, Kunio, or by every God there ever was, I'll turn you into a frog! Knock me out. Threaten me. That's bad enough, but to root through my ritual tools. Ra's beak! Have you people no decency?"

Kunio stepped back open mouthed. I don't think anyone had ever threatened to turn him into a frog before.

"Kunio, I doubt he could do it. Still, we have imposed major discourtesies upon our guest. Please put on the kettle and make us all some tea, while I explain things to him."

"Explain to me. This should be good." I finished inspecting my ritual implements and reset the closing spell on the bag.

"That is a useful enchantment you use to make the zipper stick for any but yourself. I found it most troublesome when attempting to open the bag." The old man motioned for me to exit the bathroom and take a seat.

"It's supposed to make it damn near impossible. Now you said something about explaining." I admit, I stomped to the chair like a bull in a bad mood.

The old guy smiled at me. I felt calm radiate out of him. I've been around enough to recognise empathic manipulation when it hits me. I shrugged off his spell. For the first time I saw surprise pierce that calm demeanour. I bumped up my shields in a show of strength as he spoke.

"Please indulge an elder first. Why were you following the white limousine?"

"No. I've indulged you enough by not storming out of here and calling the cops, and you can take a guess at what you can do with your empathic manipulation. I'm not out cold anymore, and no one is sneaking up behind me. You owe me an explanation."

The old guy smiled wider and shrugged. "As you Canadians say. 'It was worth a try.' You are right. First, let me apologize for Kunio. He is young and often reacts instead of thinking. I never would have condoned him taking you by force. He struck before I could intercede. He thought it best to take you quickly so that others would not interfere. Let me assure you the reason he brought you here is a noble one. I have been chasing an old foe. He was in the vehicle you were following."

I didn't know quite what to think. The pair in the room with me were a strange mix of B-rate, martial arts film, and low-budget tourist. Then again, who would believe a wizard chasing ghosties and ghoulies around downtown Toronto? I decided to play along.

"Your foe, is he a Nukekubi?"

The old man looked surprised then nodded.

"Yes, a Nukekubi, so you know what it is."

"I encountered it several nights ago. It was emerging from its kill. From what the papers have to say, it has been here a while hunting every third night."

"You are astute, my young friend. I assume you decided you must stop the beast." The old man steepled his fingers and looked thoughtful.

"Who else is there? Do you think the police would believe a spirit force feeding off peoples' terror and death energies?"

"Alas, no. You have courage, that I must give you; and it is apparent you have at least some skill in the use of the *ki*."

"I am a wizard priest of the Egyptian path." I spoke with authority and pulled my dignity around me like a cloak. Done right, with the gullible, this will transform you into a being of power and mystery in their eyes. With this crowd, I was hoping to be taken as a force not to be dismissed simply because I was different.

"Yes. Your bag's contents told me you were some kind of a mystic."

"You're learning a lot more about me than I am about you. Who are you? What are you? Most importantly, what are you going to do about everybody's favourite, flying basketball?" I slapped the mattress for emphases, but the effect was ruined when moving my shoulder triggered the pain in my neck and I grimaced.

"I will answer your questions once Kunio has served the tea."

Kunio returned from the washroom, bearing a platter with a steaming teapot, three cups and an open box of tea bags on it. He had walked up so quietly that I had been unaware of him.

"Please, everyone, be seated," suggested the older gentleman.

"Master." Bowing Kunio laid the platter on the floor and took a seat beside it.

I sat on the floor with my two 'hosts', half expecting some long drawn-out ceremony. It was gratifying when I was offered my choice of herbal teas and hot water was poured into the cups. The old man sipped his tea and smiled.

"You wished to know of us. I am Yoshida Toshiro. You may call me Toshiro, and, as I am sure you have guessed, this is my disciple, Sasaki Kunio."

Kunio gave his head the slightest of dips and said, "You may call me Sasaki."

He almost caught me, but I knew just enough about Japanese customs to know the family name came first, and I'd be damned if I was going to start calling this kid Mr. anything. "Right, Kunio. Let's keep it friendly. You can call me Ray. Now that we all have convenient labels what in Ra's name are you?"

Toshiro chuckled and Kunio went red faced but held his

tongue.

A moment passed before Toshiro spoke. "We are practitioners of *ninjitsu*. My training began before the war and I have continued my studies since.

"It was during World War Two I first encountered the Nukekubi. I was fourteen, in the infantry, stationed in the Marianas. Germany had fallen and we would soon follow. How well I remember. We were dug into our position with artillery from the American ships bursting around us, lighting the night sky with fires. The cries of the wounded sounded all about me. There were not enough medics to treat them. My best friend, Onami, was hit in the back with a shell fragment. He died in my arms. Then the American troops came. They shot. We shot back. Farm boys from the rice paddies killing and being killed by farm boys from the corn fields. Why, my sons? I pray you never see such a thing." Toshiro's eyes were far away and his voice, the pain.

Toshiro continued. "As night fell the Americans held the beaches and we were in the forest. I left my foxhole to answer the commands of nature and in hopes of finding a quiet place where I could mourn my friend. It was then I saw them. There were three of them and they were attacking a group of Americans who were trying to sneak to our rear. I had learned to open my spirit eyes before enlisting. I watched horror-stricken as the spiritual heads and hands flew at the Americans. They were screaming in terror, panicked. Their *ki* convulsed around them a sickly yellow. They became nothing save vessels of fear. The men were the enemy, but to die at the hands of those creatures seemed somehow, unholy!

"The Nukekubi bobbed and darted as the Americans shot wildly. Bullets, so deadly, but against a creature of spirit, ineffectual." Toshiro shook his head.

"One of the heads sank into an officer. He screamed then turned his gun on himself. The bullet made a hole as large as my fist when it exited the body. There was blood and gore everywhere. The officer fell as the other Nukekubi slid into soldiers causing them to turn their guns on each other. I retched as the beasts absorbed the energies of death and fear released. They must have heard me because they rose from their grizzly feast of mystic energies. They cast a sickly glow in the night and spoke to one another in hissing whispers. I will never forget what they said.

"'A sound, friends, another morsel perhaps?' said the first.

"'Like as not a scampering creature. Let us finish this tender feast,' replied a second.

"'Mayhap another barbarian,' spoke a third.

"'Or one of the children, but who will tell? In this age none of our troops would believe,' observed the first.

"'Yes, it is one of ours. I recognize him. Run away, little mortal. Today we are allies. We have no need to eat our own, but if you speak I will find you and eat you!'

"I ran back to my foxhole. The next day the fighting overran the place where the Nukekubi had had their feast. A few more bodies were not a thing for comment.

"Shortly after that the bomb was dropped on Hiroshima, killing my family, then Nagasaki, for no reason. We would have surrendered. One does not fight the *tai-fun*. The war was over, our cities were in ruins, our nation defeated and shamed.

"I took a job teaching the *ninjitsu* I had learned in my childhood, to the children of those wealthy enough to afford such luxury. Rebuilding commenced, and six years later I married my lovely Sumi. We lived in a small house, just outside the city.

"One evening, two years later, Sumi did not return from her walk in the wood that our house backed onto. It was a small wood with no large or dangerous animals. We both would stroll down its leafy trails, enjoying its peace. I went in search of her and found only her remains, face down in a stream. As I turned her over, a glowing head and hands rose from her chest. The police said she had slipped and hit her head but I knew what had done this to my wife. I vowed they would pay."

Tears touched Toshiro's cheeks and his voice trembled as he spoke of his Sumi. All those years past and you could still see the love. My heart bled for him. If there is any justice in the universe, I prayed that they would be reunited when the time comes. Glancing at Kunio, I could see concern mirrored in his features. Even then I could say one thing for him, he loved his Master.

Toshiro's voice steadied as he continued his story. "My experience in the army had sparked my interest in the spirit beasts of my land. I studied the Nukekubi and their long list of misdeeds. The blood of innocents is their only legacy." Toshiro's voice lost all softness and his face became harsh lines as he spoke.

"I began my hunt. Taking a consecrated staff as my weapon, I combed the forest by night searching for the sickly energy of fear that the beasts radiate.

"Having wandered the woods and surrounding neighbourhoods for many days, I saw a man signing for a delivery behind a restaurant that catered to unsavoury individuals. He glowed with the sickly-yellow energy of the Nukekubi. That night I waited, and the next, the third night the monstrosities took flight through an attic window. I crept to the door and smashed a window to gain entry. The place was dark, but my eyes soon adjusted. Searching, I found two bodies lying senseless upon a futon in the apartment above the kitchen. They didn't wake no matter how I shook them, and they had the runes encircling the neck and each wrist that mark the Nukekubi. I thought of hiding the bodies then a better idea came to me. Descending to the basement, I blew out the pilot light on the water heater. Using my staff, I smashed the flow regulator, allowing the gas to leak into the house. Running up the stairs to the kitchen, I turned the oven on then left.

"I heard the explosion and I joined those running to gawk at the flames. A sweet taste filled my mouth as my enemies burned. The next morning, when the flames were out, I once more hid in the bushes by the house. Two Nukekubi returned just before sunrise. They screamed and screeched as the sun crested the horizon before exploding in a flash of light. They were no more. Since that day I have hunted the Nukekubi, wherever they may be. Now I am here to continue my hunt."

Toshiro wasn't just an old man at that moment. He was the embodiment of his fight, the triumph, the sorrow, and the tragedy, but mostly a horrible sense of duty. I'd seen that look on my grandfather a few times. I could only give one response. "If I can aid you, I will."

"We do not need the help of some fool adventurer," snapped Kunio.

"Be not too hasty, my son. I am no longer young. Mayhap in this fight our guest can be of assistance." Toshiro took a sip of tea and eyed me as if I was a used car he was thinking of buying.

"Master, he has no cause to fight the beasts as we do." Kunio slammed his fist into the floor.

"Yet still he offers. Is he fool, adventurer, or brave friend? This is what we must learn."

"I offer because it is my duty to guard this plane. My Gods expect it of me, and frankly, I expect it of myself." I sat up straight and tried not to sound pompous. I probably failed, but I tried.

"That is well said. Let us speak so I might better understand how heavily we may lean upon you in our need."

"Just one more thing, how did you find out that there was a Nukekubi in Toronto? A few drug related deaths isn't exactly international news."

"We bargained with a *Rokurokubi* for the information, as if it was any of your business." Kunio was really beginning to get on my pecks.

I looked at Toshiro. "A rokuro wadda?"

"They are a type of beast akin to the Nukekubi but less evil in nature." Toshiro shrugged. "You do what you must."

"We should have killed that beast long ago." Kunio's voice was vehement.

"Kunio, Amaya kills only those who abuse women or children. You must learn that some monsters are as human as you or I. What she does is little different from what we ourselves do. Also, if we were to kill her we would lose a valuable resource in our battle. Her information has helped us often in the past."

"So this informant put you on the trail. I've watched enough cop shows to know how that works." I made a mental note to read up on Rokurokubi as soon as I could. I had too many blind spots in my knowledge when it came to the east.

We spent what remained of the night discussing theology, mysticism and philosophy. It was a pleasant way to spend the night, but under the circumstances it seemed a waste of time. That was the first thing Kunio and I ever agreed on. Just before sun up Toshiro and I were involved in a discussion of the purpose of man's earthly existence. I had just made a statement about how memories being blocked between incarnations was a system to help preserve sanity, when Toshiro smiled and interrupted me.

"I am pleased to learn The West has its own wisdom. We are indeed brothers walking different roads to the same village. Your help is most welcome in our quest."

"Master, no! What good can he be to us? He knows nothing of the martial arts. He will be a liability."

"Kunio, have you been sitting with ears closed? Our friend has other skills which may aid us. If nothing else his vehicle and courage will make him a valuable asset. Remember our foe drives. You are too young to rent a car and I have no license. We must have a car to track our enemy. Above this, he has proven he can sense the Nukekubi. He will serve as your guide as you search for the monster's lair. I have come to find such activities tiring."

There was a short and obviously heated exchange in Japanese which ended with Toshiro raising his voice and Kunio sharply bowing and going to his bed.

I then I realized that while allies in my quest probably increased my chances for success, they might just be more of a pain than they were worth. I also came to the conclusion that when it came to partners, Cathy offered a load of advantages Kunio didn't. For one, I thought she looked a lot better walking away. With a sigh, I rose to fetch my tattered sleeping bag from the back of my car so I could grab a couple of hours of sleep before our next hunt. I'd arranged to have my shifts covered, so why waste it?

– Chapter 6 –

FIRS+ LEAD

I awoke shortly after noon with a crick in my neck, dressed and crept from the room not wanting to wake Toshiro and Kunio.

Ignoring the dinginess of the hotel's lobby, I made my way to the street. Beside the hotel was a café with an all day breakfast. I took a seat in a booth opposite the counter and ordered sausage, eggs and toast, while I examined the morning paper. There was no mention of Terror, well, aside from what the crime section of the paper instils in me naturally. I often wonder if the monsters aren't better than us. Generally they're feeding, humans are just mean.

I returned to the hotel room to find my allies in the midst of their own meal, consisting mainly of brown rice. Yes, Kunio will probably outlive me, but if I have to eat like that I don't care.

Pulling my Norse Runes from my bag I spread my blue diviner's cloth and put them onto it face down. The Runes are the alphabet of the ancient Teutonic people, and while there are several varieties, I like the elder Futhark. They're more than an alphabet. Each letter is an archetypal symbol representing some aspect of life. Praying to Nephthys, Egyptian Goddess of divination, and Odin, lord of the Runes, I filled my mind with my hunt, picked five runes at random and laid them in an elemental cross pattern. Three across, one above and one below.

The past, far left, came up *Peorth* reversed, an unpleasant surprise, black magic. I was reminded of the Gods' two major attributes. One of which is a sense of humour, just look at humans for confirmation, the other a talent for understatement. The present, middle, was *Need*, delay, and the future, far right, was *Ur*, testing and conflict. Helpful influences, above, were *Tir*, courage and the warrior spirit, and hurtful things, below, were *Mann* reversed, lack of trust, bigotry.

One annoying thing about divination is how often it tells you what you already knew.

"What does your divination reveal?" asked Toshiro, from directly behind me.

I almost jumped out of my skin.

"Nothing of great use. I think our quarry managed to feed last night. We'll have to wait three more days before it strikes again."

"This is unfortunate."

"Tell me about it. I'm going to end up missing more work than I can afford over this. I'll have to get people to cover my shifts. Can I use your phone?"

"Of course. Kunio and I will be doing Tai Chi if it will not disturb you."

"Fine, can I have the floor for my Yoga when you're done?"

"Yes, then we must decide our course of action."

Kunio emerged from the washroom where he had been cleaning the dishes. "Your western stones reveal nothing. You should use a real system like the I Ching, or is it beyond you?"

I could see that Toshiro was preparing to admonish him by the way the old man was puffing up but I beat him to it.

"The Runes do tell me one thing. If we waist our energy tearing into each other like bigoted twits we'll fail, but if we try to get along and show each other some respect we might just have a shot. Ask yourself which is more important to you, being a jackass or getting the Nukekubi?"

Kunio looked as if he was going to retort but Toshiro stopped him with a fiery glance.

"We should commence with our exercises." Toshiro moved to the centre of the floor. Kunio followed him and they both started into the slow rhythmic motions of Tai Chi. I'd done a little Tai Chi, enough to know it's not as easy as it looks. I'd rather swim.

I made my calls then settled in to watch my allies. Toshiro seemed to float through the exercises, the dingy room disappearing into his concentration. Then there was Kunio, who in any other company would have been a living work of art, struggling to emulate the quiet perfection of his Master. I felt something for Kunio then. Whether he acknowledged it or not, we were brothers in a way. We both wanted to be better than we were, needed something to strive for to be complete. Don't worry, be happy, would never be our motto. Cool.

Toshiro finished his routine then had Kunio start again. This time Toshiro corrected Kunio's actions, suggesting minor alterations, noting imperfections too small for the layman's eye to distinguish. It was all I could do to keep from applauding when they finished.

Toshiro and Kunio relinquished the floor and I began my Yoga routine, which now seemed clumsy and disjointed. I finished with a short body meditation.

"Do you still believe our young friend will be a liability?" asked Toshiro as I finished my meditation.

"There are the beginnings of something there, Master, but it will not serve him in battle." Kunio laid his sketchpad to one side.

Toshiro sighed, and smiled at me. "I have been privileged to see a demonstration of Yoga before. I am pleased to see what I have. A bit rough in places, but overall the flow of your *ki* was impressive."

I couldn't think of how to reply, so I smiled, said, "Thanks," and hit the shower.

I emerged to find Kunio and Toshiro meditating. Kunio's sketchpad was lying open on the dresser. The revealed page contained an incredible likeness of me, poised halfway through the Yoga sun salutation. Impressed, I examined the piece more closely. With a silent wish that I could draw I joined my allies in meditation. Actually, I performed meditation's less famous brother: contemplation.

Prayer is said to be talking to the Gods, meditation is listening for the reply. Contemplation is letting them, or your subconscious if you prefer, direct your thoughts. Those are as good a set of definitions as any. Lying there, body relaxed and mind cleared, I let the facts I had about the Nukekubi float freely in my mind.

It had to feed regularly. It travelled in a limo, which meant money. It didn't loot the bodies of its victims, which meant it already had money and no shortage of it. Why are bad guys so often rich? Inconsequential thought, return to main line.

The limo came to dominate my musings. I had its license plate number, but I couldn't run it without police assistance. PDs James and Waite were unlikely to help me on the basis of our friendly association. The car was luxuriant and looked new. I couldn't remember a scratch on it. Was it the same one from the strip club? Maybe, a limo purchased or leased a little before the first Terror death was reported. Purchased, leasing would mean dealer maintenance; a private mechanic would be safer in case some evidence got left in the limo. We could check the places selling limos in the area and see what came up.

When I rose, I presented my insights to my companions who had also risen from the depths and were sipping yet more tea.

"Hmmm... yes. I can see how the places that sell that particular vehicle might be of use to us, but how will you know who to ask for?" Toshiro set his empty cup on the tray and stroked his moustache.

"I won't, but that car couldn't have been on the road more than a month. It was immaculate, not a scratch anywhere. All we have to do is discover which dealerships sold a car like that in the last... How long ago do you think the Nukekubi came to Toronto?"

Kunio sorted and gave me a look that called the intelligence of my family into question for six generations.

"I would say from the reports in the newspaper and other information you have not had access to," Toshiro shot Kunio a quelling look, "perhaps two months."

I slapped my hands together. "Bingo. If we can reference the license plate number against the dealer's record, we should have him."

"Would the one who sold the car have such a record?" Toshiro seemed guardedly hopeful.

"My Dad bought a new car last year. He couldn't take it off the lot until he filled out the plate number on the paper work. Believe me, Canada lives on bureaucracy."

I had barely finished talking when Kunio dove for the phone book. He practically ripped it open. A few frantic moments of leafing through the pages later he looked at Toshiro and said, "Master, there is nothing under vehicle."

"Try 'automobile,'" I suggested.

Kunio flipped through the pages muttering something in Japanese, which Toshiro diligently ignored.

I knew how Kunio felt. I was born to the English language and I dread a trip through the phone book.

Half an hour later we started calling around, trying to isolate the dealerships that had sold a white stretch limo in the last two months. Simple, right? Wrong! We had a hell of a time getting the dealers to tell us anything. Finally, we came up with a story about a business acquaintance who had just bought such a vehicle and how we were interested in doing the same. Toshiro's accent had the dealers swallowing this hook, line and sinker. Once we finished phoning we had four possibilities.

We took to the streets. Toshiro dressed in a formal suit, hoping the dealers would take him for a wealthy businessman. He looked the part, but my battered skateboard with attitude blew our cover the moment they saw us. It really didn't matter. All we had to do was determine whether or not a sale had actually been made then a greased palm would do the rest.

The first dealership was a phoney. The salesman's aura lit

up like Rudolph's nose, big, bright and red when he claimed to have sold a limo. We left with the muttered curses of the salesman behind us. The next place was better. They had sold a white stretch limo in the specified time. Passing a fifty-dollar bill to the place's girl Friday resulted in us getting a peek at the sales agreement. The plate number didn't match so we were onto contestant number three.

The salesman was a large, blond fellow with capped teeth, a too perfect nose, wearing a suit. He watched us pull up and managed to hide his annoyance in having a customer this late in the day under his inebriation.

"Hello. Can I help you gentlemen?" He spoke to Toshiro, but his breath made my eyes water. He must have had at least a three-cocktail coffee break. Mints can only cover so much.

Toshiro leaned back to get fresh air before he replied. "We are interested in a white stretch limousine. An acquaintance of mine recently purchased one. Are you aware of having sold such a vehicle within the last two months?"

The salesman smiled and nodded. "That I am. It was a honey of a car, fully loaded. It cost a packet though. If it proves a little rich we have a pre-owned division on the other side of the lot."

I was watching with my mystic eyes peeled and no red touched his aura. I nodded to Toshiro.

"Yes the vehicle my acquaintance bought is remarkable. Can you tell me more about this 'fully loaded' limousine?"

I watched as emotional energy poured off Toshiro stroking the salesman's aura. I added my own empathic push. For once it looked like something was going to be easy.

"Sure I can. I'm Tim by the way, and you three?"

Toshiro lied smoothly. "I am Mr. Yoshida. This is my son Kunio and his friend, Ray. Ray kindly offered to take over my regular driver's duties when he took ill. Unfortunately, the company insurance doesn't extend to him so we have to use his personal vehicle. Still, it is better than having someone I do not know or trust behind the wheel. I have a — how is it said in English? — 'a thing' about that."

I was impressed. Toshiro accounted for all our shortcomings and made himself a person the salesman would want to cater to. He was good. Of course if Tim was sober or we weren't playing his emotions like a baby-grand he probably wouldn't have bought it.

"It's good to have friends," commented Tim.

Kunio took that moment to scowl at me. I kept mentally stroking Tim's aura.

"I would like to confirm that this is the establishment my acquaintance purchased his vehicle from. He has been known to mislead me in the past. Something of a rivalry. Could I see the sales agreement?"

Tim shifted from foot to foot. Toshiro and I kept up the empathic pressure.

"We'll, I'm not supposed to. My father-in-law left me in charge and those records are supposed to be confidential. I could get in a lot of trouble. Does it really matter? I'll sell you a top-flight vehicle. Even better than the one I sold two months back. No, I don't think I can let you see the sales agreement, but I could copy the features section so you know you're getting everything and more than he got."

Tim dithered as Toshiro and I worked on him keeping just short of will domination.

"Maybe an added incentive, just to move things along." I opened my wallet and pulled out a twenty.

"You trying to insult me?"

I added two more twenties. "Of course not, we just really need to see the sales agreement. To be sure we're in the right place."

Tim may have been a drunk but he was a salesman through and through. I'm sure he mostly worked the used, excuse me, pre-owned side of the lot. He fit the bill. He dithered some more. I felt that he was about to crack.

"This is ridiculous! Allow me to deal with this pig, Master." Kunio moved forward in a menacing way. I almost buried my face in my hands as all the empathic manipulation shattered.

"I can take care of myself, boy. If I have to, I'll..." Tim fell silent mouth agape as Kunio belted the side panel of my car, caving it in.

"Kunio! Next time, don't help!" My car didn't look much worse than it did before, but still. I turned to Tim adding an extra twenty to the ones in my hand. Gentle was no longer an option. "Here's the deal, we get two minutes with the sales agreement, no one will ever know and we pull Kunio out of here before the day gets unpleasant. Why make life miserable?"

Glancing from Kunio to my money Tim decided discretion was the better part of valour.

"You'll leave me out of it?"

Toshiro stopped shaking his head at Kunio long enough to answer. "Without any question."

Kunio looked contrite.

There would be a stern lesson taught by Toshiro when I wasn't around to hear it. As it should be. My father would have bawled me out in front of my peer. Kunio could have done worse for a guardian.

"I'll get you a copy. Just vamoose as soon as I give it to you." I'm sure poor old Tim thought he was tied up with some organised crime feud or something. Still, it didn't stop him from taking my money. Kraft Dinner for another month. Oh yay!

We left the lot minutes later with a piece of paper telling us the limo was purchased by the Franklin Group, an investment agency that had been operating in Toronto for over half a century.

I pulled up in front Toshiro's hotel as night was closing in. All I wanted to do was get home and hit the sheets. I'd caught about four hours or so between sunrise and my waking up after noon. It wasn't enough. My allies climbed from my car and I promised to return when our foe was next scheduled to hunt then pulled away.

Home is a special place after one has been knocked out, threatened and kept up all night. I opened my door and Sekmara pounced, snagging my pant leg and demanded immediate and all-encompassing attention. This filled the next twenty minutes, before she, with tail high, stalked off in a way that left no doubt I was being punished for leaving her alone for so long. Just like a woman, only fuzzier.

I played my messages.

My father had called, twice. Since Kim, my sister, left home, my parents actually had to talk to each other. A thing they wanted to avoid at all costs. I still hoped the poor bugger would wise up and divorce my mother. I knew for a fact they'd fought constantly for the last twenty years. Before that I couldn't remember. Oh well, I was out of it now.

Tracy, a girl who lifeguarded at the same pool as I did, left a message telling me exactly what she thought of me. Surprising the language a young lady will use upon occasion. I'd filed a complaint about her when I caught her in the office eating when she should have been on pool deck.

Last but not least, Cathy had called asking that I call her back. So I did. The phone went to her machine before she picked up.

"Hello."

"Hey Cath, you said you wanted me to call."

"Ray, that is you, right?"

"Yup, last time I checked. What's up?"

"My temper you inconsiderate jerk!" I felt like a heel and didn't know why. Her voice almost broke on the phone. "You run off to hunt some beast that considers people an entrée and you don't even call."

"Cathy..."

"Don't you 'Cathy' me! I was worried sick! I did another divination and it said that thing had eaten and that you were in a difficult situation. I thought you were dead. You should have called me!"

"Sorry, mother."

"Don't get lippy with me! I'm concerned. That's why I worry. If you're going monster hunting the least you can do is keep me up to date."

"You're right." She really wasn't, but often it's easier to just say the words and move on. It did feel good to know she cared so much. "I made two allies from Japan who have been hunting Nukekubi for years. Getting them to accept me was the difficult situation. The damn creature did feed and to make matters worse, I think it's rich. I'll be going after it again in two days. I was rather busy, that's why I didn't call. I'm sorry. Did your divination turn up anything else about the Nukekubi?"

"No. When I thought you'd gone to the Summer Land I got too upset to keep my concentration.... Ray, be careful. I'd miss you if you weren't around."

"That's good to know. Do you need me over there?"

The line was quiet for a long time. "You have work tomorrow, don't you?"

"Yeah." Sekmara jumped on my lap. I don't think Cathy realized that the male voice in the background carried over the phone line.

"You should get your rest. Come by tomorrow."

I tried to stuff my heart back into my chest as the female in my life that understood loyalty started to purr. "Okay. I'm expecting a call from Toshiro. He's one of my allies, so I should get off the line. You be careful and get that leg better."

"Bye, Ray, and watch your back."

Hanging up, I breathed a heavy sigh, fed Sekmara and went to bed.

The next day was normal, except for my boss asking why I was taking so much time off. I told him as long as I covered the few hours he'd left me it was none of his business. He was pissed, I didn't care. The paper made no mention of Terror. It was past five when I dropped into my apartment to call Toshiro. I dialed, waited while it rang, then Kunio picked up.

"Hello."

"Hey Kunio, this is Ray. May I speak to Toshiro?"

There was a brief discussion in Japanese then the phone was passed.

"Ray, this is Toshiro."

"I wanted to find out how things were going."

"I called the Franklin Group. Following much effort they told me they had purchased it for their parent firm, the

Atterson Corporation, in Ottawa. I called the Atterson Corporation; they are apparently an import-export firm. They were not helpful in the least. They moved my call from office to office and finally told me nothing."

"Departmental shuffle, the best way to waste your time and keep you in the dark. I swear large corporations must have learned it from the government."

"That may be but it does not help us. I feel that this line of investigation will not bear fruit."

"Could be. Tell you what. Give me the company names and let me have a go. I have someone who owes me a favor that might have more luck."

Toshiro read out the names letter by letter, so I'd be sure to get the spelling right, and I jotted them down. This done we made arrangements to meet at his hotel for the next hunt and hung up.

Taking a deep breath to steady myself, I called Sue, Cathy's high school friend of poltergeist fame. She was doing a Masters in business administration at McMaster. On the fourth ring she picked up.

"It's your fifty cents."

"Hey, Sue, this is Ray. Ray McAndrues, Cathy's friend."

"Ray, how you doing? All's still quiet on the spooky front."

"I'm good, and glad to hear it. Um, I need a favor."

"What?" Her guarded tone wounded me. Too many people are willing to take without giving. It's why the world's a mess.

"Hey, I'm not asking for your first born or anything." Cathy got hurt helping her, so I didn't even try to keep the anger out of my voice.

"Shit, you're right, sorry. I do owe you one. What's up?"

My tone mellowed. "I need you to trace down a corporate ownership tree. The start points are the Franklin Group and the Atterson Corporation. I need a list of any subsidiaries, board of directors, major stockholders. The whole bit. I'm trying to track where something purchased by one of the branches might end up. Oh yes, the company I'm looking for would probably have a Japanese base of operations."

"That's a hell of a favor, Ray."

"Has anything tried to throw a chair at you in the last couple of days?"

"Right. You're right. I'm just not use to being the one owing. I've met too many people that take, take, take and never give back. I'm a little gun shy where favors are concerned."

And now I felt like a shit because I got annoyed. I knew where she was coming from, obviously felt the same way. "Sorry I... I know how you feel is all. I wouldn't ask except it is really important."

"No problem. I did come off, a little, as an ungrateful bitch. I... Well. You hear stories, and the stuff you and Cathy are into is kinda weird."

I hated talking on the phone. Face to face I probably would have sensed the fear in her. "No worries. For the record, I believe in the law of three. 'What so ever you put into the life of others shall be revisited into your own three times, three times good, three times bad.'"

"Sounds like the golden rule."

"Truth is truth no matter how you phrase it. I really need this favor. It's important."

"Sure. What the heck. I was thinking of going into corporate forensics. It should be good practice. Let me write down the company names."

A few minutes later I hung up and left to join Cathy for dinner. The next morning I went home, wrote out my will, gathered my strength and packed my equipment before driving to Toronto to rejoin my allies.

– Chapter 7 –

KUNIO'S STORY

J arrived at Toshiro's hotel to find Kunio sitting in a worn out, high-backed chair in the dingy lobby. The desk attendant, a balding obese man in a grubby shirt, hardly glanced away from the TV when I came in.

"We should go now," opened Kunio, as soon as I approached him.

"Isn't Toshiro joining us?"

"No. He said since you can sense the Nukekubi he would let you lead me to it. My Master needs his rest." Kunio stood, grabbed his fighting staff from where it leaned against the wall and started for the door.

I shrugged and followed him.

Once outside I had to take the lead. He didn't know where I'd parked. I swear we almost came to blows about putting his staff on my roof racks. Finally, the fact that it was the only way to carry it with my car put the argument to rest. As we drove around Toronto Kunio fell into a deep sulk. He was really beginning to piss me off. After about an hour cruising the city's sleaziest sections, I pulled to the side of the road.

"Kunio, I can't sense a thing like this. Can you drive so I can go into a more receptive state?"

"Of course I can drive." Kunio sneered at me.

"What in the names of the forty-two assessors is your problem? We're in this together, you know?"

"My Master did not come because of you. Now I must battle this beast alone. You have no stake in this. The Nukekubi are not your battle."

"I haven't seen your hunting license either bub."

"I do not wish to discuss this further."

"Fine. Just stop being a number-one, grade-A prick. We're on the same side. So what if I don't have a personal score? I have a sense of responsibility that should be enough."

"A sense of responsibility will not strengthen you against the horrors you will face as vengeance would."

"You mean Toshiro? I'm not trying to take his place. I'm pretty sure he's got you pegged for that job, if you'll just start using your head."

"I mean like myself. And save your opinions." Kunio stared resolutely out the front windscreen. I think I'd scored. Kunio was a deadly weapon, but he needed to think to become a warrior. At that point he was pretty much point and shoot.

"What? Kunio, I'm sorry if I hit a nerve." One of us had to be the grown up and I was a few years older. Oh yeah, I get to be responsible again.

"The Nukekubi have harmed me as well as my Master."

"I'm sorry. If you'd rather not talk about it—"

"No. You demanded to know my reasons, now you must listen to my tale."

I sighed inwardly. The fact that I hadn't demanded anything didn't matter. In Kunio's mind I had, so I was obliged to play along if there was to be any peace between us.

"I was only a child of five when it happened. My Otoosan...Father was a teacher and my Mother kept his house, as a good wife should. They were wonderful people, very kind and my mother was so beautiful. I have a picture of her. Here, look at her."

Kunio paused in his narrative to extract a photograph from his jeans back pocket. The picture showed a smiling Asian couple with a small house in the background. The woman was middling attractive and there was a baby in her arms.

Studying the picture I nodded, muttered something about them being a handsome couple and passed it back to Kunio who glared at me.

"We were driving from my uncle's place in the hills to our house in Tokyo when my father lost control of the car." Kunio drummed his fingers on the dashboard as he sought the word he wanted. "It was raining and the roads were slippery."

"Rain-slicked roads," I provided.

Kunio continued his story. "Yes, those are the words. We shot over an embankment and crashed into a steep-sided ravine. The car stopped and we were all alive, but the smell of gasoline was everywhere. My father asked my mother if she had seen it. He swore he had swerved to miss something then ordered us from the car. No sooner had he opened his door than a Nukekubi fell upon him. The beast screamed and we were all thrown into a panic.

"I watched that thing enter my father and take him over. He tried to fight it, but the beast was too strong. It did not just kill my father; it drove him from his body and took it over. I watched my father's form clutch my mother's throat. She opened the door and pushed me out. I ran."

"You were a child; there wasn't anything else you could have done." I tried to be soothing.

"I know that!" Kunio snapped at me. I understood better than he could know the place he was coming from. To know is one thing, to feel it deep down that's another.

Kunio took several deep breaths before continuing. "Soon I could run no more so I hid behind a boulder. By then the beast had finished with my mother. The feast of terror it must have had as she was strangled by the form of the man she loved...

"My father's body moved down the ravine. The movements were jerky and uneven. The beast was unaccustomed to his size and shape. My mother had left her mark, gouging strips from his face and arms. He taunted me telling me to 'come to Daddy' but it was not my father's voice. Not his words. He was upon me when a miracle happened. A mighty warrior charged down the ravine and struck him with a *ninjato*. I later learned the blade was blessed in the name of Amaterasu. The wounds it left in my father's form did not bleed, he was already dead, but the beast within him screeched in agony from the touch of that blessed blade.

"My father's form fought like the demon that possessed it, but the warrior was more than its match. He sliced the tendons that held my father's corpse's arms and legs, and when the beast tried to rise from its stolen body the warrior threw a powder over the broken form and it was trapped within it.

"The creature begged for its life. He called the warrior Shadow Death and said he was making me orphan. Shadow Death replied that the Nukekubi had already done that and that he gave me revenge. As the sun rose I watched my father's form scream a final time. The beast within him seemed to burn in Amaterasu's clean light. Then it was over. My parents were dead and I was alone.

"I looked to the warrior and knew my life would never be the same. I asked him simply, "teach me." My first lesson was a harsh one. I had to help burn my parents' remains. No trace could be left for the authorities to mistakenly tie Shadow Death to them."

This set a little bell ringing in the back of my head. I dismissed it focusing on Kunio instead. The man was almost in tears. I didn't blame him but didn't know how to help him either.

"Shadow Death is the name the evil beasts have given my Master. He has been father and more to me ever since. We have lived, moving from one city to another, forever hunting the tribe of horrible monstrosities that murdered my parents. Now my quest brings me here, far from my home. Now I fight for you filthy *hakujin*."

"I am honestly sorry about your parents, Kunio, but why hate Caucasians?"

"My ancestors lived in Hiroshima. The graves of my family are lost to me. Need I say more?"

"My grandfather lost a leg in World War II, and I don't hate Germans," I replied then fell silent for a time. "Kunio, you don't have to like me, but you can at least help me, for the good of our quest. Take over the driving so I can concentrate on sensing our enemy, okay?"

"Yes, I can do this, but when we find our quarry, you are to stay out of my way. I will not endanger the success of this mission to rescue you."

"Understood, now let's change seats."

– Chapter 8 –

R⊕UND ⊕NE

I dropped into a trance and scanned the area as Kunio drove. Nearly an hour later I felt the eerie, somewhat nauseous, feeling I'd come to associate with the Nukekubi. It was fleeting, less intense than my previous encounters with the beast, but there.

I told Kunio to turn north and we drove for several blocks. I could definitely sense the beast and then I saw the limo at a corner parked beside a woman, who was dressed more to reveal than to conceal. She was talking to a man in a chauffeur's uniform.

Kunio stopped. He too had seen the car. The chauffeur returned to the driver's seat, while the prostitute slipped into the back and they drove off. We followed, keeping a discreet distance. The limo came to a stop at a small factory. The sign identified it as *Party's Balloons*. The driver got out, unlocked a padlock and opened the gate. In seconds he had driven into the factory's yard, locking the gate behind him then into the factory itself.

"Let's follow them," I stated, more for something to say than because of any reason to speak.

"I will follow them. You will stay with the car." ordered Kunio, opening his door.

"Like Ammut's on a diet I will." I climbed from the car, and grabbed my ceremonial sword from the back seat.

By now Kunio was out of the car and pulling his staff from the roof rack.

"Been meaning to ask, as far as I've seen, the Nukekubi are energy and physical weapons won't—" I began.

"My staff is blessed in the name of Amaterasu. It is most effective." Kunio's tone added the insult his words didn't.

"Amaterasu?" So I have to bone up on my Japanese mythology, but there are only so many hours in a day.

"The Lady of the Sun." This time Kunio added a snort for my ignorance.

"Just checking. We should go."

"If you insist." Kunio ran, reaching the gate well ahead of me, and using his six-foot staff pole vaulted the seven-foot fence. I don't know how but he managed to land on the other side with the staff still in his hands. "Follow if you can."

I rolled my eyes. "Smart ass."

Kunio ran around the building and out of sight. Sliding my sword through my belt, I clambered over the fence. I dropped into the warehouse's yard in time to hear the first of the screams. It was a gut wrenching sound, filled with horror and desperation. Drawing my sword, I ran towards the warehouse. The screams grew louder, followed by an unnerving silence.

The silence was shattered by the deep throated bellow that served Kunio as a battle cry.

As I ran I heard a muffled thud, like wood striking something yielding. The warehouse entrance, a truck access, was blocked by a locked garage-style door.

The woman screamed again and fell silent.

I pried at the base of the door but it wouldn't budge. I noticed a pedestrian door in the wall next to me. Cursing myself as a fool, I tried the handle. It was locked. Using my sword I smashed the door's wire reinforced window, undid the latch and ran into the room.

The heat and humidity hit me like a hammer and it took me a moment to orient myself.

The young woman, whom we had seen on the street, cowered by a huge blocky vat with pipes coming in and out of it. She was wearing only a black lace bra and panties. Bloody scrapes covered her knees and elbows, and her long black hair was a disheveled mess. The limo was parked in an open space just beyond the entrance while steaming vats, interspaced by walkways, crowded the rest of the huge camber. A rail system hung from the ceiling apparently designed to dip balloon shaped forms into the vats. An open path split the room and a smashed pedestrian door was visible at its end. The chauffeur lay by the limo clutching his head.

In the middle of the open space Kunio and the Nukekubi dueled. Kunio swung his staff and the glowing head of the beast dodged, trying to close on Kunio who stepped fluidly away. Realizing that both of them were engaged, I turned my attention to the sobbing woman. Grabbing her arm, I pulled her to her feet. She resisted my attempts to move her, finally forcing me to pick her up and carry her towards the door.

"It's not that easy," hissed a horrid voice behind me.

"Ray, look out, it is after you!" bellowed Kunio's voice.

I threw myself to the ground, turning as I did, so my body would cushion the girl's fall. The Nukekubi soared over us. A burning sensation covered the back of my hand, which I wiped on my pants' leg. The girl's weight landing on my chest winded me. Rolling clear, I struggled to catch my breath.

Above me a mustard yellow hand, composed of fear energy, scooped a palm full of hot liquid plastic from one of the vats and threw it at Kunio. The hand seemed to move independently of the Nukekubi's head's location. Kunio ducked the molten plastic while taking a savage swing at the Nukekubi's head. It dodged right and down. I came to my feet, sword in hand, just as the limo roared to life and moved to block the exit. Apparently, the chauffeur had recovered.

As the car pulled around it bore down on Kunio who leapt clear. That's when it happened. The Nukekubi's head disappeared among the rafters of the room's high ceiling. Now one of its hands threw glob after glob of hot plastic at Kunio, who unbalanced from dodging the car was hard pressed to avoid them. The other hand opened a valve on another vat releasing near boiling water onto the floor behind Kunio.

Kunio stepped on the water, slipped and fell against one of the vats. He screamed as the hot metal burnt him at the same time a glob of molten plastic connected with his chest. He jammed his staff against the floor in a bid not to fall into the scalding water that soaked through his shoes.

I scanned the ceiling and spotted the Nukekubi's head. It was obviously directing its hands from above. Steeling myself, I drew in my will, pointed my sword at the Nukekubi's head and bellowed. "By Horus' might, by Ra's great light, by the spells of Thoth, I command thee be off. Be gone! Oh darksome creature of the pit. By the powers of the Gods and Goddesses of the light, I command thee be gone!"

All a non-mystic would have seen was a crazy man pointing a sword at the ceiling and spouting gibberish. To the Sighted, a beam of radiant light shot from my sword's point forming a braided pattern of white, gold, and purple, that struck the Nukekubi. The beast screeched in anguish. The sound alone almost broke my concentration. Almost, but not quite.

The creature's hands stopped attacking Kunio and moved to the head. I kept my will upon the beast, despite the fact that banishing it in this way was exhausting my reserves. An eternity later it flew towards an open skylight. I realized that its time spent in a body created a mental barrier to it passing through solids. As the Nukekubi moved out of sight its shrieks ended.

I fell to my knees, but was summoned back to the world of men by the sound of squealing tires. I couldn't let the limo escape. If the Nukekubi 's body was in the car we could still defeat the beast. Tottering to my feet, I stumbled towards the door, but I was too late. The limo was already in the middle of the room. With a squeal of tires it smashed through the garage door. The driver didn't slow down when he reached the gate in the chain-link fence; it tore from its supports and was thrown into the street. Our prey was gone.

Swearing softly, I hobbled over to the valve spilling water

onto the floor and, using my shirt to cover my hand, closed it. Kunio had managed to move past the scalding puddle before falling to his knees. Thankful that I'd worn boots I waded across and helped him to his feet. He hissed in pain and I hoped he wasn't too badly burnt.

"Come on, I have some water and ice packs in the car. I'll wash and dress those wounds for you. We can come back for the girl. I don't think she's going anywhere."

Kunio nodded and grit his teeth, letting his staff fall from limp fingers. I'll give him this, he's tough. Even so, I half-carried him to my car then used my emergency rad water and instant cold packs on his burns. With dressings from my first aid kit I bandaged him and left him laying sideways in the front passenger seat while I returned for the girl.

It was a struggle to keep my knees from collapsing. Most people never realize how debilitating the use of magic can be. Banishing is in effect putting the banisher's strength and will in direct opposition to the banshee's. This time the scales almost went the other way.

I found the girl in the room's clear area. She was standing by a vat where a blanket had been spread on the floor. A pile of clothes sat on the blanket. She'd pulled on her black miniskirt and tied a red blouse beneath her breasts. Her rabbit-fur jacket sat on one corner of the blanket, and what appeared to be an expensive man's suit, lay in its centre.

"Are you all right?" I approached cautiously.

"Don't come near me! Stay the fuck away from me! I fuckin' mean it!" The girl whipped around to face me, an open switchblade in her hand.

I froze and held up my hands. "Don't worry, I'm one of the good guys, remember?"

Dirt, smeared makeup and blood from a wound on her forehead marred her finely-sculpted, Asian features.

"Stay the fuck back. I'm warnin' you!" I watched her knife wave back and forth inexpertly.

"Relax. It's okay. Put the knife down. I was the one trying to save you. I promise I won't hurt you."

Indecision clouded her features before she slowly folded the knife blade back into its handle.

"What happened, couldn't happen, could it?" she blurted.

"It could and did."

"Oh fuck!" She looked scared. Who can blame her?

"I have to get us out of here before the police arrive. We can talk it all out when we're safe."

The girl sized me up and slipped her blade into her jacket pocket. I folded the discarded suit and Kunio's staff in the blanket and threw the bundle over my shoulder.

"What's your name?" I asked.

"Kama." She was trembling.

"I'm Ray. It's going to be all right now."

"What was that fuckin' thing?" The quaver in her voice showed how close to the edge she really was.

"Have you heard about the drug Terror?"

"I'm not high."

"Neither were its other victims."

"No, Fuckin' shit! That thing? Can't be! Can it?"

"Afraid so. That's why the police haven't been able to find the dealer. Only people who it has attacked and a few others with the Sight can see or hear it. Come on. I don't think you should be alone, but we have to get moving. That damn chauffeur is probably calling the cops."

Kama threw her jacket over her shoulders and we headed for my car. As we walked, I put my arm around her. I felt her go rigid and her hand moved towards the knife in her pocket.

"I'll not touch you if you ask me not to. I just thought you might be shaken up." My tone of voice was meant to sooth her fears and from somewhere I found the energy to empathically project reassurance towards her.

There was a second's indecision then she snuggled into me like a child seeking protection from the night. We reached my car and Kama took a seat in the back while I bungee corded Kunio's staff to my roof racks and tossed the blanket bundle into the trunk. A minute later I drove off. No sooner had we rejoined the regular traffic flow than a police car went screaming by in the direction of the factory.

I drove to a well-lit parking lot and stopped to check on Kunio. I'm not sure if he was unconscious, in a healing trance, or just toughing it out. His eyes were closed and he was slumped forward in the front seat. Second-degree burns are painful buggers. His only response to my questions was a grunt so I left him to it. Getting my first aid kit out of the trunk I sat in the back seat with Kama.

"Let's play doctor," I joked.

"Only if you've got a fifty." Kama stiffened.

"Relax, it was a bad joke."

"Oh." Was her only reply, but she did let me examine her.

"It's a good clean wound and not deep. It should heal fine without stitches." I disinfected her scalp as we talked.

"You a doctor or somethin'?"

"Lifeguard. I've got first-aid like crazy."

"Oh."

I bandaged her scalp then sat back and looked at her. She was lovely.

"Can you tell me what happened back there? I didn't arrive until things were in full swing."

"Do I gaw'da?" There was a pleading quality in her voice.

"It might help us stop that thing."

"I'll try." She licked her lips nervously. "Fuck! I need a fuckin' drink.

"I was on my corner watching out for Jeff. The prick, he's a pimp, and he's been after me since I started working. He treats his girls like shit. Says he'll kill me if I don't join his stable. Well anyway, this John pulls up in a limo; only the John stays in the back, see, and his driver does the talking. I figure the guy don't want no fuckin' pictures gettin' back to wifey or somethin'. This way he can always say it was the driver. Well, I get in and he starts talkin' to me."

"What did he look like?"

"He was big, like a body builder or something. Looked Japanese, but he talked like those guys on the English comedies. He says he likes it in kinky places. Tells me he'll pay double if

I'll do it in this balloon factory. Well, I figure with that much I can split town, get away from Jeff before it's too late. I don't like hooking, but it's better than blowing my old man every time my Mum goes out. I wanna split to a new town and get a straight job. So I goes with him and we drive to that creepy factory. Fuck, it was hot in there. All the way he's talkin' about what a treat I am and how delicious I look."

She shuddered and paused. I thought she was going to break down, but she pulled herself together.

"He gives me a couple of drinks. Seemed nicer than most Johns. I was beginning to think it might even be fun. I mean, for an old guy he was kinda hot and he wasn't all rush, rush, rush." She shuddered. "Anyway, when we got to the factory, he spread out that blanket and stripped down. He told me to get down to my undies and stop while he gets a toy from the limo. I'm thinking it's a bit weird cause this guy ain't touched me yet; but if he's paying, I'm playing. I mean maybe I can pretty woman him or something. You know, become his private play toy, gotta be better than hooking. He goes into the limo, sits there then pops out the window."

She began to shudder and I put a comforting arm around her. Again she snuggled in. Despite her outer facade she needed affection as a starving man needs food. In a moment, she settled down and continued.

"It was only his head and hands and they were all glowy. I screamed, and ran; but the fucking door was locked. That thing chased me all over that God damn factory. It just kept hissing that the fear of the prey is so sweet. It screamed and I was so scared that I fell down and hurt myself. It was right over me when that other guy comes in and belts it with that big stick. That seemed to hurt it but the stick went right through."

"That was Kunio. The staff is consecrated." I glanced at the sleeping figure up front.

"Consa whated?"

"It means blessed."

"Oh, well, I couldn't watch no more. I thought I'd seen fuckin' everythin', but I ain't never seen nothin' like that! What the fuck was it?"

"A Nukekubi. A type of Japanese goblin."

"It's gross!" She buried her face against my chest. I could tell she was holding back sobs. As hard and tough as she acted mystical monsters were just too much for her.

I stroked her hair and held her until she settled. "The next thing I knew you was pullin' on my arm."

"That's more than enough. Come with us and we'll keep you safe."

"All right." She wiped her running mascara away with a tissue.

"Good, now I'd better take you back to our hotel room before I pass out."

We reached Toshiro's hotel with the sunrise. I parked as close to the door as possible, but even doing this the three of us barely made it through the lobby and up the elevator. Fact is, the night clerk probably would have stopped a ragged bunch like us except he was busy trying to make time with one of the maids. I knocked on Toshiro's door, which opened to reveal the old man dressed in a worn bathrobe.

"Spirits of my ancestors! What happened?" he gasped. Taking Kunio's weight off my shoulders he helped him to the bed.

"That's a story, but I think we're up on points." I hobbled into the room and collapsed into a chair. "Toshiro, I would like to introduce Kama."

"Ray and Kunio saved me from that fuckin' thing." Tears filled Kama's eyes.

Toshiro crossed the room and enfolded her in his arms, holding her as she whimpered. If he noticed her momentary stiffness or how her hand twitched towards her jacket pocket, he showed no sign.

"It will be all right. You are safe here. They were right to bring you along. We will look after you. You need not worry. The Nukekubi is trapped in its human form and is no threat to you as long as the sun is in the sky."

"Like a vampire?" Kama looked at me fearfully.

"Something like that, yes," I said. I wasn't sure about the nature of Japanese vampires, and I didn't want Toshiro inadvertently scaring her more.

"Toshiro, there are some things in my car. My sleeping gear, a bundle wrapped in a blanket, my tools. Would you mind bringing them in? I'm all in."

"Of course, simply give me your keys."

I remember saying thank you, or maybe I dreamed saying it, but that was it for the next few hours.

– Chapter 9 –

AFTER THE BATTLE

J awoke huddled in the easy chair with a crick in my neck and a bedspread covering me. I was still in the remains of the clothes I'd fallen asleep in. Kama was stretched out on the floor, on my air mattress, in my sleeping bag, wearing one of my spare T-shirts as pajamas. Cathy says I'm a sucker for a damsel in distress. I'm beginning to think she may be right. Kunio lay sprawled across his bed in what remained of his jeans.

I found that my burn had been salved and a white bandage applied. "Toshiro?"

"Here, my young friend," replied a calm voice from my right.

He was sitting cross-legged on the floor beside Kunio.

"What time is it?"

"Nearly noon."

"How is he?" I could see that my dressings had been replaced on Kunio's back.

"He will recover. The burns were...How is it in English? Some just red, some with blisters, none very deep."

"First and second degree, but no third."

"Yes."

Having extended my brain to its early morning limit I

plodded to the shower to become human.

Kama was awake when I left the washroom and had just finishing her account of what had happened the night before for Toshiro.

She smiled at me. "You must be a fuckin' fish. You done now or are you growin' gills?"

Clutching my towel about my waist I smiled and bowed presenting her with the washroom. Next, I pulled on some clothes from my bag and quickly inspected the ones from the night before. The pants and undershirt I kept. With a good wash and a patch or two, they'd do for working on my car. The rest went in the trash.

The next half hour was spent telling Toshiro my version of the previous night's happenings. I finished when Kunio awoke.

"Master, I have failed." Kunio looked like someone had barbequed his dog and had him over for the feast, only telling him afterwards.

"No, my son, you have won our first victory. You prevented the Nukekubi from feeding last night. It will now be desperate and careless. You and Ray can use this to your advantage."

"Master, if it were not for Ray, I would...."

"Is that not what an ally is for? Did I not tell you, Ray might have skills useful to us? Your only faults were in not considering your plan of attack before you rushed in and in not utilizing the skills of a willing ally. Now speak no more of this imagined failure, tell me your version of our first victory in this struggle."

"Yes, Master." Kunio seemed less down but it was obvious that he was going to flog himself over his imagined shortcomings. I hoped that his self-persecution wouldn't make him less effective.

He began to speak and I listened as attentively as Toshiro.

"We stopped outside the gate of the factory that the Nukekubi had chosen as its hunting ground. What is made in such an awful place?"

"Balloons." I shrugged.

Kunio looked at me in disbelief. "Balloons? Like those used at the parties of children?"

"Yup."

He shook his head. "I exited the car and, using my staff, vaulted the fence. I moved to the warehouse and allowed my eyes to adjust. There was one large door and a smaller door at its side. Circling the building, I searched for a less obvious place to enter and found a back door. That is when the screams started. I struck the door with my staff and it burst in. The Nukekubi was pursuing the *shoufu* amongst the vats of steaming liquids. I moved behind it and swung my staff injuring the beast.

"That is when the beast's servant leapt upon me. I was forced to knock him unconscious, before continuing against my true foe. By this time my advantage was gone. The Nukekubi attacked me then left to attack Ray.

"Ray was trying to carry the *shoufu* to safety. He dropped to the ground, as the Nukekubi tried to strike them from behind. There was a screeching of wheels and I had to dive out of the path of the vehicle. My blow had been too light. The beast's servant had awakened and was now blocking the exit. My foe began pelting me with burning liquid from the vats. It drove me onto a section of wet, slippery floor and I fell against a hot vat.

"The pain! I could not think to focus my *ki*. If it were not for Ray, I would be dead. You must excuse me, Master, the rest is a blur."

"You did well, Kunio. There is something different about this beast. It is more cunning and powerful than others we have faced."

"There are more of those fuckin' things?" demanded Kama from the bathroom door. She was clad in Kunio's bathrobe, her wet hair wrapped in a towel. My blood pressure went up as my blood went south. I've said it before; I'm a guy I'm not going to change.

"Master! What is she doing here?" demanded Kunio.

"She is my guest. Given last night's events I felt it best to keep her with us. This is especially true because now the Nukekubi will have a special interest in her. She has seen it. It will wish her silenced." Toshiro's voice allowed no argument.

"What?" gasped Kama.

I leapt up and helped her to the easy chair. She was badly shaken by Toshiro's revelation. Kunio sniffed disdainfully and went to the shower.

Kama slowly recovered her composure then turned to Toshiro and demanded "Is that fuckin' thing gonna come after me?"

"It is likely. Having been its intended prey you can see it. That is something the beast cannot take back. It will wish you... neutralized. I am sorry, my child, but to hide the truth would only place you in greater danger."

"What the hell can I do? I sure as shit can't work. I can't go home. My father, the horny old bastard, said I'd shamed the family by runnin' away the last time I tried. That was before I'd even started hookin'. There's no way they'll take me back. I'm up shit's creek. What the fuck am I supposed to do?"

"You can stay at my place. I'm not using it since I'm busy hunting the Nukekubi, and with you there I can check in to collect my messages," I suggested.

"Doesn't that... What you call it?"

"Nukekubi," supplied Toshiro.

"Right well, won't that Nukekubi thing be huntin' you too? I mean, you did fuck it up pretty good."

"Probably, but I'll be here for one thing and my apartment's in Hamilton. For another, with the magical work I've done on my place, I doubt a Nukekubi could get in, in one piece at least."

"What the fuck are you, some kind of sorcerer?"

"I prefer wizard," I replied with a smile.

I spent the next half hour convincing Kama that I wasn't completely cracked and that I wasn't as bad a menace as the Nukekubi. That done getting her to stay at my apartment was a snap.

Kunio emerged from the shower wrapped in a towel silencing all discussion as Kama's attention was captivated by his well-muscled form. Burn marks crisscrossed his back while spots of red skin marked his front. He seemed to be healing quickly.

"What is it?" Kunio stood uncomfortably in the bathroom door.

"Hubba, Hubba, Bruce Lee. Honey, you are gorgeous." Kama looked like a kid in a candy store.

Kunio blushed from his cheeks to where his towel covered, and then, gritting his teeth, he focused his attention on Toshiro.

"Master, I have no clean clothes, what I was wearing was ruined in the fight."

"There's an extra set in my duffle you can borrow," I offered.

"Thank you, Ray. The sooner I am dressed the better," Kunio muttered, glancing at Kama who seemed to be sizing him up like a piece of meat.

"Don't dress 'cause of me. I like the view just fine," she flirted.

"One would think you had seen enough of the male form, *shoufu*!" snapped Kunio. Grabbing my duffle, he disappeared into the bathroom.

"*Shoufu*! I know what that means! My fuckin' father use to call me that, you fuckin' bastard!" screamed Kama.

Kunio slammed the washroom door shut.

"I am sorry, Kama. Kunio's rudeness is unforgivable. He is not used to aggressive or forward women. He has been raised in a very traditional way." Toshiro patted Kama's shoulder. "I have done my best with him, but being a father was a dream I abandoned then had placed upon me. I fear I have been less than perfect in the task."

"I ain't exactly the fuckin' girl next door." Kama's voice was sad. "Fuck, I guess it's true what he called me, but it's still not nice." A calculating smile played across Kama's lips. For a moment, I felt envious of Kunio. As I thought it over, I pitied him. The poor bugger didn't stand a chance.

Kunio emerged wearing my spare clothes, which fit like a tent. He lifted the shirt so Toshiro could re-salve his burns with an herbal concoction.

I thought of the bundle I'd brought from the warehouse

and asked Toshiro where he'd put it.

"I was wondering when you would remember that." Toshiro pulled it from under the bed.

"I've had other things on my mind."

Toshiro just smiled.

Whenever I talked with Toshiro I had the impression that he looked on Kunio and me as a pair of adolescents, who by some twist of fate had been placed in his charge. It wasn't anything he said, but the feeling was always there. Of course, all things considered, he might have had just cause to view us in that light.

"Let me see what I can sense first." I unwrapped the bundle. The suit was Armani. All the clothing was very expensive, except for the underwear. It was Fruit of the Loom. I guess even Japanese goblins put their pants on one leg at a time. The clothes were new and didn't have much of their owner's energy on them. Checking the pockets, I found a set of keys on a key chain in the form of a Chinese ideogram. Turning my attention to the jacket I received the first pleasant surprise I'd had since the situation began. Out of the jacket's breast pocket I pulled a black leather wallet. It was devoid of ID but contained an assortment of bills that added up to just over three thousand dollars.

It pissed me off. Here I was busting my ass at a pool, breathing chlorine fumes, while this ghoulish atrocity walked around with three grand in its pockets. Life's not fair.

I pulled out the cash and Kama gasped, "That wad could choke a fuckin' horse!"

"Why would one wish to use money to choke a horse?" asked Toshiro.

"It's an expression. This cash is going to be really helpful though. It means I can make my rent this month without killing my savings account," I remarked.

"No. We do not keep the monies of the enemy. It must go to a temple where it will be cleansed of the horrid stain of the Nukekubi's touch," stated Kunio.

"Shit. I don't give a fuck who touched it. A wad like that

don't fall in your hands every day. I say we keep it." Kama eyed the cash hungrily.

"You have no say in this, *shoufu*."

"Look, cutie, I'm ain't callin' you fuckin' names. I need this cash, and after last night I fuckin' deserve it."

Toshiro tried to keep the peace. "This is counterproductive. It is true that the money is befouled by the touch of the Nukekubi, but it may still serve us. Kunio, you must understand that this battle is different from the ones in Japan. There we could work and earn our way. Here the laws prevent us from doing so. So as much as it troubles me I am afraid that we must use the money to pay our way. This being the case, we must part with it quickly so the evil invested upon it cannot spread further dissension among us."

"That's no problem. I can blow three grand easy." Kama had hungry eyes.

"It is not for you to spend! It is to be used in pursuit of the Nukekubi." Kunio looked haughty.

I thought they both looked ridiculous, but there was no way I was going to donate the cash to some church so the priest could buy a new suit. "Why don't we split it evenly; and each of us can use their portion as they see fit. Personally, I'm going to pay my rent, fill my car's tank and finish paying off its insurance. That should kill my portion but good."

"What of the Nukekubi? We must use the money to hunt it," objected Kunio.

"Kunio, I've missed a week's work, burned up tanks full of gas and put wear and tear on an already old vehicle. *Believe* me, I've invested money in the search."

Kunio looked at me opened mouthed then quietly stated, "I had not thought of that."

"Yes, Kunio, it is necessary that we keep the money. I must pay the rent on this room and for the meals we eat. You also require more weapons so that you might better do battle against our foe," soothed Toshiro.

"You are correct, Master, but what of the woman?"

"Me? Well, I sure as shit need new clothes. My hotel will

have cleaned out my room by now. Probably tossed all my fuckin' stuff. I have to buy all new shit, clothes, make up... everything."

Toshiro nodded, "Then it is settled. Ray, if you could please divide the money into four we will each see to the dispersal of a portion. I suggest you and Kunio be on your way. You must take Kama to your apartment and return before nightfall. Kunio, you should purchase weapons to fulfill your needs."

– Chapter 10 –

SH⊕PPING

The drive to Hamilton was uneventful aside from the various jackasses with a deathwish I had to share the road with. Kunio rode shotgun while Kama practically lay across the back seat. This wasn't a total loss. Kama's posture allowed me to steal glances of her legs, which helped pass the time we spent at traffic lights. The funniest part was when I caught Kunio doing the same thing. He blustered and turned red. Kama smiled and shifted to a more provocative pose.

In an hour we were at my apartment. We ascended by way of the exterior stairway that led to my fire escape/balcony, in an attempt to minimize the chatter of my nosy neighbors.

I opened the door, and with a comical bow, presented the humble hospitality of my abode. Kunio entered first, followed by Kama. For a moment, I thought Kunio had been struck dumb. He made no comment about western decadence, just stood there staring at my library. His gaze shifted to take in my papyrus prints.

"When was the last time you cleaned this fuckin' dump?" demanded Kama, as she took in the laundry scattered about my floor and the unwashed dishes by the sink.

"I guess it is a tad messy, isn't it?" I agreed.

"Fuckin' right."

Kunio moved to my knick-knack shelf to stare at a grouping of amethyst crystals. My cat awoke, stretched and came running towards me. I picked her up and she began purring loudly.

"A cat. I love cats!" exclaimed Kama. "What's her name?"

"Sekmara."

Kama gave me a look composed of puzzlement, astonishment and disbelief.

"Can I call her Fluffy?"

"No."

"Kitty?"

"If you must."

"Come here, Kitty." She lifted Sekmara from my arms.

My cat is usually skittish around new people, but this time she settled in and purred as if she'd known Kama all her life. I watched the pair in disbelief. Demons, dragons, Gods and fairies I could believe in, but my cat allowing a stranger to hold her with no blood involved...impossible!

"You do understand, stay in the apartment after sunset. It's warded against all malignant forces and should keep the Nukekubi out. Feel free to read anything." I pulled a white binder and black book from my night stand and placed them by the door to take with me.

"What are those?" asked Kama.

"The things I don't want you to read, especially the black book. It makes me nervous. There's food in the fridge and I'm sure you can find the pots and pans," I instructed as Kama cuddled my cat.

"You actually got a clean pot." She gazed meaningfully towards the sink.

"Who made this?" interrupted Kunio, pointing towards a relief carving of a beautiful woman standing naked on a sea shore.

"Me. I carve as a hobby." I liked that piece, it was probably the best I'd done.

Kunio looked at me and smiled. I think he was praising my work. For him to verbalize his appreciation would cheapen it. For the first time I glimpsed the master emerging from the student in Kunio.

"I should check my messages before we go." Hitting the button on my machine allowed Cathy's voice to fill the room.

"Ray, please call me. I spoke to some of the Wiccan priesthood in Toronto. They asked me to give you their numbers and addresses as safe houses. One of them suggested that you should carry a charged citrine with you. I don't know that it will do much good, but I charged one up for you. So if you'll drop in, I'll let you have it. Take care, bye."

"Who's that?" demanded Kama.

"A friend of mine, a priestess of Bast, but don't spread it around. Most of us are a little anxious about going public."

"I can't imagine why," scoffed Kama.

Kunio glared at her from beside my bookshelf. "Maybe it is attitudes such as yours, *shoufu*, that force persons such as Ray and his friend to hide their true natures."

I was shocked. Kunio defending me was unexpected.

"Don't call me a God damn *shoufu*! I do have a fuckin' name, you know." Kama went red in the face.

The second message on my machine was a searing soliloquy from Tracy — nothing worth listening to. What the little idiot didn't get was as lifeguard one I was her boss. It's a position similar to a master Sergeant in the military, not an officer, but top of the enlisted food chain. If something happened on her shift it was my butt.

My father called next, trying to guilt me into visiting them again and that was it for the messages. I phoned my father and we talked for about three minutes before I ended the call with a promise I would visit soon. I didn't say I was immune to guilt, I just see it for what it is.

"Kama, if a message comes in, please write it down. I'll be checking in and if you could play answering service for me it would be a great help. My machine doesn't have a dial up function."

"Sure, kinda helps pay you for letting me stay here. Now, why don't you and Hunka Beefy go pick up that citrine-a-bob. I'll make dinner," suggested Kama.

"My name is Kunio. Not Hunka Beefy."

"And mine's Kama, not *shoufu*, and Hunka Beefy is a shit load nicer than what you're callin' me." Kama put her hands on her hips and glared at Kunio. I tried not to smile, but watching Kama glare up at Kunio was like watching a small cat intimidate a dog three times its size.

Kunio turned red and clenched his fist. I doubt he would have become violent but I was getting tired of the feud.

"Kunio, she's right. You have to give out what you want back. That's just karma."

He glanced at me, gave a curt nod, took a deep breath and turned to face Kama. "We must go. Kama, I apologize for not using your name."

"Some fuckin' apology!" Kama turned to the sink. Sniffing my washing sponge she deemed it useable and started in on the pots.

"Kunio, we have to go, *now*." I said before he could think up a reply.

"Yes, that is a good idea." Kunio lead the way onto my fire escape/balcony.

I caught up to him on the stairs. "We'll go to Cathy's first. She should know where to get your gear. She does Kung Fu."

"Yes. We should attend to these affairs so our thoughts will be clear and focused tonight." Kunio looked at his hand that clutched a sketchpad and a coffee table book titled *Witches*. "I am sorry; I was looking at these and with the *shou–* Kama's words, I forgot to put them down."

The pad was left over from a time when I had foolishly believed anyone could learn to draw. The few scribbles in the front of it stood testimony to the fact that that belief, in my case, was in error.

"No problem. The book's a fair telling. You can have the sketchpad; it's only taking up space on my shelf."

"Thank you. That is most generous."

A minute later we were in my car headed to Cathy's. I'd normally walk but I knew I'd need the car later.

Kunio sat in silence for a minute then spoke. "You have

some lovely things in your home. It reflects you well. One tends to underestimate you at first, but when one looks deeper there are layers."

"We're onions, me and Shrek." I replied as I turned into Cathy's building's parking lot.

Kunio laughed, "Yes, most people and ogres are." Who would have thought he was a fan of fractured fairy tales "If you desire Kama, I will not think less of you should you utilize her services."

I was pulling into a parking space which saved me slamming on my brakes. "Kunio, I don't think it's me she's interested in." I killed the engine.

"You are supplying her with food and shelter. It is only right she pay you with the coin of her profession. Historically Geisha would perform many services in my land, but Kama is no Geisha. She only has one skill to barter." Kunio had unbuckled his safety belt and shifted in the passenger seat to look at me.

I unbuckled and turned to look him in the eye. "I know you're trying to be nice, so I won't pull the offended 'I've never paid for it in my life' act. Point in fact, I haven't. Who Kama sleeps with is up to her. I'd never tell her to sleep with me or get out. That would make me as bad as a pimp."

"I do not understand. Is your order celibate?" Kunio's face was so serious.

The laugh I let out echoed against the window glass. I opened my door and climbed out. Kunio followed my example. "I'm not celibate. Talk about a deal breaker on that one."

"Then why?" Kunio looked confused.

"Kunio, I'm guessing you can appreciate the view when Kama's around. Why don't you go for her? She likes you."

"I cannot. She is... well... she is a..."

"Prostitute, *shoufu*, lady of the evening. So?" I led Kunio towards the building's main entrance keeping my voice down as we walked. The grey concrete walls of the building had stacked balconies and I didn't want Cathy's neighbours overhearing this conversation. "Kunio, she's a person, she has a past, a present and hopefully a future; a mind, a soul, and a damn cute body. Stop thinking of her as a label and find out what the rest of her is like."

"I do not know if I can."

"Try. You don't have to bed her, just treat her like anyone else. You may find she had damn little choice about hitting the streets."

Kunio fell silent.

Seconds later we stepped into the building's mud room. This had three glass walls and let onto the general lobby. I hit the button on the intercom board mounted by the mail boxes on the plaster wall buzzing up to Cathy's to warn her we were coming then let myself in. The elevator ride was spent is silence. I like to think that Kunio was considering my words. I stepped into Cathy's apartment where she lay on the couch reviewing fractures in an Edgar Cayce book.

"Hi, Ray, sorry I didn't meet you at the door. Moving's still a bitch." She pointed to her cast.

"Not a problem. I brought along a friend. Kunio, this is Cathy. She knows about our quest." I stepped into the living-room and gestured for Kunio to follow. He hesitated before joining me.

"Hello, Kunio. Relax and make yourself to home. If you want tea, coffee or anything, Ray knows where everything is, so it's no bother," said Cathy.

"Hey," I playfully retorted.

"Oh, Ray. You know I'll make it worth your while." She shot me a suggestive wink. I felt my temperature rise. She was dressed in short shorts and a T-shirt that displayed her figure well. I'm only a man after all.

It was then I realized that Kunio's eyes hadn't left her since he entered the room. A twinge of jealousy struck me, but I knew from experience Cathy considered it none of my business. She's a free agent, and Kunio was welcome to try.

"I do not wish to be any trouble," said Kunio, a quaver in his voice. He actually bowed to her.

"Don't be silly. Any friend of Ray's is welcome here." Cathy dipped her head in a sitting bow.

"You are very beautiful and gracious, dear lady. Ray is lucky to have you... As a friend I mean. I did not mean anything untoward...Not that you are not desirable...You are. What I meant to say is..."

My jealousy evaporated as Kunio tripped over his tongue. Cathy smiled at him with amused tolerance. I finally decided to come to his rescue.

"Um, look guys, I hate to break this up, but we are running against the clock here. Cath, you said something about a charged citrine and a list of safe houses?"

"The rock's on the dining-room windowsill. The safe house list is by the phone." She gestured to her end table. "I've listed who I think has a clue at the top. You know the mystical community, fifty dabblers for every one worth something, but they are all willing to help."

I retrieved the yellow, gemstone. It was the size of my palm. "It's huge."

"For the price it should be, but if it helps you it's worth it."

"How much do I owe you?" I mentally watched my share of our found money evaporate.

"It's a gift. When you finish chasing this thing you can return it or pay me then. For now, don't worry about it."

"You are most generous," said Kunio, shyly. Maybe he could be competition. He played the shy, innocent, begging to be taught, pretty well. Some women like that, I know from experience. I have mentioned an affinity for big cats.

Cathy smiled at him, which left him blushing.

"Thanks, Cath. I was wondering, could you tell me where there's a martial arts supply house? Kunio needs weapons." I glanced at the list of names and addresses. I recognized several as people I'd met at public rituals. Folding the paper, I put it in a pocket hoping I wouldn't have to involve anybody else. Risking my own neck is one thing. Risking somebody else's is something else entirely.

"Sure, there's one on Concession near Seventeenth. They should have pretty much anything you'd want."

"Thanks. Kunio, we have to get moving."

Kunio tore his eyes off Cathy and looked at me. "Wha— Oh yes... of course," he agreed.

"By the way, Cath, I have a friend staying at my place. Could you call her?" I asked.

"I'll do better than that. I'll drop in on her. I'm getting pretty mobile as long as I don't have to do a lot of corners." Her smile lit the room. "I'm almost as clumsy as you on a good day right now." She winked at me.

I grinned. "I didn't do anything. A bull came out of nowhere and went in the china shop, I swear."

Cathy chuckled then sobered. "Come here."

I went to her and she pulled me into a kiss. "You come back, safe and alive, promise?"

"I promise to do my best."

Cathy nodded. "That's as much as I'm going to get out of you, isn't it?"

"Take care, Cath. I'll be back." My bad Schwarzenegger impression didn't really lighten the mood, but it gave me a chance to grab Kunio and retreat.

"She is an exquisite woman! A China doll with skin like pearl," said Kunio as we walked to the car. "And her hair it is like red gold. You are a lucky man to call such a woman your own."

I grimaced. The last thing I needed was a lovesick puppy trailing along with me, especially if he was going to remind me of the ambiguous nature of Cathy's and my relationship.

"Cathy and I are friends. I don't own her."

"The way she looked at you? The offer to make it 'worth your while?' That kiss?"

"What Cathy and I are or are not to each other is between us. All I said is that I don't own her. We're free to date other people, I'm not crazy about it, but monogamy takes two. Even if we were monogamous, I wouldn't own her. We'd just have an agreement not to see other people."

"I do not understand this. She is a beautiful woman. You are a man."

"Kunio, you have a problem. You have to start seeing women as people. You can't avoid thinking about hitting the sheets with them, that's only healthy, but you have to see them as more than sex objects. You're not going to bed every woman you meet, so there's no use in thinking of them as potential conquests. All that does is make you nervous and then you act like an idiot. Try to see women as people first, soft, warm and sexy, second."

"You Canadians have strange ideas. The man is the master of the house. Women serve his needs. They are meant to pleasure men."

"Kunio, if that's how you feel, then all you want from a relationship is a butler and a blow up doll. Think about it."

I will, but the Nukekubi must come first."

I exhaled in relief.

A minute later I turned the key in my car's ignition. Glad that Kunio wouldn't overburden the hunt with a chorus of heartfelt sighs. He did, however, begin a sketch of Cathy as we drove.

Reaching the martial arts supply house, I dropped Kunio off and went in search of a parking spot. When I rejoined him in the shop he held a shattered staff in his hands and was screaming at a wiry, blond man with a weasely face.

"It was defective," yelled Kunio.

"What in hell do you expect if you bend it like that?" snarled the clerk from behind the counter.

"My Master has always taught me a good staff must have flexion."

"I don't give a shit what your Master said you—"

Gentlemen!" I stepped between them. I seemed to be doing a lot of putting myself in harm's way. I'd have to ask Cathy about death wishes in psychology. My heart pounded like a trip hammer. The waves of anger radiating from the two antagonists tied my stomach into a knot. "What happened?"

"This staff snapped when I tested it for stress. Now this one demands I pay for it," snarled Kunio.

"The idiot bent the bloody thing nearly double. Stinking

amateur!" snapped the sales clerk.

"I believe we can live without name calling. As for amateurs, this gentleman is the personnel apprentice of Toshiro Yoshida: a *Ninjitsu* Master from Japan, doing a special tour of Canada. I am their local liaison." I pitched my voice with just a hint of superiority.

Kunio closed his mouth and looked smug. Taking the staff, I inspected its broken ends. There was a fine dusting of powder on the wood.

"Your supplier ripped you off. Look here, the wood was going rotten at this point. They just laminated over it."

"Let me see that." The clerk sounded as pissed off as before, but I could sense the target of his anger was changing.

I passed him the broken staff and pointed out the powder.

"I'll be damned. Those bastards! If this broke during a bout someone could have gotten hurt." He turned to Kunio. "I am sorry about this, sir."

I could tell that Kunio was getting ready to snub the fellow so I stamped on his foot. His eyes widened before forcing a smile and replying, "That is well. Might I look at your other staffs?"

"Of course, sir." The sales clerk vanished through the door behind the display case.

"Be gentle with this lot and save arguing with me about your foot until we get to the car," I whispered.

Before Kunio could reply the proprietor returned carrying several wooden staffs. While Kunio inspected these, I examined the store. It was a rectangle, three metres wide and twice that in depth, with a glass topped display case running along one side. The display case was filled with oriental weapons. Other weapons hung upon the wall. In one corner was a bookshelf, and the front window displayed a variety of trophies.

"I will take this one, and two of those throwing knives, as well as three stars, if you have them? I wish a *ninjato* also, but I would like to test its balance first." Kunio's voice intruded upon my thoughts.

"Shit. You going to war or something?" quipped the shopkeeper.

"They didn't want any problems with customs so they left most of their gear in Japan. We have to purchase all the necessary equipment for their demonstrations," I said, as I sauntered towards the cash register.

"Yeah, know that one. Those boys at customs can be a pain in the ass. I don't take my stuff over the border any more. A buddy of mine keeps an extra set of gear in his basement for me. I'd better fetch those short swords. Back in a sec."

A few moments later Kunio had inspected every *ninjato* in the place, choosing what he obviously considered the best of a bad lot.

The clerk added up the merchandise. The total was over four hundred dollars. Kunio paid him and collected his purchases into a bundle.

"Look guys, if you have any extra time, I'm sure my dojo would love to see a demonstration of what you do," said the shopkeeper.

I leapt in before Kunio could open his mouth.

"I'll tell you what, our schedule is pretty tight, but if we get a cancellation while we're still in this part of the country, we'll call you. Do you have a card?"

"Of course." The shopkeeper passed me his card before Kunio and I left.

"Why did you prevent me from dealing with that fool as he deserves?" demanded Kunio as we walked down the sidewalk.

So much for enjoying a pleasant fall day. "We have more important considerations. Besides if you'd decked him, we couldn't have bought your equipment, and you'd probably be arrested for assault."

Kunio thought for a moment. "You are correct. My Master is right. I must think before I act. Why is that so hard?"

"It's only natural, Kunio. One, you're what, nineteen?" I found myself glancing up and down the quiet street looking for a white limo. Nothing.

"Eighteen." Kunio stared at the pavement.

"You're brain's still settling down, it will get easier to think ahead in the next couple of years."

"You believe it is just a by product of inexperience?" Kunio sounded offended.

"No, Cath keeps me up on a lot of psych stuff. They're finding that the brain isn't really fully developed until the early twenties. The sections that deal with foreseeing consequences take a big hit in puberty. If you want to be bored out of your mind ask her about it some time."

"So it is biology." Kunio sounded dubious and relieved. I had the feeling I might be letting him off a hook he often hung himself on.

"That and...You started training in the martial arts when you were five, right?"

"That is when my Master took me in."

"You've never really had to worry about the other kids beating the living crap out of you. Most of us have, so we learned to avoid giving them cause."

"Hmm... Maybe what you say has merit. I will think upon it, but for now let us go and eat. I am starved."

"Good idea." I opened the trunk of my car so Kunio could load in his blades.

Fifteen minutes later I stepped into my apartment, the place shocked me. The dishes had been washed, the laundry picked up and sorted, and spaghetti was bubbling in a clean pot on the stove.

"I had to wash the fuckin' pots, and if you call what you had here food, you're crazier than I thought you were," snapped Kama before I could open my mouth. "I didn't have time to vacuum, and your bag's full anyway."

"Right." I took a seat at the table, which had been cleared of its normal pile of papers and bits of junk. How I was ever going to find anything again I wasn't sure.

"What is this food?" asked Kunio.

"It's a Chinese dish with an Italian twist. Marco Polo supplied the noodles, Columbus the tomatoes and the Italians put them together with the spices," I explained.

"It's fuckin' spaghetti, and not a good one. I had to use a

canned sauce and the noodles were older than I am. Don't you ever eat in?" criticized Kama.

"Not when I can avoid it."

Kama served up two heaping plates and we began to eat. Kunio took a few moments to get the hang of twirling the noodles around his fork but then seemed to enjoy the meal. After we finished, I grabbed some clean clothes from my closet, I could now open its door without moving a pile, and we were off to Toronto.

– Chapter 11 –

FUTILITY

The sun dropped below the horizon as Kunio and I drove. A blanket of cloud covered the sky.

"Ray, I am curious. Why do you not study the martial arts? It seems a more practical way to accomplish what you do than the strange implements and actions mentioned in your books." Kunio sat calmly as we pulled onto the highway. I'll give him this; he's not a back seat driver.

"What you and I do isn't exactly the same." Swerving, I managed to avoid the old car that pulled in from an on-ramp doing about half the limit.

"How so?" I paused to collect my thoughts before speaking. This let me get around the old lady wearing a head scarf that had almost killed us.

"Okay, let me compare what I do to what you do. You draw upon your *ki* to affect you and the environment around you in accordance with your will. Is that more or less correct?"

"Yes, in basic terms."

"Good. What I do is both extremely similar and drastically different. Picture the universe as fields of energy, each of a different nature that all flow into our world at a slow rate and mingle to create our reality. The energy that relates to plant growth is different from the one that relates to the wind. In our world all the energies are mingled and dissipated. People can access the pure source of these energies, but most of us never do. I guess you could say what I do is I use my energy to create channels that direct the flow of unfiltered universal energies, to cause change in accordance with my will."

"So you are saying you are more powerful than those of us who only use the ambient energies." I was on thin ice. Kunio's shoulder chip could house a family of eight with room to spare.

"No. It's a bit like the difference between a sculptor who works in stone and a stone mason. The tools are similar, the technique alike, but the sculptor, because he's working with finer chisels, has more precise control. He can create beauty that would be impossible for the stone mason with his large, cumbersome tools."

I was forced to stop talking while I avoided a man with a cell phone glued to his ear that swerved across three lanes of traffic to get an exit. It happened to be the on-ramp where the 403 meets the Q.E.W., and he apparently didn't care that I was in his way.

"Where was I?" I asked once we were on the Q.E.W.

"The sculptor and the mason."

"Oh, yes. You have more precise control than I do. Your focus of energy is narrow, like a laser, but of lesser magnitude with a broad spectrum, whereas my focus is broad, like a sledge hammer, but of a higher magnitude though representing only one aspect of the spectrum of energies at a time. Yours is generally better suited to this world because it is more in keeping with the blended nature of this world. Think of the damage an improperly used high-nitrogen fertilizer can do to soil, it's a high magnitude pure essence, now think how much more beneficial cow manure can be since it is a blending of natural substances. Often it depends on the situation as to which is best. One thing is that with your skills you don't risk burnout, and they're less psychically exhausting."

"Why less psychically exhausting, and what do you mean, burnout?"

I smiled as we passed Mr. Cell Phone who had been pulled

off to the side of the road and was now having a conversation with a Police Officer. "Imagine a system designed to use fifteen amps of current. An average person runs about two amps through it and it never gets strained. A martial artist using *ki* is running, if he's a master like Toshiro, fifteen amps. If he's exceptionally good, like you, about ten amps. A mystic runs five or six amps until he or she casts a spell. During spell casting a master mystic, like the legendary Merlin, may channel as much as forty amps; a fairly average wizard, twenty-five to thirty. The system wasn't designed to take that kind of current. The wiring can hold out for a short time, but if the surge lasts too long, fizzle. You blow your fuses, or worse, burnout your wiring. Another downside is after channelling that much energy, it takes time to recover."

"I see what you are saying. You drove off the Nukekubi by channelling these, energies?"

"Yes, and I don't mind telling you, if it had held out a few moments longer I would have failed."

"What is the significance of the, how do you say it, incantations and the strange gestures?"

"Very little. They help me focus on the goal and choose the energy field I tap into. Also, they distract the conscious mind, so it doesn't block the energy flow. Magic really flows from the subconscious and spirit, so you have to give the conscious mind something to play with to get it out of the way."

"I believe I understand. If you may, please tell me about the stone Cathy gave you. She said she had 'charged it'."

"It's a trick anyone can do. You choose an object of a nature similar to the desired effect. Channel energy into it and the object becomes a reservoir for that force. All the magical tools are made this way, becoming batteries of magical power."

"Ah, so the bright yellow stone is like the sun, and she placed the strength of the sun within it. This is amazing, a woman who can command Lady Sun herself."

"It's more like begging a favour of the Gods, but you have the basic idea. You should know about this. Your staff is consecrated. It's just a different name for the same process."

"Yes. My Master blesses all of our weapons. I see what you are saying now."

"Figured you would. I think when a person reaches the end of either of the paths we walk; they find they've mastered them both."

"That is a possibility."

"If we survive, I'll have to show you and Toshiro the sights."

"I would like that. This is the first time I have been outside Japan."

We reached Toshiro's hotel to find him dozing in a chair. I understood why he had left the hunt to us. His age was beginning to catch up with him. He couldn't handle the late nights of hard searching any more. I also suspected he wanted to prepare Kunio for the day he wouldn't be there. Getting him to work with others and alone would ease that transition. Kunio slipped into the bathroom and changed into the clothes Toshiro had washed and left lying on the bed. Soon after we were off in search of our prey.

The minutes were like hours and I sensed nothing. By midnight I wondered if the creature had fed the night before despite our efforts to stop him. By three Kunio and I had just about given up and around three thirty we stopped at a donut shop. The place was empty except for a couple in the corner involved in a passionate embrace and a waitress who looked like an Italian wrestler in drag.

I ordered our drinks while Kunio went to the can. Taking a seat, I watched another car pull into the parking lot. It was a subcompact Dodge, maybe two or three years old. I'd seen the car before that evening. The driver stayed in his vehicle.

Kunio emerged from the washroom and moved to our table.

"I think we have company." With a toss of my head I indicated the car.

"The small car. I saw it some time ago. I am not sure of its intent."

"Thanks for telling me. We can probably assume it's been sent by Mr. Helium head to track us."

"Who?" Kunio screwed up his face.

"Our foe. You know, the flying head, like a helium balloon."

Kunio looked at me with pained tolerance. I thought it was a good joke.

"What do you want to do about him?" I sipped my coffee.

"He must not follow us to your home that would put everyone you know at risk."

"Gods of my father's! If the Nukekubi runs my license it will get my parents' address. We have to get there right away. I have to protect them." I felt all the fear, shame and panic of a twelve-year-old boy who couldn't protect the grandfather he adored.

"What you must do now, Ray, is not panic. It is unlikely whoever is driving that vehicle will have reported what they know yet. They will wait until they have all the information they can gather before telling our foe anything."

I took three deep breaths and a sip of coffee before doing anything else. "We can't just let this guy shadow us."

"Agreed. We must stop being the hunted and become the hunter. We will require a place that is quiet and isolated, but will allow us the option of several exits. Our shadow must be forced to leave his vehicle before we take action."

"I know just the place."

After driving around for a time we stopped at a mall, just as the sun was rising. We circled the building and found one set of doors that was unlocked. Parking the car, we sauntered into the building as if we had a right to be there. The storefronts were all closed but a single staff member was preparing a centre aisle coffee shop for the morning rush.

"This is good, Ray. Now we must draw our prey to us." Kunio led me away from the entrance and around a corner. A few seconds later an overweight man with thinning, brown hair, dressed in a blue shirt and slacks, entered the mall. Kunio smiled and walked across his field of vision. I followed his example. Our tail seemed to disappear only to appear behind us if we suddenly slowed or stopped. Several minutes passed and a security guard stopped us, but she let us go when I told her we were waiting for the coffee shop to open. Other people began to appear in the mall.

"We must act now, Ray, before there are too many others about. There was a washroom we passed that should serve our needs."

We turned a corner and waited for our tail to catch up before heading for the men's room. The door groaned against the spring that held it shut as we entered and the smell of disinfectant assailed us. It was a small bathroom: one stall, one urinal and one sink, all along its back wall.

"Stand where the opening door will hide you and block it closed as soon as he enters. I will deal with him," said Kunio, as he hid in the stall.

Maybe two minutes passed before the door creaked on its hinges. Our tail entered the room with a camera in his hand. I slammed the door behind him. The camera's flash blinded me as the stall flew open. A dark silhouette raced across my spotty vision. A thump, a woof and a whimper followed.

"Who are you?" Kunio's tone held a rage that was frightening to me, and I was on his side.

"Please don't hurt me. It—it wasn't my fault. I was just doing my job," blabbered the man.

"What is your job?" demanded Kunio.

My eyes had cleared enough that I could see our tail was kneeling on the floor with Kunio towering above him. One of Kunio's fists grasped a handful of his prey's thinning hair; the other was poised to strike.

"I'm a private detective." His pudgy features looked terrified.

"Why were you following us?" Kunio pulled harder on the man's hair.

"I wasn't." The private detective began to cry. So much for the Rockford files.

"Do not lie to me." Kunio twisted his hand in the man's hair.

"Please stop. Fine! This guy from head office called up and told me he thinks his nephew's turned queer. Taken up with some white kid. Wants to know for sure before he gives him a job in the company. This guy has a real problem with gays.

Please, ease up on the hair, there's not that much of it left."

"LIAR!" screamed Kunio.

"He's telling the truth." I couldn't see any red in his aura, except on his scalp where Kunio was contributing to his baldness.

Kunio released the man and turned away in disgust.

"Look, I don't care how you guys get your jollies, but I could have you charged with assault for this," threatened our tail.

"Really? Maybe we should just kill you and dump the body in the lake to keep you quiet. Don't be more of an ass than you already are. I could have a dozen witnesses account for our whereabouts right now." I had to think fast. Odds were nothing would stick because of the lack of witnesses, but police involvement could get messy.

"God no! I won't say anything, honest. Hell, I've got no problem with gays. Whatever gets you through the night. I'll just tell your uncle I couldn't find any hard evidence. Please. I'm just a guy trying to make a living."

Kunio spun around, with fury in his eyes. "You think we are...that we...I should beat you senseless for the thought."

"It doesn't matter. Let it go. We both know it's just a cover story." I sighed, another dead end.

Kunio glared at me. Our shadow cowered on the floor. Kunio snapped, "What company do you work for, and who sent you after us?"

"Dowland Investigations Limited. Mr. Yakoharo said to follow you. He said it was for your own good, with A.I.D.S. and all. Please don't hurt me." The private detective grovelled. This was a far cry from peeping into windows.

"How did you know who we were?" I kept any trace of pity out of my voice. We'd been dealt our hand and had to play it as best we could; for what we could.

"Mr. Yakoharo told me the hotel you were staying in and that you drove a beat up Hyundai Accent." He turned to Kunio. "Your uncle must really be worried about you. Why don't you just let him meet a girlfriend or two, so he calms down?"

"I do not need your advice." Kunio moved towards the man who cringed.

"Listen to me. You're going to tell Mr. Yakoharo that we lost you on the highway. You're going to forget everything that happened since we hit the off ramp. Is that clear?" I pushed empathically heightening the man's fear. I hated doing it, but keeping him out of the affair might save his life.

"Yes, but?"

"Good. Now just so you remember my instructions, give me your wallet." I held out my hand.

"What are you going to do?" He passed me his billfold.

Opening the battered leather, I pulled out a business card. I thought it was a joke at first, or a cover, but it was too stupid. As strange as it sounds, someone has to be named John Smith.

I handed back the wallet and held up the card. "Saves us having to access computer records to find you. Remember, if your client learns anything, we'll be back. Next time, I won't keep my associate on a leash. Clear?"

"Whatever you say."

"Good, go home." I wanted to have this over with. I felt like I was playing a tough from an old gangster movie and the role didn't suit me.

"One more thing, of what race is Yakoharo?" demanded Kunio.

"He's Asian. Shit! You don't know him. He's not your uncle! What's going on?" John's eyes were as big as saucers.

"Nothing you need to know about, John. Go home. Sleep in your safe bed and remember, it's kept safe by the actions of others." I turned so my back was to John and I faced Kunio. Winking, I hoped that Kunio would follow my lead. "The North Koreans must be getting desperate."

Kunio made a jerking thumb gesture at John and answered. "Yes, we must be close."

Thank the Gods for movies. We both knew the archetype I figured would impress John the most. We were a little young for the role, but he was scared enough to ignore that. John got up and practically ran from the room.

Kunio dropped the act and kicked the concrete wall. "That worm, that maggot, for him to think that we were... the thought is disgusting!"

"Not my cup of tea, but it doesn't really insult me." I shrugged.

"Do you think he will do as we told him?"

"He probably thinks we're C.S.I.S., or undercover cops, or something. John didn't strike me as too bright. He'll choose the easiest answer to the questions we pose, so yes, I'm sure he will."

"What is this C.S.I.S.?"

"Canada's spy organization. We had a national case of penis envy years ago. It motivated us to build the C.N. tower and start C.S.I.S."

"Oh? We had best return to my Master before he worries."

We drove to the old man's room where we found him fast asleep. I stretched out on the floor and in moments was unconscious.

I awoke that afternoon to Toshiro's gentle shaking and found a breakfast of instant oatmeal awaited me. Kunio and I ate as Toshiro produced a newspaper reading us an article which scuttled my appetite.

"TERROR CLAIMS ANOTHER VICTIM.

"A grisly death occurred off Clifton Hill in the tourist core of Niagara Falls, Canada last night.

"Between the hours of three and five am, William Diverson, of no fixed address, was heard screaming. Police responded to find that Mr. Diverson had ripped his own eyes out of their sockets with his bare hands. Mr. Diverson died in transport to hospital.

"This is believed to be the latest in a series of deaths involving a new street drug known only as Terror. Terror incidents have previously been isolated to the Toronto area. Police detectives fear that this latest death is indicative of the drug having a wider distribution."

"Crap!" See, I can be articulate.

Toshiro set the paper aside. "There is nothing more of use in the article."

Kunio had stopped eating and stared at the table, shaking his head.

"That's it then. We can't go hit and miss hoping we happen to be in the same city as the damn thing. Heap of good we've done." I felt nauseous.

"Do not be angry with yourself. Remember, you did save Kama," advised Toshiro.

"There is that," I agreed. My frustration was still getting the better of me.

"It is obvious that whoever the Nukekubi is in human guise, he is a man of wealth and influence. Maybe we can find him through that?" suggested Kunio.

"Yes, this is so," remarked Toshiro.

"By the way, we had a run in with a private detective last night. This talk of that bastard's influence brought it to mind." I started shovelling food into my mouth again.

"That only serves to illustrate my point," said Kunio. "Whoever the Nukekubi is, he is a being of wealth and position. In addition to this, he would have arrived here only shortly before the killings began. Using this information it may be possible to discover who he is."

"I'm going to call Kama and see how she is. Maybe my friend called in with some information on those companies."

Kama picked up on the third ring. The only messages were from my father, who wanted to chat, and Tracy, whom Kama had offered to rip apart if she didn't stop bugging me. I knew there was something I liked about Kama. Cathy had also called and Kama seemed to like her.

I hung up with a sigh.

"There was nothing from my friend who's running down

the companies for me. I'll call her in a bit and add Dowland as another starting point. This is so damn frustrating. I guess, if worst comes to worst, we can ask Cathy to divine the bastard's location for us, but it's an extra thing that can go wrong, and I don't want her in the line of fire. Damn!"

"Peace, my friend, now is not the time for wasted wrath. I suggest we all meditate upon this problem. Maybe solutions will present themselves," advised Toshiro.

I spent the next hour meditating. Keeping mentally open, I reached for my Runes and drew several for a quick update.

In the past I saw *Sigel*, the Sun, a victory Rune. I guessed the powers that be were satisfied with our progress. The present was *Is*, a Rune of delay: plans were frozen. The future was *Tir*, the Norse warrior God, keeper of oaths. This Rune suggested victory through struggle. What was helping us was *Rad*, a Rune indicating information coming from afar, possibly a phone call. Finally, the disruptive influences, *Need*, necessity, another delay Rune. The whole reading seemed to say keep plugging and victory would come. I had my doubts.

"What do your western stones reveal?" asked Kunio.

I almost leapt out of my skin at the sound of his voice immediately behind me.

"They say we have to wait until we get some information from a distance and that we stand a good chance of victory."

"They are interesting stones and seemingly useful. I will have to ask my Master to teach me what he knows of the I Ching. These systems of divination seem to have more merit than I had thought."

"They're useful tools but you always have to use common sense with them."

"Yes, that is true of everything.

"On another topic, my friend, as we must wait before we may again hunt the Nukekubi, I was wondering if we could not take my Master to see Niagara Falls? You could ask Cathy to accompany us. I know you must miss her company."

I smiled. Kunio showed a courteous side I hadn't suspected. Besides, he was asking me to help him double team Toshiro. If that didn't make us friends nothing would. The mention of Cathy's name seemed to start a bell ringing in the back of my mind, but nothing clear was coming forward just then. "Sounds good to me. Not much we can do until the bastard hunts again anyway. We should bring Kama along though. She's probably getting cabin happy at my place."

Kunio shrugged but I think I saw a glint in his eye. "If you insist, she may come with us; but I think you show her too much regard."

"Maybe, maybe not. People tend to be what they think they are."

"Such low voices, one begins to wonder what you can be discussing." Toshiro moved to join us.

"Master, we were thinking we should investigate the place where the Nukekubi last fed," said Kunio.

"Ah yes. It might be of value to do so, but it is a long drive. Should we so intrude upon young Ray's good nature?"

"I don't mind. Truth to tell, I could stand a break, and the Falls can be fun."

Toshiro smiled and I knew he had heard every word Kunio and I had said.

"Yes, Master, a break. We could also bring along Ray's friend, Cathy. She is a mystic and might sense something useful."

"Now, my son, is this to be part of our hunt, or a social outing?" Toshiro pulled on a face of severe austerity, which kept trying to crack as the edges of his mouth trembled with a repressed smile.

"Master, I do not belittle our quest, but what more can we do?"

Toshiro dropped the mask and chuckled warmly. "My son, you must think me so serious. Of course we must see Niagara Falls. It is a wonder of the world and we have come a long way. Ray is kind to supply the transport and we all need the rest. Bringing the young women along is also a fine idea. I believe I have been remiss in your teaching in that aspect. It is so easy to let the years pass and not see the changes. You have become a man and must learn to deal with the opposite sex. We should go during the day so Kama may safely accompany us."

Kunio's excitement rolled off of him like a puppy waiting at the door for its leash.

I made a couple of phone calls to arrange things with the girls. Then, for lack of anything better to do, I took Toshiro and Kunio to the *Royal Ontario Museum*. I'd already discovered the Nukekubi's energies were masked when it wore its human guise. This meant I couldn't sense it if it was more than two or three metres away therefore I couldn't track it until it hunted again. Even then I would have to be within a kilometre or two to feel the beast.

We returned to the hotel to find an envelope taped to our room's door. Toshiro opened the envelope revealing a single sheet of parchment. Sketched at the top of the page was a Nukekubi head and laying sprawled under it were three human figures. Across the bottom of the page was a sentence in Japanese.

Toshiro read the message aloud. "Death to those who challenge the Nukekubi."

"It is trying to scare us," observed Kunio.

"It's succeeding." I said. "Pass me the letter. I'll see what I can get off it."

Toshiro obliged. Relaxing, I felt the energies impregnated in the letter. The pattern was not the Nukekubi 's. It was from a vile man; a man who, if he had the power, would be another Idi Amin. This person served the Nukekubi because of his love of horror. I could sense nothing useful about our opponent, but such a one as the artist would have been drawn to certain groups I knew of.

"Kunio, can you draw me a picture of the limo driver?" I set the letter aside.

"Yes, but why?"

"There may be a way for me to track him. Using it makes me uncomfortable, but I might find something out."

Kunio took out a pencil and pad and soon had a fair rendering.

"I have to go now." Taking the drawing I headed towards

the door.

"Where?" demanded Kunio, grabbing his coat.

"To dance with the devil, my friend, to dance with the devil." I heard Toshiro calling Kunio back as I left the room.

Where I was going it was best I go alone. Defenceless as I was against Kunio's martial arts skills, so Kunio would be against many of my abilities. The occultist I was going to meet followed a different path than my own. In essence, he believed in a 'me first' way of life that would have made him at home in most corporate boardrooms. To call him a friend would overstate it, but we shared a grudging, mutual admiration. I strengthened my mystical shields as I drove, reaching his place about eleven.

The lights were on in his semi-detached house, so I rang the bell and waited. The door opened to reveal Herbert, his lean frame clad in a blood-red bathrobe and his sandy-blond hair mussed. His pretty-boy face broke into a smile.

"Ray, this is a surprise. Your timing, as usual, is atrocious."

"Runs in the family. My father keeps calling at dinner. I have something important to discuss with you."

"I assumed so by your presence. It really is a shame how old friends drift apart. Do come in."

"Yeah, verily so. You still busy raping chipmunks?"

"If you're going to insult me...You know I graduated to hamsters years ago," retorted Herbert.

"Just curious. Is it safe for me in here? Wouldn't want to set anything off, if you get my drift?"

"Safe enough. I keep my guardian on a chain."

"One of these days that damned," – literally – "thing is going to get loose, and you're going to end up an obituary before you can bind it again."

"I'm careful."

I moved through a short hall that ended in a stair and turned right into his well-appointed living room. The furniture was new, for a student, and his bookshelves were filled with hard covered books, ranging from Budge's translation of the *Pert em Hru*, to the *Koran*.

I sat on the black Italian-leather sofa as Herbert put some light rock on his stereo. A noise drew my attention to the hall. A naked woman walked down the stairs to join us. I saw her legs first and they kept me looking. Eventually, I forced my eyes high enough to see that she was bald and had a swastika tattooed on her forehead. Her nose was triple pierced with a golden loop in each hole and I didn't even attempt to count the earrings she was wearing.

"You gonna finish what we started or you wimping out on me?" she demanded in a tobacco roughened voice. Her large breasts shook back and forth as she moved.

"Shut up, bitch, and get back in there. I'll be along when I'm ready. This is important." ordered Herbert.

The woman snorted. "Yeah right. You can bring this one along as long as you don't keep him to yourself." Shooting a wink at me, she stomped back upstairs to the bedroom.

"Sometimes I think that bitch has to be taught who the master is. Why I put up with her, I don't know. Well, actually, I do. It's the hair. Have you ever been with someone who's bald?"

"No!" I managed to rip my eyes away from a buttock that was covered with a tattoo depicting a satyr and a nymph that...well...when she walked away it was a show one only expects to see in a red light district.

"You should try it. It's an utterly novel experience. You can have her if you like, as long as I get to watch."

"No thanks." I don't think I shuddered visibly. I'm as liberal as the next guy, but still.

"Pity. Would you care for a drink? I have beer, wine, and a reasonably well-stocked liquor cabinet." Herbert was the perfect host, urbane, polite, and if you happened to be in his way, capable of killing you over a nice dinner, and then order desert. I knew he'd go a long way, provided the other sharks didn't eat him first.

"You must be doing well for yourself." I took note of the big screen TV that dominated the room.

"Not bad. Granny saw to it that I was set up quite

comfortably until I finish university, then I go straight into corporate law and I'm set for life. Tell me, are you still lifeguarding?"

"Yes, and I'm doing all right with it. At least I can sleep nights."

"I never have problems sleeping."

"Most reptiles don't. Look, we could spar all night but I'm sure you want to get back to baldy minced ears, and frankly your place gives me the creeps. You still have that altar in the back closet?"

"A few additions since you saw it. Would you like to take a look?"

"No!...Thank you." With ordinary eyes his altar was creepy. With mystic sight...Let's just say peeing myself wouldn't make things better. Besides, the shields I had strengthened on the drive over were beginning to weaken from being in a place dedicated to the enemy of my Gods.

"Let's get on with this." I pulled out Kunio's sketch. "I'm looking for this guy. I have reason to believe he might be hooked up with some group on your side of things. Can you find him for me?"

"I could pass the picture on to some of the other groups. I don't recognize him myself."

"He's probably from Toronto."

"What do you want him for, and more to the point, what's in it for me?"

"Have you heard of the new drug Terror?"

"Of course." Herbert leaned back looking thoughtful.

"I think this guy is pushing it." I leaned forward in my seat. I thought of trying an empathic push, but on Herbert it would be futile and between mystics it is viewed as rude.

"Not your usual kind of heroics, chasing a drug dealer. Besides, it doesn't affect me. I believe in free enterprise."

"Do you believe in getting painted with the same brush? I think he's using secret knowledge from at least one tradition to make Terror. If he has a group, he's using it to keep them in line, and when the cops eventually catch him..."

"Hmm... Yes that would be bad. Anyone clumsy enough to leave a trail of bodies will inflame the idiot masses. To avoid heightened scrutiny of the mystical community, I believe that tracking this fellow down would serve all our best interests. The police are already trailing several of my group's known members. They think we sacrificed someone. Bit of a pain that. Stupid of the cops as well. My group only does human sacrifice symbolically. It's not our problem if the girl gets upset and runs off after a quiet, little orgy."

"So you'll send the picture around? Good. If anything turns up, you have my number, but don't spread it around. Have them get back to you, or I'll give your new number to the Baptist Reformation Church."

"That was you...you...you son of a bitch!" Herbert sat bolt upright in his armchair. "It was nine months before those idiots stopped praying for me and at eight thirty every Sunday morning for three months they were leaning on my—"

"I told you not to cast a lust spell on Casey. Courtesy only goes so far." Standing, I walked to the door. "Do be a good lad and circulate that picture for me? Bye."

Letting myself out, I started to laugh. Evangelists may be a pain, but on that one occasion they served me well.

I drove back to Toshiro's hotel, arriving shortly after midnight, and clambered into my sleeping bag. Despite the fact I'd only been awake a few hours it felt like days. That night, I dreamt of demons, hippopotami and crocodiles, but in all the dreams I was protected by a golden light, which kept the beasts at bay. Prayer can do wonders.

In other dreams I prowled the jungle as a black jaguar and soared through the skies as a golden falcon, all beneath the blazing eye of the sun.

– Chapter 12 –

DISC⊕VERIES

When I awoke I knew what the bell in my mind was suggesting. I slipped into the shower and by the time I emerged Toshiro was waiting for me.

"Did you discover what you sought last night?" he asked.

"More or less. I've left the picture with an acquaintance of mine. He'll circulate it through some groups that the chauffeur may have had an interest in."

"If all you were doing was seeking the help of a friend, why did you not take me with you?" demanded Kunio from the armchair.

"He isn't a friend, more the opposite. Trust me, the less he knows about you the better off you are."

"If he is an enemy, how do you know he will not warn our quarry?" Toshiro sounded concerned. I was getting so I could read Toshiro despite his outer calm. He was worried, I think about the quest in general. It was taking too long. There had been too many close calls. Something didn't mesh with his experience.

I couldn't help with his actual worries, so I answered his surface question. "Common cause. I implied a cult connection to Terror. Alterative religions make the cops nervous to start with; add drugs and it's very easy for them to go Gestapo. Add a couple of deaths, it's almost a certainty."

"Go Gestapo?" Kunio's face was screwed up in puzzlement.

"Act like fascists. Freedom of religion is only as good as the cops' willingness to treat people equally. The uniform isn't supposed to see race, creed or colour, but in the end it's a human being that wears it." I shrugged, truth was truth, and there was no use in being pissed off about it.

"So, this foe of yours will aid us to avoid the police looking into his own group's activities," observed Toshiro.

"Yeah, the community likes to deal with this kind of thing internally. Find the idiot and give him to the cops wrapped up in a nice, red ribbon. It's less of a hassle than being targeted because one of your altar tools happens to be a dagger."

"Is this enemy of yours, like yourself, a practitioner of witchcraft?" Kunio seemed pleased with himself for finding an English label for what I did.

"I prefer wizardry, since I'm not an initiated witch, but yes, he is a mystic. Though most of what he does I wouldn't touch with a ten-foot pole."

"It is for the best that you have started this path of investigation, but for today let us relax. While I shower you two can pack the bags and place them in the automobile. I feel it best we move. The Nukekubi obviously knows of this place," said Toshiro.

"I have to call Cathy and ask her to prepare something for me. There may be a way I can strike against our foe when he's in his human guise."

"What is your plan?" Toshiro stopped on his way to the shower.

"I can track him on the astral plane; maybe find out who he is. It's good we're taking the day off. I need to get grounded on this level of existence before I go flitting off to another."

"What is this astral plane?" Kunio looked frustrated. His English was good, but very formal, and didn't encompass a lot of speciality words like occultists use.

Toshiro spoke a few words in Japanese and Kunio turned pale.

"This is not good. I cannot follow you there. You will be alone against our enemy."

"That's why I need Cathy. She'll be my anchor. She told me she wants to help. This will let her lend a hand while staying at arm's length of this mess."

"Ray, you are not my disciple, so I may not order you, but be careful. The Nukekubi may prove even stronger on what you call, 'the astral plane.' Still, speak with Cathy and see what she says. You know your strengths and weaknesses better than I."

"I'll be careful, if things start to heat up, I'll run like the proverbial rabbit."

"I still do not like this, but if my Master thinks it is best to let you try then what can I say?" Kunio came to his feet and started packing to cover his discomfort at the decision.

Toshiro smiled. I think his disciple was growing in a way he had hoped for but not expected for several years. I can be a good influence, sometimes, I hope, maybe.

Packing up the hotel room went quickly since Toshiro and Kunio only had a small bag each. Kunio went into the shower, so I called Cathy, while Toshiro went to the lobby to check out.

My conversation with Cathy was brief and she agreed to my plan. I knew she'd been feeling left out. We were kinda a team when it came to dealing with the spooky side of life... death... whatever. Of course, up till now the worst we'd come up against was Sue's poltergeist, but still. We agreed to do the work at my place that evening after the others were settled.

Soon after, Kunio and I joined Toshiro in the greasy spoon beside the hotel. Our meal done, we piled into my car and were off. As we drove Kunio kept glancing out the back window. I was too busy avoiding madam turn and scream at the kids in the back seat and a guy with the newspaper spread across the steering wheel who would glance up occasionally to see where he was going. I was beginning to think that monster hunting wasn't the most dangerous part of my life.

Kunio reached forward and tapped my shoulder. "That red sports car, with the horse on its front grill, has been following us since we left the hotel."

"Shit!" I can be eloquent, see.

Toshiro shifted in his seat so he could observe the car.

"I believe I saw that vehicle in front of the hotel this morning," he remarked.

"Hold on to your hats!" I hit the gas.

My car jerked ahead but the red Mustang began closing the distance.

"They are gaining on us," observed Kunio.

"Brace yourselves." I swerved into a hole in traffic. Mr. Newspaper actually looked up as I wove from lane to lane, passing the slower moving vehicles.

"I still see them, but they are not so close," said Kunio.

"Ray, your driving will kill us all," cautioned Toshiro.

"I know!" I could feel sweat on my forehead. I passed a convoy of trucks and up ahead I could see where slower traffic blocked the rest of the highway.

"They are getting closer," said Kunio.

"I have an idea." Hitting my brakes I cut in front of a diesel. The Mustang moved up in my side mirror. I let off the break and swerved onto an off ramp before taping them again. We slowed and from the perspective of the highway we vanished behind the diesel's trailer. I let up on the breaks to maintain speed and took the first curve of the off ramp with tires squealing.

"There he goes!" exclaimed Kunio as our pursuer shot past us on the highway only to get boxed in where the traffic slowed.

"Hope he overheats." I muttered. Pushing in the clutch, I hit the brakes again.

My car slowed with a shudder, made the last corner onto the secondary road, then stalled.

"What is wrong with the vehicle?" Toshiro sounded as relieved as I was to have slowed down.

"I think I scared it." I caressed the dashboard. It may be small, and I'll never win any sexy car awards with her, but I like my skateboard with an attitude.

I let her coast to a stop on the gravel shoulder and collected myself before turning the key in the ignition. The engine coughed twice then purred to life.

The rest of the trip took longer than I planned, since we opted to take the back roads. We were so late reaching Cathy's place that she was actually ready and waiting. I won't say it was a first, but it was the exception. Kunio and I helped her into the front seat before stowing her crutches on the roof rack. Cathy lapped up the attention and looked spectacular in a blue dress and matching coat. We drove to my apartment to collect Kama. As Kunio descended the stairs with her I was stunned. She was dressed in a black mini-skirt and a lacy white blouse that revealed just enough to spark the imagination. I could tell Kunio was having a problem maintaining his cool demeanour.

"Are you going to sit there drooling or are we going to the Falls?" Cathy chided when she saw the direction of my gaze.

I closed my mouth as Kunio helped Kama into the car and took a seat. It was almost funny to watch Kunio in my rear-view mirror. Three in the back was tight. He started by draping his arm across the seat. Realizing this placed his arm over Kama's shoulders he pulled it back blushing. Kama added to the comedy by leaning into him, smiling coyly.

"Ray, start driving," ordered Cathy.

Toshiro sighed and smiled indulgently. He knew when to let the kids play. Of course the old dog had watched Kama come down the stairs as much as I had.

We arrived at the Falls and parked at the Greenhouse.

"We're here." I opened my door.

"I thought we were to see Niagara Falls?" Toshiro glanced around the manicured grounds that surrounded the parking lot.

"Wise man does not drive on Niagara Parkway near Falls." I said with a very bad Chinese' accent. This got a smile from the girls. "Besides, this is the first attraction on this side, other than Marine Land," I explained and moved to Cathy's side of the vehicle.

"We should go to Marine Land. The deer are great. They'll

eat out of your hand," suggested Kama as she stood.

"I don't go to places that hold dolphins prisoner!" snapped Cathy, who now had her crutches underneath her.

Kama looked like she'd been slapped. "Well, sorry!"

Cathy let it go and we followed the walkway to the Greenhouse doors, pausing to look at the beautifully manicured yards. Autumn had painted the maple trees in reds and golds, everything looked like a postcard. Reaching the double glass doors, we stepped in. The first room held a fountain bedecked with plants.

"Ray, I think I'll just sit on the bench and breathe. This place smells so good. Besides, I've seen it all before," said Cathy.

I joined her on the bench that circled the room in front of a raised, stone planting platform. Small birds flitted back and forth amongst the plants and the water gurgled in the fountain.

"Kama has a thing for Kunio you know," said Cathy, when the others were in the main room.

"Yup. I give Kunio maybe two days, if he's lucky."

"Don't be so sure. Kama and I talked on the phone a lot. She's only been hooking about a month. She's really naive in a strange kind of way."

"Won't matter to Kunio. He's old school, virgin until married and the lot."

"So you don't see a future for them."

"Kunio's a guy, his hormones will get him to sleep with her, but his head won't accept what she was." I found a dead leaf and started slowly tearing it apart.

"Too bad. I've told her I'd help her get started on the strip circuit. My agent, Kevin, is an agent, not a pimp, so she'd be fine with him, if I get her in. Trouble is she's only seventeen."

"I hope she can find something. The street's no place for someone like Kama."

"No place for anyone. Good thing is it hasn't made her hard, yet. Pity about Kunio. If ever there was a man who needed a relationship with a more experienced woman it's him."

"You offering?" I crumpled my dead leaf and found another.

"He's your friend, Ray. I wouldn't do that to you." She touched my shoulder.

The breath I released must have been audible because Cathy laughed and kissed me.

"About tonight, I've made up some flying ointment in case you have trouble getting out." She slipped her arm around my back and rested her head on my shoulder. It felt nice.

"I don't think I will. I may not be as good at astral projection as you, but this is important enough that I shouldn't have any trouble." I leaned into her and let the warm, sweet smell that was Cathy fill my senses.

"As long as you come back. You know, Ray, I've been thinking, this thing with Kunio and Kama is kind of like us."

"How?"

"Kunio clinging to an old, worn-out way of doing things, and Kama willing to have him if he'll change."

We pulled apart. She had to ruin it. "Cathy, we've been over this. As loving friends, with no commitment, I can handle you dating other guys. I won't commit myself to an open relationship... I just can't do it. It's not who I am. To me commitment is having you all to myself and me giving you all of me."

"Why, Ray? You'd be the central relationship. It just means we'd both still have our freedom." Cathy looked so frustrated. You'd think I was the one asking for something outside society's boundaries.

"I am what I am. Besides, isn't there a type of freedom in knowing your loved one is yours and yours alone?" I cupped her cheek. She nuzzled my palm before pulling away.

"Like my parents, sneaking around behind each other's backs, lying to each other until there was no trust left?"

"Doesn't have to be that way, Cath."

Silence descended. It was an old argument, like a sore spot in our mouths that we just couldn't keep from pressing our tongues against.

Several minutes later the others rejoined us and we started

walking along the Niagara gorge. This proved amusing as Kunio kept moving to place one of us between himself and Kama. Kama, for her part, kept appearing at his side.

We stopped at the power station's water intakes. This is a stone lined bay with a pair of channels that run under the road. A waist high stone wall runs parallel to the side walk making it difficult for anyone to fall into the water. There was a lull in the conversation, so I played tour guide.

"The water is taken from here and shunted through underground tunnels to the turbines, and released downstream after the Falls. You can't see the Falls the way they are naturally because so much water is drained off to supply power."

"That's too bad. They should let the water go the way it should," said Kama.

"People must have electricity and this is a clean way of getting it," countered Kunio.

"But the Falls could be so pretty."

"Pretty isn't everything. There is purpose, intelligence, moral strength." Kunio turned to face Kama.

I looked at Cathy. We both grimaced and glanced at Toshiro, who shrugged.

"We're talking about a fuckin' waterfall. Moral strength. Shit!"

"Yes, a waterfall." Kunio swallowed noticeably and added, "A beautiful waterfall," while staring at Kama.

She smiled like the cat that ate the cream.

We moved on to the *Table Rock Restaurant*. While Kunio, Toshiro, and Kama stood outside the restaurant staring at the water as it cascaded over the Falls, I went with Cathy to rent her a wheelchair.

It is a simple truth that you never appreciate what's in your own backyard. I'd seen the Falls so often it was no great thrill. So had Cathy. Kunio and Toshiro were mesmerised by the tons of water roaring over the horseshoe shaped cliff. I rolled Cathy out of the restaurant onto the observation platform and was shocked to see Kama holding Kunio's hand. As we got close enough to make out facial expressions I realized he was probably unaware of her presence. The awed expression on his face was almost comic.

"My young friend, this is magnificent! The power of this place!" breathed Toshiro, when I stood beside him.

"Wait till you see it from below," said Cathy.

"From below?" Kunio shook off his reverie. He looked down at Kama's hand in his own, blushed and released the grip.

A few minutes later we joined the line for the *Scenic Tunnels' Tour* and were soon descending in the elevator to the network of passages that led behind the Falls. The first stop was the large observation platform outside the tunnels. We all stood in our plastic raincoats, staring at the towering wall of water and feeling the spray on our faces. Jaded as I am, the sight still impressed me. The spray however stunk, a by-product of the toxic, chemical sewer we have turned the Niagara River into.

I touched Cathy's shoulder and she looked at me. No words were spoken. Her smile told me she understood, so I left her to follow the tunnels that led behind the water. As far from the crowds as I could manage, I opened my mind and heart.

To the indigenous people the Falls were considered the home of one of their Gods. Names mean nothing. The Horus of the Egyptians is the Apollo of the Greeks, the Lug of the Celts and the Thor of the Norse. Only the nature of the deity, the part of the cosmic order they rule has meaning. I invited in the lord of the place. His maleness touched mine. His will strengthened mine. I knew this God stood with me in my struggles. The sense of futility the Nukekubi's last killing had engendered fell away. I felt this deity's strength join with mine and, for a flash, I became the God. My enemy would someday fall; whether I won or lost, no evil could last forever. Like a father, creeping from a sleeping child's room, the God left me to continue my appointed task.

Quietly, I rejoined the others. I'm sure only Kunio would have commented, but he was too busy trying to decide whether he liked having Kama hold his hand or not.

We found our way to *Clifton Hill*. This steeply sloping street is lined by tourist shops, arcades, and glitzy 'museums,' promising amazing sights on every neon sign. Cafes, bars, and 'haunted houses' filled the spaces between the two-headed dog emporiums. A man dressed like a gypsy played a violin on the corner just down from the *House of Frankenstein* and up from *Dracula's Castle*. I like the place; it doesn't pretend to be anything but what it is.

Cathy paused in front of the lane that led to the *Rain Forest Café* and its attached arcade and looked up the steeply sloping roadway at the throng of people. "Between the climb and the crowd, I think I'll slow you down. You should go on ahead." She nodded towards Kama who was pale and sweating.

I'd noticed it as well. The closer we got to the site of the killing the more agitated Kama became.

"The ladies should wait here. The site of a murder is no place for delicate flowers such as yourselves." Toshiro donned a fatherly expression.

"We'll do some shopping. Kama can push the chair and I'll use my crutches. We'll meet you in front of the restaurant." Cathy gestured at the fake volcano that topped the *Rain Forest Cafe*. From the strained look on her face, I could tell she was choking on her feminism.

"I could go with you," offered Kama.

"Someone has to look after Cathy," I replied adding to Toshiro's inadvertent jibe.

Kama nodded and moved to stand behind the wheelchair. Cathy wore an expression that promised that I would be getting a long talking to in the not too distant future. It was worth it!

Kunio, Toshiro, and I followed the street to where a lane cut past the *Mystery Maze* attraction into the casino's parking lot. The casino is a grey, multi-storey building with glass doors at the ground level. A long L shaped delivery ramp forms a sloping trench with the building down one side then hugs its edge ending against a wall. A two-metre plank fence closes off the long side of the ramp while a wall rises up on each side of its shorter leg. The sloping access ramp is half filled with cardboard crushers and further down a collection of picnic tables. Judging by the tattered police tape around the picnic tables that was where the Nukekubi had taken a life. None of the casino staff were sitting out when we arrived, the aura of death and fear the Nukekubi left behind probably put them off without them ever knowing why.

I tried to imagine what it had been like for the victim. What would cause a man to dig out his own eyes? Was he terror stricken, running like a rabbit between that wall and fence? Half seeing his pursuer in darkness, not sure what pursued him, knowing only that it held his death? Maybe he tried to wrench open the locked doors in that tall, grey wall. Maybe he'd screamed in a vain hope that someone might help, or did he scream hopelessly from the fear? How long the game of cat and mouse had gone on, or where it started, I couldn't guess. In the end all that was left was a blood stain, marking where our foe had driven a man to blind himself before it fed.

We moved to that stain and I closed my eyes, mentally reaching out, while Toshiro and Kunio searched the area. I could feel the horror of the Nukekubi; the fear of its victim. It was faint, already blending into the background static of the place. I tentatively opened my psychic shields so that I could better sense the area.

It hit me like a sledgehammer. Our foe was smarter than I'd given him credit for. Under the blood, embedded into the asphalt, was a psychic landmine. A concentration of fear. In a week or two it would have dissipated, to a non-sensitive it would make them feel uncomfortable but nothing more. To me...

It ripped across my senses plunging me into a vision.

I was chained to a tree on a beach. Cathy and Sekmara were in the water drowning. I pulled against the chains that held me. I had to reach them! I had to save them! I couldn't! The chains were too strong.

"*Merrow, merrow, merrow.*"

"*Help us! Ray save us!*" *they cried for me. Years of training and I couldn't save the one's I loved! My beloved and my cat went under* and didn't come up.

My grandfather, looking like a rotting corpse, rose from the sand, and was gutted by a large, shaggy, steely-clawed beast. He looked at me with pleading eyes.

"Why did you let me die? Why didn't you save me?"

I tried to focus, but I felt my fear building like a tide. I couldn't save anyone. I'd fail. People would die. The one's I loved would die.

My father lurched in front of me clutching his left arm. He collapsed. I attempted to perform C.P.R only to watch his spirit rise, glare at me with accusing eyes and vanish.

I couldn't stand it. I couldn't watch anymore. All the beings I loved were suffering, dying! I wasn't good enough to save them. I reached for my eyes but something held my arms. I struggled, but my arms wouldn't work. Some part of me knew this for what it was. A hallucination powered by my enemy's deadliest weapon, fear. It was making me live my greatest fear. It was the fear that made me train so hard. The fear that made me cherish the ones around me. I'd used it, but never defeated it. I chose to use it. I set my will behind that small, sane part of me and focussed on that fear. Sekmara would, barring the unforeseen, die before me. Then, drawn by love, she would return to me in a new body. Would I sacrifice the soft touch of her fur or the trusting love and support she gave because of nature's clockwork? Would I stop living because all stories end in death? Everything ends in death, but death is not an end, it is a transition. I would not sacrifice life because it would bring pain. Pain is life as much as bliss. One without the other is meaningless.

I stopped trying to reach my eyes, and the pressure on my arms lessened. The chain released and Cathy appeared in the arms of another man. I watched, apart from the scene, as I burst into view and beat her.

Another fear, a fear that I would become that which I hate. I laughed at how ludicrous the scene was. The fear recoiled from the sound. Given her training, Cathy could probably beat the crap out of me. I knew this fear and denied it. I choose to be the man I am. I would not change those fundamental choices for the sake of temper.

The image evaporated, replaced by the zombie version of my grandfather.

"It's your fault!" The rotting lips formed the words, but the voice was off. It wasn't my grandfather's, it was my own.

"I'll see you and raise you." By now the hallucination was getting thin, the energy driving it exhausted. I was almost back in the real world. I remembered my grandfather and he was there. A gestalt made of my memories and as true a representation as a twelve-year-old boy joined with an adult's perspective could make.

"Nice work. You're almost out." The voice was his. A voice I'd longed to hear for fourteen years. "Do I need to say it? You've done me proud. You should let go of that, it doesn't serve you." He gestured towards the corpse version of himself.

"Easier said than done." I looked at my grandfather. Silver haired, broad shouldered, though a little chubby. It struck me how much alike our faces were.

"Keep trying." He smiled.

I was kneeling on the loading ramp with Toshiro holding one of my arms and Kunio the other.

"I'm back. I'm okay." My voice was breathless and a crowd was gathering at the end of the ramp.

"We must leave," said Toshiro.

A uniformed casino security guard came out of the crowd and approached. "What's going on here?"

I was exhausted but listened when Kunio whispered in my ear. "You were screaming."

I nodded and forced myself to focus on the guard. "I'm sorry. Epilepsy is a pain in the ass. With a little warning you can get someplace private. This is at least out of the way. My friends can look after me."

The guard's demeanour changed to one of concern. Most people are decent given a chance. "I'll call an ambulance."

"There's no need. I'll be all right if I can just take a nap. The back of the car should do." I directed the last to Toshiro.

"I must insist," began the guard.

I pulled myself up to my full height. "I appreciate your concern, but I must refuse." Wrapping myself in as much dignity as I could, I walked away. Kunio and Toshiro shrugged and followed. We met the girls at the back of the crowd.

"We heard screaming," said Cathy who was on her crutches. Kama was pushing her empty chair.

"Ray went mad. We had to hold his arms so that he did not gouge his eyes out," explained Kunio. I decided I needed to talk to him about not trashing another guy's image.

"Ray?" Cathy stared at me in that way that said she was checking my aura.

"Psychic landmine keyed to pull out your worst fears and make you experience them. I didn't think a Nukekubi could do that."

"Nor did I. This is not a typical beast." Toshiro stroked his moustache.

"That's high level shit!" Cathy's brow wrinkled in thought. "I can map out how to do it, but I don't know if we could pull it off. You need to be more careful."

"No argument, I don't want to do anything like that again anytime soon." I looked at her. Seeing her alive and well was the best medicine. Cathy blushed under my scrutiny. I think she guessed part of what I saw. I also wanted to hug my cat, but that would have to wait.

"What did you see? I mean you were screaming like a little girl and you're still fucking white. I mean like, you hunt fucking monsters." Kama patted my arm offering support.

"Kama, one's fears are one's own. You ask for an intimacy few have ever known." Toshiro's voice was gentle. I felt like hugging the old man. He was right, and I don't know if I could have been so diplomatic at that point.

We descended to the *Rain Forest Café* where Kunio vanished into the arcade while Toshiro chatted with the girls, giving me time to recover my strength. We were just beginning to wonder what Kunio was up to when he emerged and presented Kama with a plush toy fish almost as large as she was.

"I..." Kunio blushed. "I won this for you. It took many tickets but the games to win them are not complex."

The smile on Kama's face was golden.

"We should eat." Cathy gestured to the *Rain Forest Café*.

"Cath... I—" I began. My wallet is a little thin for eating

at some establishments.

"My treat. A lot of dancers I've lent money to paid up when they heard I got hurt. I think Jessy's been pestering them. " Cathy sat in the wheelchair.

I shrugged and moved to push her chair. I'm evolved enough to let the woman pay and not feel unmanned. Really, I am. I can do it. My subscription to Neanderthal Weekly is on its way, but I didn't have a choice, Cathy paid. Sometimes you just bow to the inevitable.

The *Rain Forest Café* was bedecked with artificial foliage and an animatronic snake that made Kama jump straight into Kunio's arms when she happened to walk under it. We sat beside the fish tank. Kama was almost child-like in her delight each time the animatronic gorillas and elephants did their show. I don't think there had been much whimsy in Kama's life up till that point. Kunio blushed several times as we ate so I assume some footsie was being played. Toshiro, Cathy and I sat back and enjoyed the show. The food completed my cure and I was ready to drive home.

There were three good reasons I drove. First, Kunio was completely distracted by Kama. Second, my car's a stick and Cathy had a leg in a cast. Third, Cathy's driving would make Evil Knievel nervous.

Toshiro was quieter than usual. About the time we were passing Beamsville he spoke. "Ray, do not take this poorly, but will it not be crowded at your apartment with four of us sleeping there?"

"I hadn't thought of that, but it will be," I agreed.

"You can crash at my place. I have a foldaway couch and a spare room. Ray and I can do our thing in his apartment," offered Cathy.

"What about the Nukekubi? It's still hunting me, ain't it?" asked Kama.

"My place is warded every bit as well as Ray's. Maybe better. I'm less susceptible to a pretty face. Oh, yes, have you seen Amanda lately, Ray?" Cathy smiled at me.

"How was I supposed to know she was only interested in

stealing my power? I stopped her." I grumbled as the others listened, too polite to ask.

"We should accept Cathy's offer, Master. Her home is much larger than Ray's," said Kunio.

"Yes, my son, you, Ray and Kama should stay at Cathy's after they have performed their ritual. I will sleep at Ray's so as not to disturb you."

"Master, I did not mean you should not be with us."

"Kunio, I am an old man and age brings some wisdom. Young people must spend time away from their elders. Besides, I am weary and have much to consider. Our foe is posing many questions for which I must discern the answers. It has skills I have not seen before. I will sleep at Ray's and you four will stay at Cathy's. I am certain it will be better for Ray to stay up and practice things of this Earth after his journeys in the spirit world."

From the smirk on Cathy's face I knew she'd conspired with Toshiro. Sometimes I'm glad Cathy and I aren't exclusive. With her mind I wouldn't stand a chance.

– Chapter 13 –

DANGERS ⊕F SPIRI+

J left Toshiro, Kunio and Kama at Cathy's place Cathy and I went over to my apartment. Kama had transformed it.

The clutter had been put away and the laundry washed and hung in my closet. Sekmara lay on the neatly made bed and looked at me as I stepped in. I rushed to hug and pet her. She purred and nuzzled my face.

"Should I leave you two alone?" Cathy's smile took any sting from the words.

"Be happy your major competition is furry. Of course you're both female, so there is much of a sameness. Manipulative, conniving, demanding ..."

"This from a man who wants me to act as his anchor?" Cathy hobbled past me and laid her bag on the bed.

"Let's set up and get this show on the road." I started clearing the floor for the ritual.

Preparing the temple area took only minutes. My coffee table, draped in a deep-blue cloth, served as an altar. The crook and flail, the Egyptian tools for commanding and persuading mystical entities, sat crossed in its centre. The sistrum, chalice, winged disk and mirror of Hathor, lay at the compass points around the altar.

"Which God forms are we using?" asked Cathy.

"Anubis, God of travellers, is a definite. I need guide energy to find my quarry. I lean towards the Amun aspect of the God Ra for the warrior force. He can really kick butt. We could use the Goddess Bast or Sekhmet if you'd prefer gender polarity."

"I would. Amun's too testosterone heavy without a female presence. I'll call on the cat Goddess, Bast. You may need catlike stealth to get close enough to do any good. Besides, Sekhmet is too uncontrolled an energy for me. I'm a pussy cat, not a lioness."

"Hmm yes, you are manipulative and vicious, not just vicious."

"Someday, McAndrues, someday."

"I hope you have the chance." I collected the statues of the jackal headed and cat headed deities from the top of my book shelf. Two candles and a salt bowl followed.

"Remember your first rule, Ray. If a magic act scares you, you're not ready for it. We can stop now."

"New rule. Some things scare you because they're scary. Let's get started."

Cathy moved to my side before the altar. Casting the protective spells and invoking the Gods went smoothly then I lay on the floor, my head in her lap. The candles on the altar flickered, sending dancing shadows across the ceiling and I focussed my mind upon them. Vibrations coursed through me and my eyes slowly closed. My breathing steadied and I floated towards the ceiling. Looking down I saw my physical form. A golden glow emanated from Cathy, encompassing us both, and the altar shone in rainbow hues. I checked the thin, golden line that tethered me to my body then left the circle. Floating around my apartment, I examined my surroundings. So far I was on the physical plane, a living ghost, able to go anywhere unseen.

Cathy stroked my body's brow and looked at my apparently sleeping face.

"Be careful McAndrues, come back to me. I love you."

I knew she never would have admitted it if she thought I was still there, but it made me feel ten feet tall. I felt like I could conquer the world. Which was a good thing considering what I was about to attempt. I've said it before, in magic attitude is everything.

Getting back to work, I pictured the Nukekubi in my mind's eye and willed myself towards my foe. Blackness engulfed me like a rising tide of fetid water. Screams echoed on all sides and the stench of decay filled my nostrils. Jagged rocks bit into my feet, and the air felt slimy and thick. Blood-red lightning streaked, revealing the horrors of an abattoir. Fear rose up from the depths of my being. The sporadic light revealed hideous things creeping towards me. I could taste the terror that permeated the place.

"Keep your head, Ray. This is the lower astral, that's all. You can ascend from it. Now how in the name of Ra did I get here?" I spoke to myself.

"Help me," wailed a figure that approached in the half-light. I stared at it. It was female, Asian, middle-aged and dripping wet. Bubbles frothed from its lips when she spoke. She was drowning where she stood. My heart lurched. I knew her. I didn't know from where, but I knew her and had felt affection for her in some other life.

The wraith released a gurgling howl, giving off an explosion of sickly, mustard-yellow, fear energy that permeated the air. It staggered then stood again.

"Help me!" it whimpered. The call was echoed by others like it. Glancing around I saw shambling, corrupted, human forms on all sides. Each one's appearance mirrored a hideous, terror-filled death.

I focussed my mind on an image of the Amentet fields, the Egyptian heaven, and willed myself there. Nothing happened!

"Help us," screeched the shambling wraiths that now surrounded me.

"How? I can't be kept in the lower astral!" I muttered to myself as I tried again to leave that darksome place.

"You sought me, wizard. Now taste the fate of those who would challenge their betters." The voice was feminine and could have made a fortune doing phone sex

I spun to face the voice and saw a blood-soaked, human skull. Tentacles of shining red energy writhed beneath it, like some obscene jellyfish. I realized with a disgusted jolt that the tentacles were loops of intestine. The wraiths halted in their progress, hovering in a circle less than two metres away.

I willed myself away from that place, trying to return to my body.

"You cannot escape, human. This is my place, walled in with my power. None may depart without my leave." The sultry tones made the threat and horror of the beings appearance more terrifying.

"An astral pocket, bracketed by the fear and despair of your victims?" I made the connection. It's a good thing I was on the astral or I would have had to change my underwear.

"You are quick, mortal, but you are also dead. I would have preferred that my earthly child feed upon your flesh, but I will at least taste your spirit." A red tongue darted from the skull's mouth and swept across its teeth before it vanished and the wraiths about me rushed forward wailing. A line of glowing Nukekubi floated beyond them driving them on.

"NO!" I screamed and drew upon my heart chakra. Golden light exploded from my chest. The wraiths fell silent and halted as the energy enveloped them. It was the first comfort they'd known since their deaths.

"By earth and air and fire and sea, an orb of protection form round me." I spoke the words to focus my thoughts. A moment later a glistening orb of energy surrounded me.

"More," cried the wraiths who rushed me. Mutilated bodies crowded against the orb of protection and cracks began to cover its surface. Stalling them was taking all my concentration.

"I am not your foe. Turn against the beast that attacked you!" I screamed, praying that at least one of the wraiths might listen.

"Help us, please," they moaned.

I realized they couldn't help themselves. They'd been locked in terror for too long, their minds were almost gone, their essence of self shrivelled. All they had left was the terror of their last moments of life. The astral responds to emotion, taking on the shape of the feelings projected into it. This whole pocket dimension reflected the last tortured seconds of the Nukekubi's victims. It was a gross perversion of the natural order that strengthened my foe at the near eternal expense of the innocent. How the Gods could permit this I didn't know. Then I realized they didn't, not unchallenged. They'd sent me. I knew what had to be done.

"I hate this!" I murmured as I braced myself and let my shields fall. Wraiths fell upon me, threatening to smother me by sheer weight of numbers. Reaching with my will, I touched them, taking the fear and despair that bound them. I became one with the energy, its consciousness and centre. How many wraiths I pulled into that merge I don't know, but when I could barely stand against the force of their terror, other wraiths still littered the ground.

The terror pulled at me like a tide of dark blood. My awareness of self was drowning in it. The astral form I wore became a giant shambling thing. Mustard-yellow blood oozed from every pore, my arms and legs stripped of flesh. Everything hurt and screamed for relief. It was different from the fear landmine in that the fears weren't my own. Spiders, snakes, secrets revealed, hidden appetites, a collage of the fears that torture humanity paraded across my mind, most finding no place in me to relate to. Only the fear existed, and fear was a kind of energy, and energy I could use.

Screaming for the wraiths and myself, I released the pent up fear and despair that had been my attackers'. It became a laser of mustard-yellow force that struck the sky of my foe's pocket dimension. The energy tore at the barriers that held so many captive. The blackness parted. I felt the wraiths around me hurtle towards that opening. Now, free of the fear energy that bound them, they were drawn to the sections of the astral that best reflected their own natures. I sent a single word hurtling out with them. "*Cathy!*"

The last of the wraith energy dissipated and my astral form crumpled, whimpering in emotional turmoil and exhaustion. I curled into a foetal position, unable even to think.

"Impressive," observed my captor's voice. "Though it will do you no good. Still, credit where credit is due. If you had faced one of my worshippers you might have escaped. It will be quite some time before I fully replenish the screen protecting this aspect of my being, not to mention my larder."

I huddled, whimpering as a burning red tentacle stroked my back. From nowhere Sekmara appeared, only now she was the size of a tiger. She leapt against the Nukekubi's skull, sending it careening away.

"Ray!" called a voice that sent a soothing balm over my shattered psyche.

"Cathy," I moaned.

Energy touched me and I staggered to my feet. She stood beside me. Her broken leg meant nothing here. She was even more beautiful than in her physical form.

"We have to get you out of here," she snapped.

"Sealed dimension," I tried to explain.

"I saw you spring the trap and came in with my eyes open. I know the way out."

"Sekmara."

"She wouldn't stay behind. She heard you call and went astral before I could stop her. Damn good familiar."

Sekmara had kept our foe busy and was now entwined in those awful burning intestines.

"Too good to lose!" Closing my eyes I did the only thing I had energy left to do. The astral is shaped by mental energy, so letting the image of me as a man fade away I reshaped my form into one better suited to my current need. In less than a second a black jaguar stood beside Cathy. Leaping, I dragged my claws across the intestines. Acid-like blood spewed forth, but as the beast writhed it released Sekmara. We both leapt to Cathy's side. Grabbing the fur of our necks, she closed her eyes. For a moment, we moved freely through the astral then everything halted.

"Going so soon?" asked our foe. We were at what I conceptualised as a large sealed gate in the dome of mustard yellow that encased this region of the astral. The skull with its dangling intestines hovered before us.

"Step aside, bitch," ordered Cathy.

"I am queen here, witch. You will all stay."

Sekmara and I hissed at the floating skull.

Cathy pointed a finger and bolts of blue light lanced towards our foe. It fell back, stung, but remained blocking our way.

"Ray, I can't hold it back and punch through the barrier."

I tried to speak, remembered I was a cat, tried to become human, found I lacked the energy and growled in disgust.

"Shit!" was all Cathy said then, "Shit, shit, shit! Shit!"

Glancing behind us I saw more wraiths closing in.

"Any good chess player knows when to sacrifice a pawn to save a more valuable piece," spoke the skull. All it had to do was keep us from leaving. The terror of long-dead victims would do the rest.

Cathy began weaving a spell as Sekmara and I crouched ready to spring. The energy that formed the gate behind the skull swirled then split as a force from beyond that darksome realm drove against it. A gold dragon with a pretty Asian woman at its side appeared through the gap. It belched fire that sent our foe reeling. Seeing our chance, Cathy and us cats leapt through the open gate before it slammed shut behind us. In seconds we were back in my apartment, mystically exhausted, but otherwise unharmed.

"Ray, don't you ever do anything that stupid again!" snapped Cathy, as soon as she was settled enough to speak.

Sekmara added her comment by swiping her claws across my bare arm.

I moved to butt my head against Cathy in contrition, remembered I was human, and spoke. "I wasn't expecting an astral temple about the damn thing!"

"Ray, didn't you sense it?"

"I was rather busy in there. Sense what?"

"That wasn't your Nukekubi. That was the spiritual embodiment of Nukekubi. It must be where all astral travellers seeking the beasts get drawn to."

"Shit, you mean?"

"That thing's the Goddess of the Nukekubi. The embodiment of all their spiritual natures combined."

There was no way to thank Cathy or Sekmara enough. To walk open eyed into what they did is beyond words. I hugged Cathy and rubbed my cat's belly.

"I have one question, though. Who were the dragon and that woman?" Cathy rested in my arms. We both needed the comfort.

"I bet if we ask we'll find out that Toshiro took a nap at your place. A gold dragon seems a likely enough animal form for him. As to the woman." I smiled. "A lot of spirits were freed when I made my call. Old victims of incarnate Nukekubi. I can't be sure, but I think that when Toshiro's time comes, he'll find his Sumi waiting for him."

"Maybe this wasn't a waste of time then, but you're still never to be so careless again."

I kissed Cathy in answer.

Closing the temple went quickly and before we were finished Sekmara was asleep on the bed. Cats are so lucky.

I called Toshiro at Cathy's and he insisted on walking over. The old fox said he needed to stretch his legs after his nap and refused to say anything more.

Once Toshiro was settled in my apartment Cathy and I went to pick up enough takeout food for ten people and joined Kunio and Kama at her place.

– Chapter 14 –

MISINTERPRETATIONS

Once the meal was over and I washed the dishes – Cathy was really milking the leg – Kunio and Kama settled on the couch to watch *Shrek*. *Shrek* is, in my opinion, the best date movie ever made. Cathy followed me into her spare room where I was making up the sofa bed. Taking a seat at her computer desk she swivelled her office chair around and watched me.

"I am exhausted." She stretched and stifled a yawn.

"Me too. The food is helping."

"Did you feed Sekmara?"

"Oh yeah. A whole tin of tuna. She's earned her treats for the month."

"Just don't overdo the fish, too much isn't good for kitties. Change of topic. What do you say about Kunio and Kama now?" She smirked at me.

"What should I say? I think you're pushing by having them here without Toshiro. Kunio has a lot of ground to cover before he's ready for any relationship, let alone one that flies in the face of his moral training."

"Toshiro likes Kama. It was his idea that we young folk spend some time alone."

I shrugged. "He isn't infallible. Look, what I say doesn't

matter now. I just hope neither of them gets hurt."

We rejoined Kunio and Kama in the living-room and Cathy settled in her easy chair. I sat on the floor at her feet. Sitting next to the couple on the couch seemed out of place. Come to think of it, Cathy seemed to enjoy our relative postures. Women!

Things went smoothly until about midnight when Kunio excused himself to use the washroom, which was at the end of the hall beside the spare room. A couple of minutes later Kama went to the spare room.

"Love is in the air," sang Cathy.

"The shit will hit the fan," I replied, and we both concentrated on *Shrek Three*. It was a marathon, so sue me.

Maybe twenty minutes passed before we heard the scream. Kama, wearing a black, lace nightie that belonged to Cathy, came running up the hall. A confused Kunio dressed in a robe and holding his sketchpad, followed her. Kama almost flew into Cathy's arms.

"Kama, I am sorry. What have I done? I am sorry." Kunio moved towards them.

I intercepted him. "Not now, later. Come on." Taking his arm, I led him back into the spare room.

I sat Kunio on the bed then asked, "What in Tartarus happened?"

"I do not know. All was going well. I listened to you, Ray, and treated Kama as a person, not a *shoufu*. She is very warm and funny. When I left the washroom she called me into the bedroom. She looked so beautiful in that silky lace. We kissed. I desired her. I have never been with a woman, but she told me what to do. It was exciting and frightening. I realized I had no money to pay."

Gritting my teeth at what I knew was to come, I let Kunio continue.

"I told her I had no money but offered to sketch her in return. She screamed at me, calling me a 'fucking asshole' then ran from the room. What did I do wrong?"

I rubbed the bridge of my nose. "She wanted you as a lover.

You made yourself just another John. Kama had sex for money. She wanted to make love with you. There's a difference. I knew something like this would happen. Damn Cathy! Rushing in where Horus wouldn't dare go.

"Look, I don't know if this can be salvaged. If it can, it won't be tonight. Try and get some sleep. I'll do what I can with Kama. Never offer her money again. That makes you like the others. Be special or be nothing."

I left the room and rejoined Cathy and Kama. From the expression on Cathy's face, I could tell this was no place for a male of any species. I went to her bedroom and settled onto her queen-sized bed to meditate. An hour later, Cathy entered the room.

"Feeling at home?" Her voice could have frozen a polar bear.

I sat up in bed. "This was the only empty room. I figured you didn't want me around."

"Men, you're such scum!" She clumped to the side of the bed threw her crutches on the floor and sat down.

"Yup, we're all insensitive, selfish louts who are so foul and cruel because we make human mistakes and can't always read women's minds."

The main light was out or I'm sure I would have seen rage redden Cathy's face. A minute passed in charged silence before she spoke in a tired voice.

"It could have been so good for both of them."

"It still might be. Kunio didn't know the rules of the game. He's so confused it's pitiful."

"Kama's a mess. She's convinced she'll never live down her past."

"We'll work on them, but it's late and we're both tired. Given the fight we had, I'm lucky I'm still conscious. The social stuff has me grounded enough so I won't drift off in my sleep. Should I go home?"

I felt Cathy shift position and watched in the dim glow of the bedside lamp as her shirt hit the floor.

"Help me get undressed."

I rushed to oblige.

I awoke to Kunio whispering in my ear. Opening my eyes, I stared into the back of Cathy's head illuminated by the daylight that leaked in around the window curtains.

"Kunio, if this isn't good, I swear, if it takes me a lifetime, I *will* turn you into a frog."

"It has struck again! While I wasted my time here, it has killed again, see?"

My first reaction was to brush away Kunio's hand, but slowly his words penetrated. I rolled over and took the newspaper he was waving about wildly. Wiping the sleep from my eyes, I forced them to focus on the headline:

TERROR GRIPS THE REGION

"Call Toshiro. I'll get dressed and bring him over." I sat up, all remnants of sleep gone.

Kunio stood staring past me, his mouth open.

"What?" I glanced around expecting something horrible.

"Probably me." Cathy said behind me. Rolling over I could see she had sat up in bed, reaching for her robe, which was draped over the footboard.

"Cathy, a little modesty please." Cathy has a different view about nudity than most of the world. I can accept it, but sometimes I need to remind her that generally society views clothes as an essential part of most group activities.

"Why? For the price of a beer he could see it all anyway. Besides, if he's going to wake me up, he deserves to be embarrassed."

"I...I am sorry," breathed Kunio, finding his tongue at about the same time Cathy closed her robe.

She laughed. "No problem. Nudity isn't one of my hang-ups. My faculty adviser says I'm an exhibitionist. I didn't tell you that, did I, Ray? Old Prof McDowell caught my act. Hasn't been able to look me in the eye since."

"Cathy, I find that interesting, but I think Kunio should

call Toshiro now."

"Yes. I must not lose sight of what must be done." Kunio left the room. He did glance back just in case though. Neither Cathy nor I laughed, what hetero man wouldn't?

"Think I got him back a bit for what he did to Kama." Cathy belted up her robe.

"You're wicked." I was pulling on my robe when Kama's voice intruded from the doorway.

"Don't bother for me. I've seen enough of those fuckin' things," said Kama.

"What? Oh!" I'm sure I went five shades of red. So maybe I'm not as evolved as Cathy. "I'm sorry we woke you."

"Fuck that. What's up?"

"It's right here." I picked up the paper and passed it to her.

I got back to Cathy's with Toshiro to find that the coffee and tea were ready and a big bowl of pancake batter awaited the stove. We took seats at the kitchen table and Toshiro had me read the article aloud. Kunio tried to sit beside Kama but she arranged it so that Cathy was between them.

"This is most odd." Toshiro accepted the cup of herbal tea that Kama offered him. I was left to collect my own coffee.

"It's out of pattern, it hasn't been three days," I poured my coffee and added water. Cathy always makes it too strong to drink black.

"That is not the only abnormality. Tell me, Kunio, what do you think of this article?"

"Master, I have not fully read it. I do not read English that well. I saw the headline at the store and thought it imperative to call everyone together." Kunio looked downcast. I envied him. I've tried to learn a second language. My brain just doesn't seem to work that way. He spoke three fluently and two well enough to get by.

"You must learn to be less hasty when there is time to spare." Toshiro's look included me.

One good point about not having a teacher: there's no one to rub it in when you screw up.

"My young friends, I ask you, what is the rush? Even if this had been a new killing by the Nukekubi, there is little we can do until evening."

"Forgive me, Master, but why do you doubt that this is a killing by our foe?"

"Did you not listen to the description of the victim? She was a high school student, with family and friends, hardly the fare that our current foe has shown a fondness for. She was coming from a gathering. It is a sad truth that many young people experiment with hallucinogens. Some even slip them to their peers unbeknownst to the person taking them."

"If the person was on a bad trip, PCP or LSD could have a fear reaction like the Nukekubi's." I supplied.

"Ray, you are such a nerd." Cathy smiled at me across the table. I could see love in her eyes. It made it all worthwhile. "It was probably a party mix. Blend together two or three drugs and let 'er rip."

"A sad and dangerous phenomenon to be sure, but hardly something we should become involved with. This is a case better suited to the police." Toshiro nodded to himself. I think he'd seen too much in his life. Too much change for the worse and too much waste.

"Master, I feel a fool."

"We all do foolish things, my son. Now since we are together, and there is a park across the street, let us go to it and perform our Tai Chi, in preparation for today's endeavours."

Toshiro and Kunio downed their tea then left with Cathy, who wanted to watch their technique. This left Kama and me alone.

"Do you think you'll catch that fuckin' thing?" Kama started washing the dishes.

"Yes, I do. I have to. I can't stop looking until I do." I stacked the dry plates from the draining board in the cupboard making room for the new load.

"Somethin' about that screwy wizard stuff?"

"Maybe." I grinned at her. If my sister and various girlfriends were examples, it was about to come out.

Kama looked into the sink of dirty water. "I wish I could do somethin' instead of being a stupid whore."

And there it was. She wasn't just worried about her existence. She wanted to live. "Did you know that the priestesses of Ishtar in Babylon rented out their sexual services? It was considered an act of devotion to lie with them. The client was believed to be lying with an incarnation of the Goddess."

"That's fuckin' weird. Everyone knows hooking's bad."

"Who's everyone? Prostitution doesn't hurt anyone. No one should have to do it, but as a choice, what's the harm? I say legalize it, unionize it, and get rid of the pimps. In places where prostitution is legal, rape drops by around 90 percent."

"Fuck really? Kunio sure don't think that way. People will never fuckin' get over what I've done."

"First, how are they going to know if you don't tell them? Give yourself a chance, you might not believe this, but Kunio wasn't trying to hire a prostitute. He likes you, not just your body. He's pretty naive about a lot of things. He thought the only way you would sleep with him is if he paid you. He doesn't understand the difference between having sex and making love."

"He just wanted to get his rocks off!"

I shook my head. "You need not be Aldonza, my Dulcinea. Live as you desire to live."

She looked at me as if I'd said the moon is pumpernickel.

"It's from *Man of La Mancha*, my favourite musical." I leaned against the counter top.

Kama smiled sadly and tried to tease me. "Does Cathy know you like musicals? There's a guy I know you'd look just adorable with."

I stroked the side of her face and smiled. "Spare me. I hate that cliché. So what if I like musicals and can't stand team sports? It doesn't mean I'm about to dress in taffeta."

Kama snorted with laughter then went back to washing the plates.

"What I'm saying is, you are what you believe you are. Ra's beak, think about it. I hardly know you, and I'm acting like you're my kid sister. Cathy likes you enough to try and help you get a job that doesn't put your life at risk. Toshiro treats you like a granddaughter, and Kunio, believe it or not, really likes you as a woman. You have to have something going for you."

Kama's eyes filled with tears and she sniffled. I don't think she was use to hearing much good about herself. I put my arms around her and just held her. Later she pulled away, kissed me on the cheek and disappeared into the bathroom.

Toshiro and Kunio returned and I phoned Sue to see how her research was going.

She insisted I drop by the university to pick up the information. She was T.A.-ing classes but had a couple of hours between them.

Kunio and Toshiro came with me in case they spotted something in the description I might miss.

We arrived at McMaster University and it took me a moment to get my bearings. I'm accustomed to being there at night. McMaster is a mixture of classical and modern architecture, with young ivy trying hard to give it an aged appearance. It's actually a pretty campus, made only slightly terrifying by the fact that there's a nuclear reactor on the premises.

We met Sue at the main entrance rotunda. She was dressed in her typical blue jeans and a sweat-shirt with, "Accountants do it by the numbers," emblazoned across her breasts. She wore her dark hair in a short and sassy style that really suited her.

"Hi, Sue. I'd like you to meet Toshiro Yoshida and Kunio."

"Hi. Ray, I have that information for you." Sue smiled at my friends and the smile reached her sparkling blue eyes. Her looks are certainly drool worthy. Surprisingly, she seemed to have no affect on Kunio. My guess, he was too hung up on Kama to notice.

"That's great. If I could just take your notes and run we're kinda pressed for time."

"Not so fast. I want to know what all this work is for. I'm thinking of using it as the foundation for my doctoral thesis." She made no move to hand me anything.

"Sue, you wouldn't believe me if I told you. Can we just

leave it that it's important?"

"If you say so. I need to talk you through the notes or they won't mean anything to you. There are some empty classrooms just down the hall. We'll take one of them and go over what I've found."

"That may be for the best, Ray. Sometimes I find your explanations difficult to follow when you speak about what you fully understand. Following you when you are trying to guess at something's meaning may prove too much for me," observed Toshiro.

"I would welcome a change of scene," agreed Kunio.

"Lead on, McSusan." I joked and bowed.

Sue rolled her eyes then led the way to a classroom with blackboards on two of its walls. Grinning from ear to ear, she started scribbling with a piece of chalk on one of the boards.

"First you told me it had to be a company with a strong Japanese connection. That didn't narrow the field much until I added high-ranking executives newly arrived here from Japan. That narrowed the field to these four firms. Then came the tricky part."

Sue began drawing what looked like a complex family tree, overburdened with incest. She started talking and soon lost me in a maze of companies that owned percentages of other companies that were subsidiaries of other companies that were divisions of firms.

Finally, she stopped talking. I stared at the web in confusion and noticed that my mouth was hanging open. Glancing at my allies, I could see that Kunio gazed out the window, longing reflected in his features. Toshiro had fallen asleep.

"So you see, it is obvious what has happened to the item you wanted charted," finished Sue.

"What? Obvious? Sue, you lost me. I can't even find the starting points I gave you."

Toshiro woke up, said something in Japanese, looked to the chalkboard, and added, "Thank you, dear child, for your most interesting talk."

Sue looked at the lot of us as if we were dolts.

"It's simple. Try listening this time. Both Dowland Limited and the Atterson Corporation have places in this corporate web. In fact, Dowland Limited owns ten percent of Atterson Corporation which has five members on the board of directors of the Franklin Group as well as a seventy-five percent ownership. This means that—"

"Sue, I understand that the really big companies buy up any small company that begins to threaten them and form a monarchy unto themselves. They control the world markets for their own benefit. Hades, they even own governments. The principle isn't beyond me."

"That's an over simplification. And they don't own governments."

"We'll agree to disagree. All we need to know is where that limo ended up."

"I wish you'd tell me what you want this for."

"We are hunting a Nukekubi that feeds upon human fear and death at night and masquerades as a Japanese businessman during the day." Kunio's limited patience was exhausted.

Sue stared at me for a long moment, but I made no comment. "Yeah right. Your friend has a weird sense of humour. It has to be the Suwa Corporation. It has majority ownership in a group of companies from the Franklin Group up. Their Toronto office is new and the firm is Japanese based. The company fits your criteria."

"I appreciate what you have done though it amazes me that the vehicle could have travelled up this twisted pattern to its summit." Kunio shook his head. I think he was apologising for his earlier impatience.

"What bothers me more is the number of these companies that produce similar products. Competition in the marketplace! What a crock!" I griped.

"It's not that bad, Ray. Anyone can start a business," said Sue.

"And be shot down by the big boys working in tandem to preserve their monopoly."

"This has nothing to do with our quest. This strange web of business, as complex and confusing as it is, has told us where our quarry must be. I thank you, Susan. Your efforts are greatly appreciated." Toshiro stood and bowed to Sue.

"*Arigato gozaimashita.*" Sue bowed back deeply.

Sue's accent was awful, but Toshiro smiled approvingly at the effort to use his mother tongue.

Glancing at her watch Sue hurried to scoop up her notes. "I have to go. I have a class in five minutes. Bye." She almost ran from the room.

"Bye." I called out as she left. "So what's our next move?" I turned to my allies.

"Tomorrow, you and Kunio must go to the Suwa offices and search out the lair of the Nukekubi ," said Toshiro.

"That shouldn't be too difficult. Only the first few floors of the building are finished and just a handful of executives will be there," I commented.

"You know this place?" gasped Kunio.

"I applied for work there. It's the new skyscraper in the downtown core."

"You applied for work with our enemy?" growled Kunio.

"How in Hades was I supposed to know? They're going to have a gym with a pool, and they're unionized."

"You are blameless, but it would seem the fates have entwined your destiny with that of this Nukekubi." Toshiro steepled his fingers as he thought.

"I... I was beginning to suspect that. Old business. Well, at least we've found the haystack," I commented then yawned. "I vote we put the rest of this on hold until tomorrow and head back to my place. I could stand to catch some zees."

"What is a zee and why should one wish to catch it?" asked Kunio.

"It just means get some sleep. It's..." I noticed Kunio's grin and rolled my eyes. "Right, good one."

"It is a good suggestion," said Toshiro. "You must both be rested for tomorrow."

– Chapter 15 –

C⊕VER+ AC+I⊕NS

I awoke the next morning to the sound of my phone ringing and managed to bash my arm on my night stand as I fumbled for it. Wondering why I was sleeping on my apartment's floor I scrambled for the phone and managed to pick up before my answering machine.

"Hello." I wiped sleep from my blurry eyes as my brain tried to catch up to my body. I vaguely remembered telling Toshiro to take the bed when we turned in, and sure enough the old man was stretched out in front of me. Kunio lay on a camping mattress in front of the door.

"Ray, how good to speak with you again," smirked the voice on the other end.

It took me several seconds to do the necessary mental gymnastics. "Herbert?"

"Yes. Did I wake you? Sorry? You see, I had to be up for an eight-thirty class, so I thought I'd give you a ring."

I grunted then managed to form a sentence. "What do you have for me?"

"Sadly, no names. Your hunch was correct, or at least seems to be. Very clever that, considering its source. The fellow whose picture you showed me was a member of a Satanic group up until about six months ago. He was expelled for selling drugs through his lodge. He was a cabbie, but at last report was driving a limo for a major corporation."

"Expelled for dealing?"

"Ray, we are not savages or fools. I know as well as you that to master the universe one must master oneself. You should grow beyond your own bigotries."

"Sorry." I actually was. Despite the fact that there are a lot of drugs in some of the more fly by night sections of the occult community, what Herb said was true. While serious practitioners might use drugs to get past a mental block, it is always controlled, ritualized and a last resort. No matter what I thought of Herb he was a serious occultist and he wasn't alone on his side of things. "Can you tell me anything more? Like the company's name."

"No. The fellow's old high priest takes his secrecy oath seriously. He wouldn't have told me anything except he is concerned about Terror. It would seem he had a sister that died of an OD. He practices zero tolerance amongst his lodge members. He did know that your man is driving for the president of the company."

"Are you sure it was the president?"

"The fellow dropped in on his old group to boast. He made it obvious he had come up in the world."

"Don't you just hate people like that?" I was waking up. It felt like a full three brain cells were firing.

"Quite! Well, that is all I could find out. Oh yes, you owe me twenty dollars for photocopying and faxing expenses. Goodbye."

I signed off with "Break a leg," and really felt all the warm wishes implied by the remark.

Two pairs of eyes were staring at me with a mixture of curiosity and sleepy annoyance.

"The long version or the short?"

"Tell us all that is of importance." Toshiro sat up in bed looking like he'd just stepped out of *A Nightmare Before Christmas*. Boney with a pale, puffy face. It was nice to know I wasn't the only person in the room who considered mornings a form of cosmic torture.

"That was my contact from the unpleasant side of the art. The chauffeur drives for the president of the company. This, plus what Sue told us, equals, gentlemen, I think we now know our enemy."

Over breakfast we decided to return to Toronto. Kama had stocked my fridge. I'm almost embarrassed to say it; I washed the dishes before I left. I didn't want her thinking I was taking advantage.

During the drive my mind filled with trying to find a way around the problems we faced. Problem one, how could we get into the Suwa Corporation headquarters to confirm our quarry's identity? So far we had only strong circumstantial evidence and we didn't want to waste time on a red herring. Problem two, if our suspicions proved accurate, what could we do about them? Slaughter a few prostitutes and homeless, it hits the papers and gets an investigation to keep the public happy. Especially if a cover explanation like a new drug can be put forward. Do in the head of a major corporation, or a political leader, and they will catch you. I didn't relish the thought of playing wife to some guy named Slasher for the next fifteen years at taxpayers' expense.

We reached Toronto by eleven a.m. and found a motel a short way from the highway. Dropping Toshiro at the motel, so he could establish our temporary base of operations, Kunio and I drove to a mall. Kunio insisted we pick up baseball caps and sun glasses before proceeding to the downtown core. With difficulty we managed to find a parking space. It was now nearly two in the afternoon.

"Any ideas on how we're supposed to get in?" I asked, as we walked to the Suwa building.

"There is an ancient saying. Do not change your colour to match the walls. Act as if you belong and the walls will change to match you. We will try that first. Put on your hat and glasses and remember to keep your face down. There will almost certainly be security cameras. "

I looked at Kunio dressed in jeans, an old denim jacket left over from my hippy phase and a baggy T-shirt. I wore my comfy jeans, T-shirt and brown suede jacket.

"I guess I've been thrown out of worse places than the Suwa

building," I said.

The outside of the building showed no sign of its incomplete status as I followed Kunio through its large, glass doors into its ornate lobby. The lobby took up nearly half the ground floor and the twin elevator banks faced each other across a hallway that branched off its back. The front entrance was glass and the walls and floor looked like marble. A closed fire door pierced the wall to my left when I entered. Kunio paused at a computer screen that was built into the front desk. The desk was a huge affair, again in marble, behind which sat the concierge, a middle-aged woman with mousy brown hair and too many Twinkies under her belt. Her blue and black dress suit made her look washed out and even heavier than she was. Kunio scanned through the office directory then led me towards the elevators.

"Hold it!" snapped the concierge in a high pitched voice. "You stop right now or I'll have to call security. This building is private property." This stopped us before we even got past her desk.

Kunio turned so his back was to the ceiling mounted camera took off his glasses and flashed her a dazzling smile. Speaking in English far less fluent than his regular, accented but proper, pronunciation, he explained why we were there.

"So sorry, honoured mistress. Gracious uncle, Yakuta Hiroki, has said about jobs for my friend and I, how you say... um... making walls. Honoured uncle said they need people here."

The woman from the counter rolled her eyes. "Your uncle should have told you to go to the contractor's office. I can't let you go up without work passes. I could call Mr. Yakuta and ask if he wants to see you, but I think you'd do better to check with the contractor directly. I can get you the address and phone number. I'm sure they'd be happy to have you, everything from four up is behind schedule."

"Thank you, the address and number would be most, how is it... appreciated." Kunio bowed and shot her a vacant smile.

A minute later we left the building with Kunio clutching a

sticky note with an address and phone number on it.

"That was a waste of time." I commented.

"Not so, my friend. We have confirmed that there are workmen in the building. There was also the possibility that the receptionist would be the type to avoid offending those in higher authority, even when it requires disregarding the rules. Many people are like that."

"Okay, I think we need to check out the third floor." My brain was finally kicking in.

"Why is that?"

"The directory showed a lot fewer names on the third floor than the second. Top executives get bigger offices."

"Ah, yes. This makes sense to me."

"Great, now how do we get in to do it?"

Kunio sighed like I had said something stupid. "First we find a door then the closest refreshment shop."

"What? You're hungry?" Kunio had lost me.

"It is clear you have never worked construction." Kunio chuckled. He was leading me in a slow circle around the building.

"I qualified as a lifeguard when I was seventeen. If it wasn't for my Dad's home handyman projects I wouldn't know a hammer from a wrench."

Kunio walked right past the first pedestrian door we came to. No one on the street paid any attention to us. Just two more people in the busy city.

"I believe from television and movies that what I have observed with construction crews in Japan holds true in the Americas." Kunio stopped at the second door we came to. The ground around it was littered with cigarette filters and the pavement was stained with brown streaks. There were some scratches in the paint at the door's edge. "This is the one we want."

"For what? It's as locked as any of them."

Kunio smiled as he led me towards a *Tim Horton's* sign visible down the street. He chatted as we walked. "I worked a summer as a painter's assistant when I was fifteen. The painter's wife was having an affair with a Nukekubi that Toshiro and I were hunting. Working the job allowed me to get close to the beast by pretending to befriend the shameful woman. It was common for us to disable a security door to facilitate bringing things in and to allow people to take smoke breaks."

Minutes later we were positioned up the street from the door holding a box of mixed donuts and two cardboard trays laden with eight coffees.

"Now what?" I asked.

"Wait," said Kunio.

The minutes passed then the door opened and two men in jeans and battered jackets stepped out. One of them lit a cigarette then they started towards the *Tim Hortons.*

"Keep your hat and glasses on and follow me." Kunio walked up to the building, then pulling one of his concealed knifes pried at the edge of the door. It opened and I followed him onto a barren concrete landing. A locked steel door was to my left and a short flight of concrete stairs in front of me let out into the underground parking. As I passed the door I noticed that someone had used duct-tape to secure the latch in the open position and along its top a short piece of wire bridged the leads connected to the alarm.

"Face down and shuffle! Remember you are going back to work. If we are seen on camera they must see only two workmen bringing refreshments." Kunio's voice was a whisper.

"It's called a coffee run." Feeling chastised I did as I was told.

Kunio led the way across the dimly-lit garage. It was almost empty and in several places there were wire boxes for cameras that hadn't been installed yet. Reaching the level's centre Kunio hit the button for the service elevator.

"It probably needs a key..." I trailed off as the doors opened. Kunio and I piled in. Kunio looked smug.

"It did need a key, see." I pointed to the key in the console.

"Yes, Ray, it needs a key, and without question the key is supposed to be removed when the elevator is not in service.

Also without question the workmen are not supposed to use the emergency exits to facilitate going for a coffee or a cigarette. Convenience often defeats rules. It is human nature. Now, prepare yourself. We can stop only briefly on the third floor."

I nodded and Kunio hit the button for third. The elevator ascended. I kept my face down in case the camera on the ceiling was hooked up. The door opened and we stepped into a smallish foyer with a uniformed, security guard seated behind a desk across from the elevators. He was reading a paper, which he looked over as we entered. Beyond him was a small, cubicle village presumably full of secretaries and the like.

"You guys shouldn't be here." The guard set his paper down and regarded us with calculating eyes.

"I know, coffee run. I thought you might appreciate one." Kunio stepped onto the floor and presented his cardboard coffee tray to the guard while I held the elevator.

"That's nice of you guys. Between you and me, the office swill they have here, I wouldn't give it to my mother-in-law. You'd think the big wigs could shell out for something decent. Course, I bet they have good stuff in their private offices." The guard took a paper cup marked DD and Kunio opened the donut box and offered him his choice. I was pushing my senses to the limit.

"So how soon do you think you guys will be done on the fifth?" The guard took a long swallow from his cup.

"Two, maybe three days," said Kunio.

"Well, thanks for the coffee, but you'd better get off the floor before one of the bosses sees you and makes a fuss." The guard picked up his paper.

Kunio returned to the elevator and hit the buttons for the fourth and fifth floors. We slipped out on the fourth entering a nearly-finished office area. Corridors formed an H pattern with the elevators opening on the cross over line.

"Did you sense the beast?" Kunio hurried from one set of hallways to the other checking that we were alone.

"No. If it's here, its energy is masked too well when it's in its human form. I'll have to get closer."

"As I thought it would be." Kunio led the way down the hall.

We walked the entire H twice, with me expecting to get caught every step of the way. Finally, I sensed the beast's energy. It was a faint echo of what it was when it was manifesting as a Nukekubi, but it was there. "I got it. He's below us and towards the building's centre."

"Good. We will take the stairs down to confirm our prey's location." Kunio was in hunt mode. Nothing extraneous would get in the way. I envied him; I was doing a running count on how many criminal offences we were committing.

We reached the stairs and I was relieved to discover the doors were of a variety that could be opened from either side. Kunio led the way down as I tried to ignore the tremor in my chest. Slipping into the hall on the third floor, I paused, struck by its beauty. The walls were painted to resemble Japanese blinds, with minimalist nature scenes. Tinted shades softened the fluorescent lighting's glare, while the floors were covered in a deep-pile carpet of grass green. The hall formed a box with a set of outer offices with windows and a large central office opposite the elevators beyond which was the cubicle village and security guard. The stairs opened onto a short hallway connecting to the inner access hall.

"This hallway is nicer than my apartment." Of course there were public rest rooms nicer than my apartment, so perhaps the comparison wasn't the best.

"The beast has wealth, but its facade of beauty is built upon blood." Kunio's voice was hushed.

I looked at Kunio wondering if Toshiro had somehow smuggled along with us. The anger I had come to associate with Kunio was gone, leaving only a grim determination. His prey was in sight and nothing else mattered.

We walked along the hall, listening to the murmur of a busy office then I felt it. The aura was masked but definitely there. I moved towards the door it radiated from. The nameplate read Mr. A. Suwa, President. I was reaching for the handle when I heard a voice from the floor's foyer.

"A couple of men tried to con their way past the front desk. The security office thinks they might be wandering the building. We're supposed to find them yesterday. One Asian, one Caucasian, both wearing baseball caps and sun glasses. You seen them?" someone demanded.

"Christ! They stopped here, I thought they were just a couple of guys from the construction crew doing a coffee run," replied the guard's voice.

"Don't sweat it, so did the guy in the video room. Where'd they go?"

"They said they were heading to fifth."

A heavyset man in a blue suit rounded the corner from the foyer. He stared at me like a startled rabbit then yelled, "They're here!"

"Run!" snapped Kunio.

We bolted towards the stairs.

"Go up," ordered Kunio when we reached the landing.

I climbed the stairs as quickly as my legs could move. My heart throbbed like a trip hammer in my chest. On the seventh floor we left the stairwell. My lungs felt like a hot bellows. Kunio led me into a half-finished office, where I found myself thrown to the floor and a smelly drop cloth tossed over me.

Minutes passed before I heard voices.

"They didn't go down. Jim would have caught them. They have to be up here someplace," said a man's baritone.

"Any idea what they're after?" asked a base that almost shook the floors.

"Probably just some college prank, but the chief is afraid they might be some sort of industrial spies. He wants their asses bad."

"We should really let the cops handle this. It's what they're paid for."

"We called them. They say they can't spare the manpower to search the building. They only sent one man over, so it's up to us."

"Why do they think they're here anyway?"

"Way I heard it, Milly, from the front desk, mentioned to

Mr. Yakuta that his nephew had dropped by. Mr. Yakuta doesn't have a nephew."

"So she reports to security."

"Who remembers seeing two workmen coming in with coffee and donuts that he didn't see leaving?"

"Shit, who trains these guys?"

"Hey, with the way those construction guys waltz in and out of here, who can blame them? This place shouldn't have been opened for at least another couple of months. Everything is half assed."

The voices faded beyond hearing.

"What do we do now?" I whispered.

"Come." Kunio stood up and led the way back to the stairwell. We descended a floor and started searching. In moments we discovered a paint encrusted pair of overalls.

"Put these on and go out the front door. I will take care of the rest," he instructed.

"But?"

"They are looking for two men, not one, and not a painter. Do as I tell you." Kunio rummaged through some empty paint cans then said, "Close your eyes."

I followed his orders and felt a smattering of sticky drops across my face and hands. I instinctively tried to wipe the paint away, smearing it all over the place. Kunio put a few spatters on my hair for realism's sake and replaced my baseball cap with a paint-encrusted headscarf.

"Carry these cans and slouch. If anyone stops you, you were working and the searchers ordered you down. You took the stairs because the service elevator was busy," instructed Kunio.

"But?"

"Good luck. I will take a cab to the motel." He slapped me on the back.

"But?"

"Go now." Kunio left the unfinished office and quickly disappeared from my view.

I started down the stairs. On the ground floor I was stopped by a uniformed security guard with brown hair and a mean expression.

"Where're you going?" The guard was huge; at least seven feet with a Mister Universe build.

I swallowed hard before answering. "I was told to come down here, and the elevator was taking forever." I felt like he could look right through me and tried not to sweat.

"Hmm. Which floor were you on?"

"The sixth." Honestly, the guard might not have been as huge as he seemed, but at that moment I was five years old with my hand caught in a cookie jar. I was where I shouldn't be and he had me dead to rights.

"We've checked up to the eighth," said a small Asian man in a suit, who stood behind the guard holding a cell phone.

"All right, get out of here." The guard waved me on.

I didn't have to be told twice. In fact it was all I could do to keep from bolting out of the building. Hitting the latch on the one-way fire door beyond the guard, I stepped onto a landing identical to the one I'd entered through. Resisting the urge to bolt through the alarmed door, I descended to the garage level and slipped out through one of the official exits. I hit the street and dumped the paint cans and coveralls in the nearest garbage before finding a public washroom where I could clean up.

Rid of the worst of the paint I walked to my car and circled the block several times in hopes of spotting Kunio. Finally, I gave up and headed towards Toshiro's motel room. Driving, I contemplated the meagre sum in my bank account and wondered how much the judge would set as Kunio's bail, or if they'd cut out the middleman and just deport him. I arrived at the motel with a heavy heart and sat in my car for several moments before going in to break the bad news. Steeling myself, I walked to Toshiro's door where he greeted me.

"My young friend, you look distressed. Where is Kunio?"

How could I tell him we were screwed with all the bells and whistles? "They realised we were trespassing. Kunio disguised me so I could escape, but stayed behind as a diversion. They've probably caught him by now." I stepped into the room, slumped into a chair and put my head in my hands.

"Oh. Was it police searching the building?" Toshiro's voice reflected mild concern.

"No, there was a cop at the door, but they had office staff looking for us."

Toshiro sounded utterly at ease now. "Would you like some tea, while we await Kunio's arrival?"

I looked up. "Didn't you hear me? There were searchers everywhere!"

"I heard you. You do take honey in your tea, do you not?"

I was so taken aback by Toshiro's nonchalance I simply replied, "Yes."

"Ray, I know you have surmised that I have hopes that you and your lady friends will teach Kunio things I cannot. He is blocked in his growth and you can relate to him as an equal moving around those blocks." The old man held out a teacup to me.

"Toshiro, I—" I took the cup.

"Please let me finish." Toshiro took a seat in the room's other chair. "That being said, I do feel there are things Kunio can teach you as well. I say this openly to you because you are a little older, and I trust it will not offend you." He took a sip of his tea and set it on the dresser that half filled one of the room's walls.

"I'd love to learn more martial arts, but I don't have the time to dedicate to it."

"I understand this, what I speak of is an ability to trust others to do what they do best without your interference. You can be...what is the term, ah yes... a control freak. You have faith in your own abilities and limitations but often fail to see others' strengths, thus you do not extend them the faith they deserve, your efforts to keep Cathy to one side of our conflict being an example. Granted, she has a broken leg, but she is still a formidable woman. There is no reason she should not help you search mystically for our foe.

"I'm getting annoyed, so what you're saying is probably right. But Kunio is—"

Toshiro chuckled and shook his head. "Trust that Kunio

overshadows you in the art of evasion. He is my student. He will shine. You will see."

I took another sip of tea and examined the room. It had all the standard accoutrements, bed, dresser, armchairs, night tables and in addition a desk and chair set. Everything was two or three years old but in generally good repair.

Toshiro began discussing techniques Kunio might use to avoid the searchers. I listened. Who knows what will come in handy one day. Nearly an hour later the door opened. Kunio sauntered in and casually poured himself a cup of tea before sitting on the bed.

I looked at him opened mouth then stammered "How? How did you manage to get out of there?"

"There was minor difficulty." He cracked his knuckles.

"You remember your lessons well, my son." Toshiro's voice held a note of pride.

"I did as you taught me, Master." Kunio bowed.

"Could you expand on that?" My astonishment was becoming respect tinged with curiosity.

"It was nothing really." Kunio grinned at me.

"Please, for my benefit."

Kunio looked to Toshiro, who nodded.

"Very well. Following your departure, I returned to the stairs and climbed to the ninth floor. Having waited several moments, I pressed the elevator call button and took it to the fifteenth level, which is as high as it goes. There I pressed the button for the fourth and, entering the other elevator bank, took it to the eighteenth level. From there, I took the stairs to the fourteenth floor. By the time I reached my goal the elevator had stopped at the fourth. Pressing the call button, I ran for the stairs as the elevator rose to my level. This time I climbed to the sixteenth floor and once more pressed the button. The machine's silence told me it had been shutdown in an attempt to trap me.

"Returning to the stairs, I leapt down them until I heard footsteps. Hiding on the sixth floor, I allowed my pursuers to pass me. I had directed all the searchers to where I was not and knew there would be few if any on the lower floors. Descending to the second floor landing, I called to the guard at the base of the stairs. He climbed towards me. As he drew near, I dropped from the side of the stair to the steps behind him and ran through the fire door then onto the street. By then it didn't matter that the alarm sounded. Everyone searching for me was where I was not. The guard chased me onto the street, but it was easy to lose myself in the crowd. I walked a few blocks then hailed a cab to bring me here."

I nodded. "Kunio, you have to teach me how to do that. Just, less running on stairs, okay? I've got a bad knee." Kunio seemed to swell. Toshiro was right. I try too hard to protect the people I care about and end up being controlling. Kunio had things to teach me and doing so would help him grow as well.

"With my Master's permission I would be happy to."

"You see, my young friend, I told you not to worry. Kunio is a good pupil and the art of misguiding the untrained is not a difficult one." Toshiro stood and began to pace. "Now that we know the identity of our enemy it is time to finish this chapter in our struggle. We must destroy it."

"That won't be easy." I wanted to pace, but if two of us were wearing out the carpet it would look too much like an old comedy routine so I stayed seated.

"It might be more than that. The fact that our opponent was able to so long resist your banishing, as well as leave a 'psychic land-mine,' not to mention nearly killing Kunio speaks to me of something. This member of the race of our enemies seems different from others I have faced. It is more malignant, more powerful." Toshiro started making another cup of tea. I swear the man's kidneys will be alive six months after he passes just to deal with the backlog.

"So what are you saying? We're fighting a Nukekubi from Krypton?" I quipped.

Toshiro looked puzzled then his face cleared "Krypton... oh yes... Superman, quite amusing."

I stood. "Well guys, turbo charged ghouly or no, I'm hungry. Can I pick anything up for either of you?" I moved to the door.

There was a chorus of no's, so I exited in search of an establishment peddling fast and palatables.

– Chapter 16 –

THE HOME FRONT

Walking down the street, I noticed that the sun was beginning to set. Counting the days, I realized it was the third night since the Nukekubi had struck. Soon that horror would once more stalk the streets and I would have to try and stop it. I also kept thinking on Toshiro's words. My control freakishness might come from a good place, but I'd worked hard not to become my father. It bugged me I hadn't been more successful.

I found a *Wendy's* not far from the hotel, ordered my meal and took a seat to watch the people around me as I ate. The place was full of teenagers, mostly couples. They seemed so carefree, unaware of the evil that the world held, secure in their illusions of immortality. In my life I had seen wonders most would never dream of and in the last two weeks I had touched the face of evil. My illusions, my innocence, were gone. Maybe that's part of growing up; maybe that's the beginning of enlightenment. Who knows?

The other thing I saw was how convinced they were of their own rightness. I hated that. I had to analyse so much, think through things to be sure I was doing the right thing. Was I so bad for wanting to protect the ones I loved? Keep them at arm's length from some of the nastier aspects of reality.

I ate slowly, letting my depression roll over me. It dawned on me that my mood might not be totally my own doing. Calculating the days since the last full moon, I realized that it was dark of the moon.

The dark of the moon is a time for destructive magic. Notice I did not say evil. Destroy a tumour and it's called healing, knock down an old building and it's urban renewal, destroy a bad habit and it's self improvement. The time is what you make it, for me, though, it's a time of low ebb, when my moods and powers both hit rock bottom. So not only did I have to fight the Nukekubi, I had to do it with the metaphysical equivalent of the flu. Who says the universe doesn't have a sense of humour. Oh well, it gave me an excuse not to worry about being a control freak for a few hours.

I finished my meal and walked back to the motel room, trying all the way to remember something funny, and failed miserably.

I opened the room's door only to discover that Toshiro and Kunio had sent out for Chinese food. It would have been nice if they'd told me they were going to do that. I love Chinese food.

Finishing his mouthful of rice Toshiro spoke. "You have returned. This is good. We must decide how best to deal with the Nukekubi, since he is hunting further afield."

"If we wait outside the creature's office tower, we could follow it," suggested Kunio.

"That would work, so long as the beast is leaving from its office. It is equally probable it is already driving the streets," said Toshiro.

"I can call Cath. Since our little trip on the astral and she's in this up to her neck anyway... Besides, if I've got a problem it would be a start." I kept thinking that if I got Cathy hurt I'd never forgive myself. Add something else to the list.

The phone rang and Kunio answered it. As he stood listening, his face turned white then grew hard. He barked, "We will be there immediately," into the receiver and slammed it down. "That was Kama. She said you received a phone call.

The beast said to tell you he knows who you are, where you live and who your family are. He says he will make you pay for your interference."

"No, sweet Ra and Isis, no!" I gasped. "That S.O.B. must have bribed a cop to run my plates." My mood grew blacker, but not more depressed. This was a deadly, cold blackness, shot through with the red of anger. With this blackness I could kill easily and without hesitation. If you remember my fear, you know why. There are rules of engagement. You don't threaten my friends or family and I'll leave your non-combatants out of it. Try to harm those I love and I'll hunt you down and see you suffer in the darkest pits of Tartarus. Death itself will not stop me. Not even the innocents you hold dear will be safe from me. If that makes me a monster then so be it! I would never throw the first punch in that kind of a war, but by the Gods of light and dark, I will throw the last one. A man has to protect those he loves. In short, don't fuck with my family!

In minutes I had everything in my car and was barrelling down the highway with Toshiro and Kunio sitting white knuckled in the passenger seats.

"I'm not as worried about Kama. The wards on my apartment should keep the damn thing out. It's the henchman who could cause problems there. I'll leave you two at my place and go on to my parents' house. My sister and friends should be safe enough. They wouldn't turn up in a quick search. Call Cathy and leave a message, she may not be in, she said something about visiting her mum," I planned aloud as I drove.

Kunio and Toshiro looked at me with concern, perhaps tinged with a bit of envy. If only they had been warned before their loved ones had become prey to the beasts.

We reached my apartment in just over half an hour, though how I did it without killing the lot of us, I don't know. I stopped only long enough to drop off Kunio and Toshiro and pick up my camping gear then I was off.

The camping gear was important. I had to have an excuse to satisfy my parents or they'd be at me so much I'd be hobbled even worse than I was. Testing my new dome tent would serve that function. I wanted to deal with the Nukekubi outside of the house, to minimize the chances that Mum or Dad might stumble into the line of fire. If Dad ever found his balls and started studying again he might be of some use. Mom would scream, and then freeze solid. I couldn't count on either of them, not unless I wanted to go the route of my grandfather. So what else was new?

I drove like a maniac the rest of the way to St. Catharines and was pulling into my parents' suburban driveway in forty-five minutes. My arrival sparked a mixture of bewilderment, surprise and pleasure. They didn't have to talk to each other for an evening. I explained that I'd be testing my dome tent in their large backyard and the bewilderment vanished. My parents accepted the fact that I would be sleeping outside with only mild disapproval. They had long before decided that their blue-eyed boy was a little cracked.

Erecting the tent, I laid my mystical tools within its confines. Keeping my staff with me, much to my mother's disapproval, I joined my parents inside for the evening.

I sat in the house my father built one room at a time from lumber scrounged from the dump and bought at end of stock sales. The final veneer of good carpets and nice wallboard hid its many flaws, despite the fact that no two rooms had floors at the same level. The places' one advantage was lot size. He'd bought the land when it was sandwiched between the city dump and a swampy woodlot. Now it was a quarter acre property backed by a fashionable housing development and fronting on the municipal golf course. The fates had been good to him on that one.

I knew I could be hard on my parents. Ultimately, they were people with good points and faults. They had raised me, and the idea that some inhuman beast was threatening them because of me sent a shaft of cold steel down my spine.

Night deepened and I went to the back patio to slap some temporary wards over my folks' bedroom windows. This was exhausting work and the results were nowhere near as strong as I would have liked. It was the wrong time of the month and year for that kind of magic. Finished, I scanned the area covered by patio-block. A mature tree grew up in the middle of it. I'd pitched my tent in the grassy yard behind the patio. Finished with my precautions, I went to my tent and waited.

My nerves were jangling like a bell choir and every sound made me start. I spent the time studying every banishing spell in my grimoire. Time crept on and my eyes grew heavy then I felt it - the eerie, unpleasant feeling that accompanied the Nukekubi. The clock beside me read four thirty-five. Taking up my sword, I climbed from the tent and crept towards the house. My father's wood box supplied cover while I waited for the beast to come into view.

It was circling the house, looking for an easy entrance. The Nukekubi moved closer to the study's windows. It hovered there then backed up as if about to take a run at the glass. I leapt from my hiding place, sword in hand, and swung at the beast, but I lacked Kunio's skill. The monstrosity went straight into the air and hovered there out of reach.

"By Isis in mourning, by Osiris and Hades, by Hecate the witch queen, by my hard cutting blade *Be gone! Be gone! Be gone!*" I commanded, while feeling the energy flow out of my arm and up my sword. A cloud of black and crimson swept up from my sword point, encasing the Nukekubi.

It hissed and sputtered.

"Not this time, little wizard. My will is stronger and I have not been weakened by Shadow Death's apprentice pummelling me with his stick," hissed the beast, neither advancing nor retreating.

I could only stand there feeling my already low energies beginning to ebb. The beast began to drift closer. I let my concentration lapse and dove away from it. I didn't want to trust my personal shields if I could avoid it. I rolled, gained my feet and started to run. The Nukekubi was hot on my trail as I bolted down the driveway and turned onto the sidewalk.

"That's right, little wizard, run. It has been an age since I have feasted on your kind, but I remember the fear was so sweet. Much better than the street tramps I have been obliged to dine upon," breathed the Nukekubi.

I had to hit the dirt twice to avoid it hitting my shields. The beast must have thought I was running in panic. He wasn't far from wrong, but a clear part of my mind had a plan. Less than half a block from my parents' place is an entrance to a deep wooded ravine. My plan was to get into the dense foliage it offered. The life energy would strengthen me and hopefully hamper my foe. I hit the edge of the gully at a full sprint and tumbled down the first three metres of the steep slope, twisting my left ankle before regaining my feet.

Ignoring the pain, I descended the rest of the way, finally splashing into the stream at the gully's base. The Nukekubi flew at me and I ducked. Its momentum carried it into a thicket of trees.

"Help me my childhood friends and teachers." The words did nothing, but I projected the intent with my mind. Remember, I said life creates magic. For a moment it seemed like the beast was entangled in the branches. The life force of the gully recognized me. My enemy freed itself but not before I dashed into the cover of a clump of young trees. I fought to calm my panic. I knew the beast was striking at me through my fears and I mustn't let it.

The Nukekubi swooped down at me, but with a swift upward jab of my sword, I fended it off. As quickly as the underbrush allowed I scrambled to a trail I'd used as a child, emerging from the thicket scratched and bleeding. A large percentage of the trees in the gully are hawthorns. They had earned their reputation on my skin. The scent of blood seemed to drive my enemy mad.

I charged down the trail, which was overgrown in many places, sending a myriad of young whip-like branches slashing back into the Nukekubi. The beast kept up a hissing, sputtering tirade of what sounded like Japanese curses. Nukekubi heads are spirit in form, but having a living branch pass through the beast seemed to hurt it. The curses reached their most fervent when I pushed back a hawthorn branch, as thick as my thumb, and let it go. It whooshed back seeming to cut my foe's twisted face in half. I turned; ready to thrust with my sword at a hopefully disoriented opponent. Before I could drive the point home, the Nukekubi flew back and away. The beast's energy was less intense and it seemed to be moving slower. It hissed and flew towards me. I ran.

The trail ended in a clearing that left me exposed to aerial assault. I sprinted across, but somewhere in the pursuit I'd wrenched my bad knee, and between it and the ankle neither of my legs was working right. Before I was halfway across the beast was free of the bush and bearing down on me. Out of nowhere a sparrow hawk flew up in front of the Nukekubi. The beast could have simply passed through the bird, but its aversion to passing through matter showed itself and it paused. This gave me enough time to disappear into the brush. I thought a short prayer of thanks as I ran. More importantly it made me notice that the sky was getting lighter.

The trail crossed the stream that bisected the gully and doubled back. My wind was gone and I had a stitch in my side, but to stop was to die. I reached the end of the valley I'd started from and had a slight lead on my assailant. Here a culvert ran under the road to a similar valley on the other side. This valley formed the rough of the municipal golf course. I hadn't gone through the tunnel before because it was small enough that the Nukekubi could move faster through it than I. My desperation had given me an idea.

Splashing into the water that flowed through the culvert, I scrambled to the other side and waited, sword poised. When the Nukekubi appeared through the culvert, I'd skewer it with the consecrated blade.

"Shit!" I swore when the glow of false dawn, backlit my enemy flying over the road. Diving for cover in a bramble I lay still, trying to be silent while obeying the commands of my burning lungs.

"Come out, little wizard, and I will make it quick. You have brought this on yourself. One should never interfere in the affairs of one's betters."

The Nukekubi's voice had a bit of a breathless quality,

almost as if the chase had wearied it. It made a snuffling sound as it drew nearer, like a dog on a scent.

"I sense you, little wizard. You are in that bramble. Come out, the *ki* of mere plants cannot stop me. Come out and it will be an easy death. I will allow your spirit to go where it will."

"Is that what you wanted to give Kama, Mr. Suwa?" I played my delaying card. If I could only keep him talking.

"You know!" hissed the beast then it paused. "I guess it was unavoidable. You have been a worthy opponent, so I will be honest. The tramp would have had no easy death. Their horror strengthens me as much as their deaths and I owe a debt to my Mistress who made me."

"I know," I replied, standing up, sword in hand. If die I must, it would be as a man.

"You are mine!" snarled the beast as it flew at me.

I am no master with a sword, like Kunio or Toshiro, but I did fence for a time, and a long sword is little different from a sabre. Flicking my wrist to the side at the last minute, I deflected the Nukekubi, who hadn't expected me to know even this simple parry. I slashed out, catching the beast with my sword tip, leaving a gash of glowing golden energy across its hideous face.

A spectral hand tried to grab my throat, but my personal shields held it inches away from my flesh. This is what I'd been saving them for. My breathing was easier now. Mustering my remaining strength I pictured a white, sun-like radiance filling me, bursting out on all sides.

The Nukekubi hissed and spat as it backed away from the light. I added the hoarded power of my shields to the spell. It was my weapon of last resort. The energy involved in the procedure is enormous, and in the shape I was in I could maintain it for only a few seconds. I was hoping seconds would be enough.

The beast hovered unsure of itself about three metres away. Sword raised I stepped towards it. The birds at the other end of the valley started to tune up in preparation for the new day. My dear feathered friends screeched and squawked, making an ungodly racket. My enemy's eyes went wide.

"Surprise, my Dad's coming, and he doesn't like you!" Ra, Egyptian sun God and my primary divinity, knows that I'm a wise ass and doesn't seem to mind.

"It is not yet finished!" growled the Nukekubi, who shot into the air and disappeared from view.

I collapsed against a tree, my resources exhausted. If it were not for the fact that my damp clothes were growing crusty with the first frost of the season I probably would have slept then and there. Scrambling painfully out of the gully, I hobbled to my tent. I shed my wet tattered clothing before I crawled into my sleeping bag and plummeted into unconsciousness.

I didn't awake until afternoon and then only because my father was shaking me. I had a phone call that sounded important. Crawling from my sleeping bag, I discovered that while I slept the Blue Jays had used me for batting practice. If it didn't hurt, it was dead and my legs were in business for themselves. I paused to pull on the clean clothes I had in my travel bag. A quick inspection of the ones I had been wearing revealed that I had a new set of wiping rags.

My mother smiled when I entered, said something that deserved the groan it received as answer, and I proceeded to the phone.

"Hello," I opened.

"Ray, are you all right?" demanded Kama's voice.

I winced, "Gently, gently, I feel like I went eight rounds with Mike Tyson."

"Can you talk?" she asked.

"No."

"Did... it, show up there last night?" There was a tremor in her voice.

"Yes."

"Fuck! When?"

"About four thirty. Why?"

Kama sighed "There's only one of those fuckin' things then. It showed up here about twelve."

"Are you okay?" I demanded, my concern conquering my

pain.

"It was fucking scary but yeah. Kunio and Toshiro fought the fucking thing. I'll give you the four-one-one later."

"Right. I'll be there as soon as I can. Are Kunio and Toshiro okay?"

"Kunio got hurt, but Toshiro said he'll be all right."

"Good. Toshiro would know better than anyone. Look, I'm going to sign off now. I'll see you later."

I hung up the phone as my father entered the room, his square face with its hawk-like nose, ruddy complexion and mischievous blue eyes pulled into a suggestive leer.

"Who was that?" He arched his eyebrows to imply something risqué.

"She's a friend of mine."

"A friend?" He echoed in a way that said he didn't believe it.

"Father." I looked at the floor and blushed. How he does that to me I don't know; it's some power of his. I was innocent.

My Dad laughed so hard it made his wiry frame shake and slapped me on the back, an action that sent swords of pain lashing through my body.

"Well I'm just glad that you've come to your senses and are seeing someone other than that prostitute." My mother entered the hall where the phone was. She's a handsome, mid-fifties woman with dark out of a bottle hair, blue eyes and the remains of a figure type that Hollywood seems obsessed with. Looking at old pictures, I could see why she caught my Dad's eye. Why he didn't run when she opened her mouth I don't know, but she was my Mum.

"If you mean Cathy, she isn't a prostitute, and I'm still seeing her."

Mother looked like she was sucking lemons but knew better than to push it. "Lunch is ready. If you don't hurry it will be cold." She stomped from the hall.

"I'm sorry, son. You know what she's like." Dad followed her into the dining room and I trailed him trying to decide which side to limp on.

Following lunch I took down my tent and packed everything away. A hot shower furthered my recovery to the point that I felt almost human.

I spent the next hour on my parents' patio soaking up the late autumn sunshine and placing semi-permanent wards around the house. The wards would stand up to the Nukekubi long enough for my Dad to realize something was wrong and call the police. The cops might think they were nuts, but at least they'd be alive. Once the wards were set I drove back to Hamilton.

Opening the door to my apartment I found Kunio lying on my bed with an impressive display of bandages wrapped around him.

"Kunio," I called softly so as not to waken him.

"Ray, I have failed again." Kunio, gasped in pain as he shifted his position up onto his elbows so he could look at me.

"I didn't do much better. Where are Toshiro and Kama?"

"They have gone to purchase some herbs. My Master exhausted his supply upon my unworthy person."

"Stop whipping yourself. I'm sure you did your best." I hobbled to my recliner and half fell into it.

"It was insufficient," he replied through teeth clenched against his pain, then allowed himself to sink back onto the bed and rest.

My legs felt like Tartarus incarnate and the scratches that covered most of my body were aggravated by my clothes. Leaning back in that recliner was heaven and I took a deep breath before I asked him. "What happened?"

"I will tell you that you might see what a fool I am."

"No fool in my eyes. Kama and my parents are both still alive."

"Little thanks to me, but I will tell you what happened.

"You dropped us off, and we took up our vigil, not knowing if the Nukekubi would strike or not, we prepared for the worst. We called Cathy, but contacted only her answering machine. Kama and I spoke. I believe she has forgiven me, though I am not sure. That was the only thing I did correctly last night."

"Get use to not knowing. Women never let you know when you're forgiven. If they ever did, it would mean they couldn't bring it up six months from now to torture you with." Hey, my life experience is as valid as the next guys.

I heard Kunio shift position and groan before he continued.

"In that case I think I am as forgiven as I will ever be." He remarked before continuing with his narration. "Shortly after midnight I felt something odd, sickly. If that is what you and my Master feel when the beast is near I do not envy you. My Master and I peered out of the windows. Our foe appeared before my eyes. There was only glass between myself and the Nukekubi. I leapt back, but the Nukekubi did not enter as I expected. It simply hovered outside the window, issuing threats and insults. Kama shook with fear, but was struggling to regain her composure. She is brave and worthy. I wish I had not been such a fool the other night."

I hoped for Kunio that things really were mended on that score. Being with Kama could help him to become the man that was emerging from the youth, and I don't mean that in a sexual sense.

"Listening to the threats made my blood boil. My Master has always warned me about my temper. Why did I not heed him? My Master tried to calm me, but my rage built.

"Finally, I threw open the door and like a mad man, charged to the attack. I turned to strike, but the Nukekubi had disappeared. Then I felt its fear. It had dropped upon my... What is the English word, the shell of spirit energy that encases us all?"

"Aura, or - if you've purposefully channelled and strengthened it - shields."

"Thank you. It dropped upon my shields. They stopped it from entering me, but I could feel the fear it was projecting towards me. I spun, striking with my staff, but the light from the parking-lot lamp dazzled my eyes and I missed. Something struck me across the back of my knees. Then I was tumbling down the stairs. Hitting the ground I clambered to my feet, but now my legs were injured.

"The Nukekubi swooped towards me just as I heard something creeping up from behind. I tried to strike them both but my ankle gave and I fell. The beast's servant swung at me with a baseball bat before I could rise, striking my shoulder. I avoided the worst of the blow or my bones would have snapped, but it still numbed my arm. Then the Nukekubi descended onto my shields. The pain of it. The fear. It was breaking through my protections. I believe it intended to enter me. Use me like the one..."

The dread in Kunio's voice was almost a living thing. He took a deep audible breath then continued.

"...use me like the one that killed my father used him.

"All I have said took but moments to occur. I would have been destroyed, except for my Master. He descended upon my foes, sending the beast's servant to the ground with a kick as he struck the head of the Nukekubi with a *ninjato* he had spent the evening blessing. The beast turned to face my Master, who was by this time dragging me towards the apartment. Our foe flew towards us, but on the stair was Kama. She held the cup you keep with your altar tools. She threw its contents into the Nukekubi's face. The water passed through and fell on the step, but the beast flew away screeching."

"A face full of holy water can give a lot of nasties a bad day."

"Evidently. Kama was so brave. I was foolish to ever think myself above her."

"Her heroism cost her though. The beast's servant roused himself and rushed Kama, knocking her down on the stairs. My Master was still busy with me. That brute raised his fist to strike her, but before he could she pulled her knife from her pocket. She held the weapon all wrong, but still she swung it at her attacker. He blocked it, twisting her wrist, forcing her to drop the blade. This delayed him long enough that my Master finished dragging me into the apartment. He leapt out and with a kick sent the beast's servant tumbling down the stairs. Grabbing Kama's hand, my Master dove through the doorway.

"By then the Nukekubi had recovered from Kama's attack. It flew at the open door and slammed to a stop before it. Your wards defeated it where I could not.

"The beast's servant approached, pulling a pistol from a holster hidden beneath his jacket. My Master took my staff and struck at his arm, smashing it between the staff and the fire-escape's railing. The chauffeur's muscles must have tightened when he was struck, because the pistol fired into the wall, spraying plaster everywhere. My Master reversed the staff and brought it down on the chauffeur's wrist again. This time I heard a cracking sound and the gun was dropped.

"The beast's servant bellowed like a bull and charged my Master who drove the staff into his assailant's stomach, pushing him down the stairs. As this was done, the Nukekubi grasped the staff in its hands and pulled. I could hear it screeching as it touched the consecrated wood. It was trying to drag my Master beyond the protection of your wards. He released the staff and the Nukekubi flew back into the night.

"My Master closed the door before the beast could return. It threw itself against your wards but it could not force its way in. It retreated when we heard police sirens."

My neighbours must have heard the shot and called them. Hold on, what did Toshiro tell the cops?" There was dread in my voice for the last.

"My Master said that Kama was his granddaughter, a prostitute trying to leave the business, and that the gunman was her pimp, trying to force her to go back. He said that you were trying to help us by letting us use your place. He said you were the son of a family friend who happened to live in the city. He refused to pursue charges for fear of angering the pimp enough that he would follow Kama to Japan to take his vengeance."

"Glorious! Now the cops have me pegged as consorting with hookers," I groaned.

"Is it not a deserved label?" queried Kunio.

"Not in the way they'll think."

"We could do little else."

"I know. What else happened?"

"There is little else to tell. The police left, my Master treated me and I slept until this afternoon when he, Kama, and Cathy left to purchase herbs to aid my healing. They would not have had to if I had been less of a fool."

"Kunio, there is little difference between courage and foolishness. It's all a matter of perspective. If you had been successful, our problem would be over."

"This is quite true, my son. Release your anger and simply learn from your mistakes."

I nearly jumped out of my skin hearing that voice behind me. How Toshiro could open a squeaky door, walk across my creaky floor and not make a sound I didn't know, but he did it.

I groaned as I settled back in my chair. "Toshiro...please...among friends, make some noise when you move."

"I am sorry, my young friend. I did not mean to scare you."

I swear he had an amused twinkle in his eye.

"That's all right." I made the mistake of standing and sank back into the chair. I decided not to do that again anytime soon.

"It would appear that Kunio is not the only casualty from last night's endeavours." Toshiro moved to the kitchenette and began putting away herbs and groceries.

"I'll live; I just won't enjoy it much for a while. Hey, Cath, Kama." The girls entered the room.

"About time you got here. What have you been doing all day?" Cathy glared at me.

"Contemplating my damn navel. What in Hades do you think I've been doing?"

Cathy looked miffed then she quieted and almost whispered, "Sorry."

"That's all right, thanks for doing the shopping."

Once the groceries were stowed I was obliged to tell my story. Later Toshiro went to work with my mortar and pestle, making some horrible tasting tea that made me hurt a lot less. I added a couple of cold beers to my pain control program.

"Neither of you may hunt the Nukekubi tonight." Toshiro's tone made this a statement of fact. Noticing that both Kunio and I were trying to rise so that we could deliver a standing protest he continued.

"I know the cost will be great, but in your present conditions you would both be easy prey for the beast."

"But—" I began.

"Your courage does you both credit, but, Ray, you can barely walk let alone run, and Kunio, if you were to use a weapon you would only succeed in aggravating your injuries."

"But—" began Kunio.

"In addition, I believe it would be of little use to search for our foe tonight. There was another Terror death last night. This time a young woman in a place called Fort Erie. Do not distress yourselves. I believe it was another death mimicking our foe's killings. The situation is tough. All the area police will have been alerted to watch for any signs of Terror. Our opponent will go far a field for this night's hunting. In fact, I am sure of it. In today's business section, there was a piece on how Aritoshy Suwa would be personally inspecting a building in New York. Apparently he wishes to lease it as a distribution centre for the U.S. branch of his company."

"Did it say when he would return?" I asked.

"He was quoted as saying it shouldn't take more than two days," replied Toshiro.

"Why give us a respite?"

"I believe, my friends, that he was injured far more than either of you suspect. While it is true the Nukekubi have amazing powers of recuperation, it still takes time for damage to be repaired. Features on the physical form heal quickly, it would seem from my experiences, but damage to the energy form takes time and energy. Keep in mind you have succeeded in disrupting our dishonourable foe's feeding schedule. You are, how is it said, wearing him down." Toshiro smiled at both of us, and I couldn't help but feel a rush of pride.

"Very well, Master, if there is nothing we can do."

"Sure, I don't really want to get up anyway. On the bright

side, I can make it to my evening class tomorrow."

"That might not be wise. You should rest and allow yourself to heal," objected Toshiro.

"I can sit in a classroom and be miserable as easily as I can sit here and be miserable. Besides, we're starting on Hindu philosophy this week. I don't want to miss it."

Toshiro nodded resignedly as Kunio and I lapsed into somnolent states.

– Chapter 17 –

HIGHER EDUCA+I⊕N

J grimaced and leaned against my doorjamb as my downstairs neighbour stood on my fire escape/balcony ranting at me. Finally, I'd had enough.

"Mrs. Lefont, I assure you that I did not invite those 'lowlife thugs' to visit. Good day!" I closed the door and hobbled back to my chair.

"She seems excitable..." Kunio broke off into a series of Japanese curses, as the effort to roll over caused his battered muscles to seize.

"She's a pain in the ass." I picked up the novel I had been reading. Kunio gritted his teeth and turned back to the television.

"Hello my fellow crips." Cathy pushed open the door and clomped in on crutches.

"Cathy, cheerful is not welcome here right now," I growled.

"Grouchy!" She moved beside me and gave me a kiss. So the day wasn't all bad.

I reached for the beer that had been frosty when Mrs. Lefont knocked and took a swallow of the fast-warming brew.

"You know what I'm like when I'm sick."

"Big macho man retreats to his cave and chews berries till he feels all better." Cathy smirked.

"Hi, Kunio, Ray. I have the new bandages for you, Kunio," said Kama, as she followed Cathy into my apartment, closing the door behind her.

"Thank you, Kama. Your aid is appreciated." Kunio shifted to look at her, hiding his pain better than when it was just us guys.

Kama moved to Kunio's side and began peeling off his dressings.

"I am not macho," I objected.

"Let's see. You work as a lifeguard. You chase monsters for a hobby. You refuse to take it easy when you're hurt. You get jealous of other men." Cathy ticked her points off on her fingers.

"I'm not macho. I'm just male."

Cathy and Kama shared one of those glances that no man can possibly understand and shook their heads.

"Where's Toshiro?" I asked.

"He stayed at my place to take a nap. You ready for class?" Cathy took a seat on my kitchen chair.

"Shit, is it that late? I just had a beer; I can't drive." I forced myself not to grimace when I twisted to see the wall clock.

"One won't put you over the limit," said Kama who took a seat on the bed beside Kunio and held his hand. Kunio seemed happy.

"With the pain pills I've been popping, it puts me over my limit." I slumped in my chair. Truth to tell, I really didn't want to go. I still hurt too much.

Cathy glanced at Kunio and Kama then smiled. "I'll take you."

Dread entered my voice. "Cath, I wouldn't want to impose and with your leg."

"It's no problem. One advantage to driving an automatic, you only need one good leg. It's a beautiful evening; I'll put the top down." She looked pointedly at Kunio and Kama and then at me like I was lacking in the brains department. I got her. I just thought she was pushing again.

I knew I wasn't going to win this one. When Cathy plays matchmaker the Gods themselves would be hard pressed to get in her way. "Okay, let me get my books."

Minutes later, I hobbled down the exterior stair of my building, cane in one hand, and notebook in the other.

"You really do look like shit. Maybe we should just go to my place and you can lie down." Cathy reached the parking lot and waited for me to catch up.

"I should get to class, besides being cooped up is driving me nuts."

"Short trip." Cathy opened the door of her *Volkswagen Beetle*. I took the front passenger seat, positioning my cane between my legs.

"That's new, isn't it?" she pointed at my falcon headed walking stick.

"Yup. Just started work on a mystical shaft for it. Um, you will be careful driving, right?"

"I'm always a careful driver." We all delude ourselves in some way.

The drive to McMaster was harrowing, not because anything strange happened, but because Cathy's driving could make a cabby's hair turn white. We arrived at the tollgate to the parking lot and I climbed from the car definitely shaken, not stirred.

"I'll be back around ten to pick you up." Cathy leaned across the seat. No woman makes shorts and a tank top look as good as my Cath.

"Appreciate it, I think. You do keep your insurance paid up, don't you?"

"That's gratitude." Cathy made an illegal U turn and sped away.

Leaning heavily on my cane, I hobbled through the campus to the cut-stone building where my class was. I'd never noticed before how macabre the evening shadows at McMaster are. They offer a thousand hiding places and give the sprawling campus an eerie quality.

Arriving at class, I settled into a chair behind a table in the dingy, utilitarian room.

I felt it. A pinprick at the outer edge of my awareness,

coupled with a slight increase in my discomfort.

More annoyed than threatened, I closed my eyes, relaxing as I reinforced my defensive shields. Occasionally some dabbler gets upset over nothing and takes a pot shot at another mystic. Thus start witch wars, a childish waste of time. This foolishness goes on enough that I put the mystical poking off as an unimportant overture to an amateur's temper tantrum. My mistake.

The pinprick repeated itself. I tried to focus on it, but it was fleeting.

"Why does it always have to happen when I'm doing something," I muttered.

"Are you all right?" asked a matronly middle-aged woman sitting two seats over from me.

"Sorry, just talking to myself." I gave her one of my most winning smiles.

"Sometimes the only person who really understands," she observed, turning back to her textbook.

A deluge of mystic energy crashed against my outer shield. It fell over me like black, sticky tar, clinging to the reflective energy of my outer defence. I inhaled sharply and focussed my strength into my inner shields and clamped down on the physical nausea that accompanied the attack.

"You don't look too good," observed the woman from two seats down.

"Probably something I ate. Can I copy your notes next week?" I stood, leaning heavily against the table.

"Of course. You go home and get better."

Ignoring the pain in my legs, I headed for the door.

I stumbled out and I mentally scanned the attack against me. The energy clinging to my mirror shield was pure malice. Curse energy thickened into a sticky tar. A mirror shield reflects energy back to its source.

The glop attacking me was too thick to be bounced back. The good news was whoever was casting it wasn't anywhere near my class. The bad news was I was already depleted. As well, my foe was using ritual to heighten his or her abilities and

I couldn't get to my tools. I wondered who hated me enough to cast the spell. A curse works by generating negative emotion and throwing it out at a target.

Exiting the building, I found a shadowy place and leaned my back against the wall. Forcing my mind to clear, I spoke a single word. "Who?"

My own energy quested out through the sticky glop and followed the line of force back to its source. I saw the chauffeur, dressed in black robes, in a circle of power. I could make out enough detail to see that the ritual implements were an eclectic mix, belonging to no single tradition.

"Damn, fly-by-nighters." I muttered. My outer shield was almost gone. "How to get out of this?" I had to lose the curse energy quickly, before it attracted human avatars to fulfil its intent. A curse like this is like wearing a sign reading 'mug me'. Violent individuals are drawn to it like flies. It works the same way for any nasty bacteria that may be near.

"McAndrues, is that you?" demanded a voice I didn't want to hear. I tried to ignore it, but it moved closer.

"It is you. Afraid to talk to me?"

I groaned inwardly. The curse hadn't penetrated my inner shields and it was already taking effect.

"Hello, Tracy." I opened my eyes and stared at her. She could have been pretty at five foot six with an athletic body and a heart shaped face. The way she spiked her dark hair and dressed in torn jeans and leather hid her good looks.

"I want to talk to you. Do you know the trouble you got me into? You owe me a week's pay, that's how much they docked me."

"If you'd been doing your job, you wouldn't have been docked."

"It was a bunch of fuckin' adults. Besides I could see the pool."

"Adults can drown too, and you couldn't see the right side of the deep end."

"Fuck you! You had no right. Who's that bitch at your place? Do you know what she told me to do?"

I ignored Tracy's tantrum. The darksome energy around me continued to build. I tried to ground it, forcing the energy into the earth where it would decay harmlessly. Problem was it was keyed to my pattern. The chauffeur must have obtained something of mine to form a link. Every time I brushed the darksome force off it rose back up around me.

"Are you listening to me? I said I expect you to pay me back or I'll have my boyfriend, Bruce, drop by to talk to you about it."

An idea struck me. I grabbed at the last remnants of my mirror shield and tore it open, folding it in on itself so it enveloped Tracy. I also tied it to the anger that radiated from her. My shield fed off her aura, like a parasite. It used her energy to hold its pattern and decoy the attack. Drawing in my inner shields, I cleared my mind, trying to lose my sense of self.

"You should fuckin' mind your own...." Tracy fell silent and staggered back.

"Tracy, you are a 'pain'. This need you feel to blame others for your failings is a 'sickness' that I hope you 'recover' from. Goodbye!" I dropped the tone of my voice and increased the volume slightly as I spoke the key words. The suggestion they implied would direct the negative energies, now trapped around Tracy, into channels that would do no permanent harm.

"You...I...Gotta go," said Tracy, as what little colour showed through her heavy makeup drained from her cheeks.

She started towards the parking lot. I took a moment to think. Depending on my foe's skill, and Tracy's natural psychic talent, I had maybe ten minutes before he realized the target he was hitting wasn't me. Desperation dragged a plan from my throbbing brain. I started across the campus to where it backed onto a wooded area.

My knee ached and I could feel every brush of my clothes against the partially healed scratches covering my body. Finally, I reached a place where the ground sloped steeply downward, forming a natural amphitheatre. I stumbled down the bank and paused in front of the trees at its base.

Holding my cane by the shaft, I pointed it at the ground and slowly turned in a ring four times, starting in the east.

"By the power of Geb, Earth Lord, nature Lord. By Osiris, green God, growing God. I do scribe this ring, a fortress proof against all malignancies. Blessed be the green!"

I repeated the charge until the circle was done. I took a breath and turned to the East to call the element of fire. Before I could start, the circle I had scribed shuddered like a gong being struck. I felt the energy reverberate into me and out through the trees and grass around me.

"Caught on quicker than I'd expected," I muttered, lying on the grass.

I reached with my mind into the life around me: the trees, the grass, the things that crawled beneath the soil. Their life essence joined with mine. The wards reverberated again. Circles are strong, but not impenetrable, and mine had been cast in the most impromptu of styles.

I felt the energy attacking me shift. The malice gone. I guess even a man as reprehensible as the chauffeur could only maintain that level of hate so long. Now it was a controlled elemental attack. Water energy sloshed against my circle, fetid waves of suicidal depression and despair.

I stood and drove the base of my cane against the ground. It was little more than a stage prop, but it made me feel better and sometimes that makes all the difference.

"Undines, spirits of water, twisted, drawn from thy realm, heed my will. Green is the life force. Green is the seed. Roots that reach deep, drink, grow and feed."

I felt the life force of the trees behind me reach out and grasp the fetid water energy. They drew it to themselves, the same way their roots drink up ground water. The area around my circle cleared.

Rushing, I summoned forth the four elemental kingdoms. I would have given much to have had my crook and flail, or even my sword, but they were back at my apartment.

With the elements summoned, I started thinking of ways to strike back. My temper began to boil. That some piss ass, half-cocked, under trained, Crowley wannabe, would dare attack me? My rage flashed like lightning across the landscape of my mind. I'd teach this fool. Driven by anger, I prepared a devastating blast of psycho-emotional energy then caught myself just before I let it fly. The blast I readied would have shattered the weak wards of my impromptu circle as it left me.

"Clever bastard," I muttered, as I took the twisted fire energy my foe had been sending me and gradually added it to my wards. As I did this, the rage subsided and my mind cleared.

A pair of students appeared on the top of the rise and saw me. I pretended to study the trees at the slope's base, staring into the darkness. They left without bothering me.

"Now, to stop being a punching bag." I drew energy into myself, filling my heart chakra to bursting. I thought of Cathy, Sekmara and, a little disturbingly, Kama, Kunio and Toshiro. I built the emotion as another attack broke against my circle then let it fly. The purely benign nature of the love energy I sent forth passed through my enemy's shields. The attack was no threat, no danger. It was actually healing. The golden energy filled his ritual space, displacing the anger, hatred, rage, and cruelty that were his driving force.

I shifted my focus, leaving my foe to try and ground the positive energy that now blocked his attempts to raise a malignant force. Mentally, I grabbed the elemental forces about his circle and tore them apart. I sent them, earth, air, fire and water, all spinning like crazed eggbeaters, ripping free of the structure imposed upon them by my enemy's ritual. I imagine that the backlash must have hurt considerably.

I felt my foe's pain cascade down the energy lines he'd cast towards me, but I snapped them with a wave of my cane and a visualization of blue energy leaping along its shaft. It was over, at least for the moment. I stood breathing hard for several minutes, getting my bearings then I took down my wards. I had just finished when a voice hailed me from the top of the slope.

"Hey, what are you up to?"

I glanced up and saw a campus cop starting towards me.

"Nothing, officer."

"Then move along."

"Why?"

"I said move along."

"I'm a student here. I have every right to be on campus."

"If you're a student, get to class."

"I needed a break from class."

"Then go to the cafeteria."

"I'll go where I damn well please!" I caught myself. The tag ends of the attack were still clinging to me and were causing this.

"I don't need any of your mouth," commented the guard, who stepped closer.

"You work for the university, I pay tuition, don't push, I won't take it. I'm going now anyway but in future have some manners when you speak to me." I started up the slope, staying out of the guard's reach.

"I want you off campus," he snapped. He was an older man, probably retired, with a paunch that made his uniform look ludicrous.

"Why?" I asked as I hobbled away. The aftermath of the attack was beginning to hit me and all I wanted to do was close my eyes and sleep. I probably wouldn't have even argued with him, but I'd long ago had my fill of campus cops who thought they were storm troopers. The next guy he went after might be some insecure teenager.

Cathy found me propped against a lamppost at the corner where she'd dropped me off.

"Hey, sailor, want a date?" she joked, as I moved to her car door.

"Only after a good night's sleep."

"Trouble?"

I took my seat before replying. "The chauffeur knows just enough of the art to be a royal pain in the ass. By the by, can you spot me fifty until my next pay check?"

"Sure, why?"

"I need to make an offering to Geb and Osiris."

"*World Wildlife Fund* wild spaces campaign?"

"Lot more practical than some mouldy bread and wine in a bowl. Anyway, the *World Wildlife Fund* will give me a tax receipt."

Cathy smiled. I closed my eyes and don't remember anything until she woke me in the parking lot beside my building.

– Chapter 18 –

WHAT PRICE A SOUL

Three more days passed as Kunio and I recovered. The only thing of interest that happened was when a coworker of mine dropped by with a card that everyone was signing for Tracy. She had a horrible flu. I felt almost guilty as I scribbled my name next to the get well soon message. I also felt a little hurt that no one bothered to get me a card. Then again, I didn't go out drinking with my coworkers and consider most of the modern pop sensations to be immature, spoiled brats. I'm more of a Beach boys, Beatles kind of guy.

Kunio and I were still in rough shape. I could walk, but my knee was tender, and Kunio was favouring his right side. We needed to stay in bed, but we both knew the hunt must go on. We went out for a walk to limber up. We returned to find Toshiro, Kama and Cathy crowded into my apartment wearing grave expressions.

"What now?" I think I managed to keep the dread out of my voice.

"That fuckin' thing called. It wants to talk to you. It said it had an offer for you. It wants you to meet it at the Suwa building, tomorrow at two o'clock," explained Kama. She was pale and obviously shaken. I could guess who took the call. Kunio pushed past me and gently touched her shoulder. It wasn't a hug but for him it was as if he'd offered her the world.

"Am or pm?" I limped to my chair and sat.

"During the day, my friend," said Toshiro. "It seeks audience with you while it is in its human guise, though it wishes to see you alone. The beast said it had set aside an appointment for you. It left a number so you may confirm. It also said to tell you as a gesture of good faith it would be in New York City tonight, beyond our reach to stop it." Toshiro brought me a cold beer. I was breaking him of the habit of offering me his horrible-tasting, pain-killing tea when he saw me grimace.

"You shouldn't go. It's too dangerous." Cathy got up from her seat on the bed and clumped to my side.

"I'm not thrilled about the idea, but maybe I can work it to my advantage." I squeezed Cathy's arm.

She rolled her eyes. "I give up! Get yourself killed, go ahead. Just don't come around haunting me because I'll only say I told you so."

She's beautiful when she's exasperated.

"Look at it this way, right now; we don't have any way of reaching our prey. If I go, maybe I can spot some weakness we can exploit." I put on a brave face. To tell the truth, I was thinking of sucking my thumb and pulling the covers over my head.

"I do not like this. The Nukekubi are devious tempters of the heart," warned Toshiro. "Once one of their number sought audience with me. It was a female, in her human guise, lovely and petite. She offered much if I would relinquish my quest. I was tempted, but she has not killed since that meeting."

Kunio and I looked at Toshiro with surprise.

"Did you think I was born an old man?" He scowled and shook his head before continuing. "Even now, I can appreciate beauty in the female form. Young ones, the passions do not die with age; they simply become more easily ruled."

"You know, Toshiro. I do have a thing for older men," flirted Cathy. Toshiro blushed and Cathy giggled wickedly.

"I'll go and see what it has to say." I shot Cathy a quelling look, it just seemed wrong to tease Toshiro like that. Besides, there was a slim chance the old dog might take her up on it.

"Be careful, and keep to your beliefs," cautioned Toshiro.

"I'll call and confirm the appointment. I won't object to another night to heal."

The next day's drive to Toronto was uneventful, if driving on the Q.E.W. can ever be called uneventful. We took a room in a seedy dive. Once Toshiro was settled, Kunio drove me to the Suwa building. I'd dressed for the occasion, in my one and only blue weddings/funerals/graduations and job interviews suit. I'm sure the people who saw me must have taken me for a nervous bridegroom. I admit it. I should let Cathy buy my clothes. Don't tell her I said that.

I arrived at the Suwa building at about one-thirty. The same concierge was at the desk, but this time I had a legitimate reason to be there, so I walked right up to her.

"I have a two o'clock appointment with Mr. Suwa." I tried to sound businesslike.

"You're one of those two who snuck in here a few days ago. I don't know how you got away, but I'm calling security."

"Madam, please check your appointment roster. My name is Ray McAndrues. The appointment is for two pm," I returned in my best, you are irritating me and I am extremely important, voice.

"That's it," she picked up her phone.

"Go ahead, call security. It might cost you your job. Maybe I'm a member of a firm that specializes in checking the effectiveness of private security forces and systems. Examining them, testing them, and then making recommendations as to how to improve the system. Maybe, because you stopped my colleague and myself that first time, you avoided the black mark that coloured the rest of the security staff. Perhaps, not letting me pass when I do have an appointment, would affect my high opinion of you."

As I spoke, I added an empathic push and watched as the receptionist began to sweat. It took about thirty seconds for her to break down and check her day calendar. I guess the decks had been cleared since Kunio's and my fact-finding mission because as soon as she saw my name she started fawning.

"I'm so sorry, Mr. McAndrues; it appears that you do have an appointment with Mr. Suwa. Please, when you speak with him, if you could—"

"I will be making some recommendations, but you did your job in a courteous, polite and effective manner. I will emphasize that," I interrupted.

"Thank you, Sir. If I could just check your identification before you go up?"

"Certainly." I pulled my driver's licence from my wallet and handed it to her. She scrutinised the picture then passed it back.

"Thank you. Mr. Suwa's office is on three."

I started towards the elevator with the bright enthusiasm of a man walking to a gallows.

Stepping off the elevator on the third floor I was stopped and my I.D. checked against an appointment list by a uniformed security man. This guy was different from the one I had seen last time. I took my time walking down the hall enjoying the prints on the walls. Finally, I came to the door labelled "Mr. A. Suwa, President". The Nukekubi presence radiated from it. Knocking, I turned the knob and entered an outer office, four-metres square, with diplomas and certificates on the walls. The floor was covered with a gold carpet, while a sofa and coffee table formed a sitting area in one corner. Opposite the door was a mahogany desk, behind which sat a classically beautiful brunette. She had long luxurious hair, a largish bosom, and a face that belonged on the cover of Vogue.

"May I help you?" Her teeth were brilliantly white. She looked about twenty-five, but it was hard to tell.

"I have an appointment with Mr. Suwa. I'm Ray McAndrues." I saw the woman for what she was. The first line of Suwa's defence, she was meant to fluster me and cloud my judgment. Thing was, while I appreciated her classic beauty, she wasn't my type. I'm hooked on the girl next-door type. Give me Maryann over Ginger any day.

"Oh yes, the two o'clock. Mr. Suwa will be with you momentarily. Would you care for a coffee while you wait?"

I almost said yes, but I caught myself. It would be simplicity itself to drug me here and make it look like I partied a little too hardy later on. Just another tragic, drug related, death. No one would notice.

"No, thank you." I smiled. So she wasn't my preferred type, she still looked good. Besides, I doubted that anyone who earned less than six figures stood a chance.

"Please take a seat." Her voice was honey and cinnamon. She walked over to sit on the couch opposite me.

She should be in pictures, her legs and hips were perfect. I couldn't tell if she were some plastic surgeon's fantasy or a gift from the Goddess of beauty, to all lovers of the female form. I could tell that Suwa had good taste, fortunately not my taste.

With an effort, I managed to keep my mind on the conversation. It was a pleasant surprise to find this beauty had brains. I'm sure Suwa scoured every university campus in Canada to find her. We were discussing the pros and cons of nuclear energy, when the intercom on her desk buzzed.

"Please, send in Mr. McAndrues," requested a deep, clear voice, with an Oxford accent.

"Mr. Suwa will see you now." The secretary opened the door to the inner office and motioned me through.

I stepped into an adjoining office where I was grabbed, thrown against the wall and frisked.

"What in Hades is this?" I demanded when I was released.

The second office was smaller, well appointed but functional. A handsome, Asian woman, of late middle years sat behind a desk with a computer screen and keyboard on it. Immediately to either side of me were classic examples of Neanderthal man, dressed in security guard uniforms. The Nukekubi's driver stood between them scowling at me.

"He's clean, buzz him through," grunted the driver.

The woman at the desk smiled at me and gestured towards the door at the far side of her office. "Please forgive any inconvenience. Mr. Suwa will see you now."

I pulled my lapels straight and strode through the indicated door.

The office beyond was bigger than my apartment, with a rich burgundy carpet. Its walls were dark-stained redwood and several expensive, but tasteful, prints hung on them. The ceiling was a full-spectrum-light panel, while the room's furnishings were all antiques, or at the least, damn good reproductions, from the Victorian era. The two exceptions to this were the desk and executive office chair, which sat in the corner opposite the door. The desk was made of oak, stained a deep brown, with two phones and a computer screen on it. Beside the door was a bar, in front of which was a sitting area, with a couch and several chairs, around a low, dark coffee-table.

"You have good taste, in women and furnishings, I'll give you that." I closed the door behind me.

"I am pleased you find them both attractive." My foe rose from his padded leather swivel-chair behind the desk.

Suwa stood maybe six foot two inches and was built like a tank. His face, so grotesque when in the Nukekubi form, was now quite handsome, in a strong Asian way. A red mark cut across his features from his right eyebrow to the left corner of his mouth. It was more like a scrape than a sword wound, but I knew its source. He walked towards me and proffered his hand palm down.

I hesitated, reached out, locked my thumb with his and raised my forearm, which forced his hand to angle flat with mine. We shook hands as equals. For a second he looked surprised by this then he smiled.

"You invited me here," I prodded, trying to prompt our discussion.

"Yes, of course. Please take a seat. May I offer you a drink?"

"No, thank you."

"I can understand your caution. You are, as it were, rather in the enemy camp." He collected a tumbler, added ice and poured amber fluid over it. "Pity really, this scotch is an excellent single malt."

"I'll play it safe, thanks, and you must realize I didn't come minus precautions." I settled on the couch.

"Of course, now that we have finished blustering, why do we not talk? I believe we are much alike, you and I. It is seldom I have the opportunity to speak with one worthy of respect." Suwa sat facing me and leaned slightly forward. He might be a murdering monster, but he knew how to use body language.

"Come again?"

"Don't be modest. Three times you have faced me and you still live. Indeed, I believe I suffered more than you from our last encounter." He brushed the discoloured area on his face.

"As above so below. It is an interesting phenomenon how the body manifests damage to the spirit." He was being civil. What should I have done, gloated? I don't like being out classed.

"Yes, I had to let it be known that I'd walked into a half open door while half asleep. Your sword's enchantment is quite strong."

"For threatening my parents, I'd rather have used it to disembowel you, slowly." Okay, maybe not civil, but this thing tried to eat me and my family, there are limits. I did smile when I said it.

He nodded and looked mildly contrite. "I regret that action, it was dishonourable to involve non-combatants. Sometimes when the hunger comes, one can lose control."

"Sometimes?"

"You haven't considered my position, young human." He was trying to sound paternal. The SOB deserved an *Oscar* for his performance. "I must feed. I have no choice. Like the wolf, I must hunt and kill or cease to be. In a way, I serve your kind."

"Really?" I leaned back in my seat. I suspected I knew what was coming and had an argument ready.

"You understand the balance of nature. One such as yourself must. The wolf hunts the deer, but he takes only the weak and the sick, thus he culls the herd, making it stronger. That is my function. Do you truly believe any of those riffraff I feed upon would help society? They are leeches, spreading diseases of ignorance, poverty, apathy and perversity. I prune them away, as a farmer removes dying branches for the improvement of the tree."

"You take more than the old and the sick," I countered. "You take the young who have gone astray, and you spread terror, a sickness worse in itself than the others combined." He did have a point. Does the rabbit consider the fox evil because it eats rabbits?

"It may be true that some of those I feed upon, might reform their natures, if given time," he concurred. "How many? One in a hundred, a thousand? Balance this against the good I do. I create jobs; I help feed those willing to work. Let me be brutally honest. Your race are little more than herd animals to me, and the wolf must hunt."

"And the herd must defend its members. The law of nature applies to the hunter as well. If the wolf attacks the buffalo, the buffalo will form a circle and protect the young and weak. The wolf might find itself impaled upon the buffalo's horns." I smiled showing teeth. Let my foe be reminded that I was a member of a predatory species, no matter what he thought of us.

"This is so. You do understand the balance." Suwa looked like his scotch had turned to lemon juice.

"As I must. Do you really think that if people knew the truth about you they would want the jobs you offer?"

Suwa laughed. It was a cold, harsh sound. "Oh yes, do not delude yourself. Your race is full of self-serving hypocrites. There are many who would bring me my meals if they felt it improved their chances of promotion. In ancient times, many a tribe welcomed me amongst them, so long as I only fed upon their enemies. It was little different from when I was war chief of my birth tribe."

That caught me by surprise. I knew a lot of creatures were twisted human spirits, but I hadn't thought of the Nukekubi in that light. I'd been too busy trying to kill it to wonder about its origins.

"You were human once?"

Suwa took a swallow of his scotch as a nostalgic look filled his face. "Long ago, before Japan was Japan. I was war chief of my village. I had a wife, her name was Chou, it means butterfly, she was lovely in her youth, but didn't age well, and a daughter, Hana, my flower, that had lived past infancy." He smiled a little when he mentioned Hana. I felt the name resonate with me.

Suwa poured himself another drink. "It was a very different world. Imagine yourself on a camping expedition that never ends. You humans have made life much more comfortable, I will give you that. Modern plumbing is glorious."

Suwa seemed to warm to his topic. I got a sense that he was lonely. I could understand having a large part of your life that you couldn't talk to others about. My view of his driver is that the man just wasn't bright enough to be more than a pawn to Suwa. On another level the beast was trying to humanise himself in my eyes. He undoubtedly felt I would find it harder to kill a man than a monster. He couldn't know I'd read enough history to know that some men are monsters. Still, I felt a strange connection, almost affection, for him. I was beginning to suspect that Suwa was a piece of long unfinished business.

"I'll agree with you there. Plumbing has probably saved more lives than all the doctors combined." I nodded at him hoping he'd continue. The longer he talked the more likely he'd let slip something I could use.

He tipped his glass to me and smiled. "If not to friends, to civil foes and cease fires."

I nodded again. "Was your tribe Neolithic?"

Suwa smiled, I think he approved of my vocabulary. "We used some copper, mostly for ornamentation. We lived in pit-houses, though *The Hobbit* sadly romanticised the whole dirty process of that. We did farm. In my father's time we'd learned how to grow rice from a new group that came from the mainland."

"Do you miss your wife and daughter?" I'd found a chink in his armour. As he sought to manipulate me he had to engage me. That meant sharing information. He undoubtedly thought the details of that time long past couldn't hurt him. As a wizard I know that beginnings always hold the seeds of the end.

"Strangely, no. My Hana, perhaps a little, but they have little to do with the being I have become. My mistress however played a pivotal role. Her name was Satomi, that is at least what I knew her as, and she was lovely, much like the street whore you have been sheltering. Our chief, Daisuke, brought her from another village to replace his dead wife. Petite, a voice that caused a man to dream, adorned with the most intricate tattoos, they formed blood-red patterns all over her. It made my blood boil to see her with our chief who could have been her grandfather.

"One day I was cleaning hides and she rose from her weaving, a skill she had brought to us, I could see in her eyes she wanted me. I followed that gaze from the village. She waited for me in a clearing where she had spread a deer skin. The taste of her skin on my tongue. The feel of her ripe, young breasts. I could not deny my passion and we joined. I think I may have seen it then in her eyes, a spark of the magics she held, but I was hers to command from that moment on.

"We were at war with the village up river from us. They were twice our size." Suwa laughed. I must have looked confused.

"They numbered nearly two hundred and they were twice our size. They were the largest village we knew of. It was a different world, Ray. I am sorry, I presume. Do you mind if I call you Ray?"

He was playing it well, be polite and then add the trappings of association. I saw through it, but appreciated the work of an artist. It wasn't surprising he was rich. He knew how to work people. "Not at all."

Suwa gave that ingratiating smile. "You must call me, Aritoshy. As I was saying, it was a different world. Daisuke had negotiated a peace with the upstream village, but I didn't trust them. Daisuke was an old man and had no fire left in his belly. Satomi spoke against the peace to me. She told me I should seize control of the village. Lead our people in war. It would have been a glorious defeat and I knew it. We could not win without allies. She promised that if I overthrew Daisuke and lead us into battle she would become my wife. I told her we needed more warriors or better weapons.

"That is when she offered me the gift. She said she could make me a god, undying, eternal, powerful, able to strike fear into all who opposed me." Aritoshy's face nearly glowed. He savoured the memory like a fine wine.

"That night she led me to our clearing. The moon was dark and thunder rumbled in the distance. Her fingernails became like sharpened pins and she used them to place the marks upon my neck and wrists."

Aritoshy rolled up his sleeve revealing a line of red symbols tattooed about his wrist. "Part of me wished to flee when Satomi revealed her true nature. She was a creature not of this world, but she promised power. The power to be more than a man!

"She dipped her nails into the marks upon her own flesh and drew the ink from there. The pain! You cannot know it's like, Ray.

"In the depths of the night I stumbled to my hut and rose the next morning. All seemed as it had. Many looked at the marks about my neck and wrists and whispered. All suspected that I had taken Diasuke's woman, but much is allowed to pass if one is circumspect. The marks were a blatant declaration. The scandal tore the village apart. My wife wept all day and my daughter would not speak to me, but I didn't care. I no longer cared about many trivialities.

"That night I rose beside my wife, I was Nukekubi and I hungered. Chou was the first to die screaming. She ran from our dwelling. I pursued her. She leapt into the stream and drowned herself. The fear, the death. It was sweet!"

"The next night Diasuke followed her into death. The old man was not as much a coward as I thought; breaking his courage made the kill all the sweeter. I became chief. Satomi vanished from the village; I felt nothing. The next night I attacked the upstream village. I returned to find my Hana standing by my empty shell. She was scrubbing at the marks upon my neck and had drawn blood. I drove her into the woods but before I could devour her she tripped on a branch and fell over a cliff."

Aritoshy talked about murdering his family as if it was no more than changing a flat tire. As creepy as the whole affair was, this was the creepiest. Well, the fact that I was now convinced that the dream I'd had of a woman's hands scrubbing flesh was no dream but a remembrance from a past life, was a close second. Hana was long gone, but a spark of her essence lived on in me. My dad this time around has his faults, but I figured I'd traded up.

Aritoshy seemed not to notice my upset. "With my path to power in my village cleared I restricted myself to killing the men of the upstream village until they were weak and ready for conquest. It was my first hostile takeover." Aritoshy laughed. I felt nauseous.

"And you felt no guilt?" I wanted to run, to call Cathy, to touch something human. It wasn't so much what Aritoshy said, it was the way he said it. So matter-of-fact it wasn't cold, or hot, or anything. He sounded like someone recounting a trip to the market.

"No. I have always been puzzled by that. I was surprised how little it mattered when Satomi vanished after transforming me. I guess her gift gave me clarity."

"She tore your soul to shreds. The spell that made you Nukekubi separated your top three chakra from the bottom four and turned the chakra energies in on themselves. Your heart chakra, your moral centre, is disconnected from your head. Your connection to the Divine was destroyed. Gods, it's, it's..." I rubbed my temples. That demonic bitch had made a metaphysical sociopath and left it to run rampant.

"Impressive?" Aritoshy steepled his fingers and smiled.

"Horrific! Can't you see, you steal others lives? You destroy hope. You've been made into a twisted abomination that spreads and feeds on fear. Even predators give something back. You're like a black hole, sucking in life and producing nothing.

The ones you feed on have real lives. I'll grant you, a lot of them are throwing them away, but they could still straighten up and do something."

"You are being foolish and emotional. The world is for the strong. If you have the power to do a thing that gives you the right to do it."

"No matter the consequence to others?"

"If they were strong, you could not treat them so, Ray." Again with the paternal tone and demeanour, in a twisted sense I guess it applied. "We both understand power. We've both worked for it. I am what you might call a Duke of my kind. I am stronger than those who follow me, and I have had the courage, over the centuries, to accumulate great wealth. Money is simply another form of power, one that allows me to move through your world with impunity. Why throw your life away fighting a foe that has you so overmatched?"

"Aritoshy, do you have beef interests in South America?"

He looked startled at this change of direction. "The price was right."

"Nuclear energy interests?"

"Mostly uranium mining. It's the wave of the future."

"Stock in oil tankers?"

"People need oil."

I went for the *coup de grace*. "Interests in solar energy start-ups?"

"Pie in the sky." His tone was dismissive.

"Wind power?"

"Unreliable."

"Carbon fixing technology."

"Global warming, who cares if the ice caps melt?"

I shook my head. "Shall I go on? Can't you see? Your nature, due to your selfishness, can be nothing but destructive. You are a predator outside the natural order. You do not improve your prey. Your killing leads to no greater life. You take from the cycle and do not return to it. It is my duty as a servitor of the Neters, the keepers of the natural order, to stop you in any way I can."

Aritoshy took a deep breath and considered before replying. "You speak of the abstract. Because I have come to respect you, I can offer you something concrete. I will agree never to feed within the province of Ontario again. In addition, I will place you in a position as a junior executive. You can oversee the recreational facilities my companies own or manage. Shall we say two hundred thousand a year plus benefits and six weeks paid vacation, with good promotion opportunities and a full twenty and out retirement package? This is yours, if you will cease hunting me and persuade your friends to return to Japan. Those fools can satisfy their compulsive need for vengeance on the lower beings of my kind. The young one will only last, at most, another sixty years. Shadow Death is nearly finished anyway. I regret that I never faced him in his prime. That would have been a challenge. Well, Ray. It is a very fair offer, what do you say?"

"No." Was I tempted? If you haven't got it yet, rich I ain't and have never been. I'd like a new car and a nice house, who wouldn't? Sometimes the price to others is just too high.

"I will also make arrangements for Susan, my outer office secretary, to be your personal secretary. She is a lovely creature, and she is single."

"Too small a price for my soul." I think I kept regret out of my voice.

"This is unfortunate. I was becoming fond of you. It is seldom I meet a being that can challenge me, especially among your kind. You have such short lives. I have to admit, I took some pleasure in how you punished my idiot chauffeur for attacking you. I told him that he had no chance against one who could withstand me, but he did not listen. The headache made him wince in a most amusing way.

"I'm sorry that I will now be obliged to kill you and your allies."

"I hope you don't mind if we try and prevent that eventuality." I stood, prepared to fight or flee if my foe's truce proved to be less than solid.

"Yes, sadly, I believe we have exhausted the possibilities of this conversation. You will understand if I do not wish you well." Suwa was still the urbane gentleman. I have often wondered if at some level he felt a connection with me, sensed that Hana and I were manifestations of the same soul. I was probably the closest thing to a friend, to family, he'd had in years. That is a sad commentary.

"Yes, of course. Until next we meet." I held out my hand and we shook as equals.

"Until next we meet." Suwa smiled and added in a flat voice. "I'll have to have you for dinner."

I walked from the office, passed the two secretaries and took the stairs to ground level. In minutes I had left the building and was walking down a busy street, crowded with my own living, breathing kind. The feeling of the sun on my face was tremendous. More than this though, I now knew how to finish my foe and walk away a free man.

— Chapter 19 —

PLAN OF ATTACK

Kunio had taken my car so I was forced to use the subway. The Toronto trains may be clean and well maintained, but I have never cared for public transit. The journey seemed to stretch on forever as I watched everything from drunks to men in business suits board and depart the car I rode in. The contrast struck me and I couldn't help but wonder how like the Nukekubi we humans really are.

The rich prey on the poor to gather more wealth than they can use. For a second, I had a mental image of two-hundred grand a year flying out the window. I wondered what my father would have said, and then I recalled an old photo of him. Long hair, tie dyed shirt, carrying a *Green Peace* sign. That was before my mother. I knew what he'd say if he knew the whole story. I smiled, knowing I'd made the right choice in continuing the hunt.

It was nearly four-thirty when I rejoined my companions. I entered Toshiro's room to find him and Kunio burning incense and chanting as they passed Kunio's weapons through the smoke. The details were different from the one I use, but I recognized a consecration ritual when I saw one. I took a seat until they were finished then spent the next few moments telling them about my meeting with the Nukekubi. Kunio was shocked when I mentioned the incentives I'd been offered. It surprised him I had turned them down. Toshiro greeted the news of my steadfastness with a gratified smile; I had not disappointed him.

Lying down to meditate, I focussed my mind on the problem of catching the Nukekubi. With the deaths from the drug party-mix the sons and daughters of upstanding citizens now seemed to be at risk. That meant that the cops would be searching for the Terror connection in earnest. It's a sad truth that in this world some citizens are viewed as more than others. Hookers and homeless don't rate high on the official radar and there are only so many investigative man hours to go around. The result of the added scrutiny was that the beast's style would be cramped.

My foe's problem was twofold. Where to get victims and where to hunt? The former was simple, escort services. Thing was, he could only go to that well so many times before someone got suspicious. In addition, I was sure he'd used them in the past to try and cover his tracks.

It was while I was pondering this that the phone rang. Toshiro answered it. Kama's voice issued from the speaker, but it was too quiet for me to make out the words. A brief, quiet conversation ensued before Toshiro hung up. I figured that if it was urgent Toshiro would let me know, so I stayed in my trance state.

I finished meditating and took out my runes to ask where the Nukekubi would strike next. Drawing a single Rune, I looked at it. The Rune was *Beorc*, a birch tree, with the meaning of family, home, children. Discarding the first and last possibilities, I focussed on the home. My home or its home, I asked, pulling another rune. It was *Othel*, a possession. My intuition told me it was the creature's home.

"I have it," I said.

"Your western stones reveal something?" asked Kunio.

"I can't be one hundred percent sure, but I think the beast will next strike in its own home."

"That does not make sense," objected Kunio.

"Maybe it does, my son," interjected Toshiro. "Tell me, Ray, when you visited the Nukekubi did you by any chance see indications of a struggle? Damaged walls, furniture, things of that nature."

"Nada. Though with all the unfinished floors in that building... That article on Suwa in the business section of the paper. Wasn't he quoted as saying he oversaw the construction of each of his branch offices?"

"Yes, I assumed it was just a convenient excuse to move from place to place. It also said that each completed office tower contained a penthouse dwelling for his use when he visits the branch." Toshiro stroked his moustache as he thought.

"Master, what are you thinking?" Kunio was about half a step behind, but I could see he was coming to the same conclusion I had.

"*Beorc* and *Othel* both have connotations of home." The final piece clicked into place in my head. "Home is where the heart is. Its office! Home must be its office!"

"Why do you say that?" Toshiro was taken aback by my exuberance.

"I met the bastard. He's a power junky. He lives to increase his dominion over others. He's the type who'll work night and day, neglecting everything else, because his only real satisfaction is gaining power. My mother's father was like that, a complete asshole. All the things we associate with home, emotional gratification, personal triumphs, happiness, come from the workplace. It must be his office."

"It is possible, but our foe would risk much by bringing his victims to his place of business." Kunio started to pace.

"Think about it. Who are his biggest pains in the ass? Us. The security guard will keep us out. All he has to do is have his chauffeur block off the finished levels and freeze the elevator between floors. Simple, if you know the building's circuits. That leaves him the rest of the building, nearly thirty floors, to play his sick game of cat and mouse."

"What of the body?" I'm sure Toshiro had come to the

same conclusion as I had, but needed to play devil's advocate to vet the theory.

"He could put the corpse in an unfinished wall then finish it. If he wrapped the remains in plastic the smell would be contained. It could take years to find the body, and by then it would be nearly impossible to link him to the death," said Kunio. His brow was wrinkled in concentration, but he was finally putting himself into the head of his foe.

Toshiro seemed to puff up and when I opened my mouth he gave a little shake of his head as he watched his disciple with pride.

Kunio continued, "Or the beast's servant could butcher the victim and carry the meat out in garbage bags. Emptying the trash would be a suitable job for Suwa's man Friday." Kunio smiled like the cat that ate the canary. I'm not sure if he was prouder of his reasoning or the proper use of the saying. "Another possibility is if there are doors that open to the roof to simply drive the victim to jump. An apparent suicide. Though too many of those would become suspicious."

"How, my son, does our enemy arrange for a victim?" Toshiro had the answer I'm sure, but Kunio was finally thinking for himself. His father, what else would you call Toshiro, wanted to bask in the glow of success for a few moments more.

"How is it said... dating... no, escort, yes escort services, or have his servant pick her up. If one bribes most security guards, they will become conveniently absent. Or simpler still, Suwa has an access card to the parking lot. He would not even have to face the guard. I only wonder that our foe has not used this system exclusively." Kunio's fingers beat a rhythm on the arm of his chair.

I came to his aid. He'd done well, but it took time to see all the angles. "Probabilities. The risk of getting caught at something increases directly with the number of times you do it. Maybe a security guard decides to check the underground garage and sees a girl being snuck in. Happens once, it's passed off as the boss having a cheap thrill, so what? If it happens too often, and the guy keeps reading about hookers ODing on a new drug, he might get suspicions."

"That fits with what we know of our enemy. He is cunning and devious." Kunio nodded and ran his finger across his upper lip in a way so reminiscent of Toshiro stroking his moustache that I had to smile.

"This does present us with a problem, my young friends. How are you to enter the building to challenge our foe?" Toshiro wore a look of pride and relief. Kunio still needed him, but now that he was thinking things through it wouldn't be for much longer. What good father could ask for more than a strong, self-sufficient son?

"We could bluff our way in. The woman at the front thinks I'm some sort of security inspector." I didn't sound too confident.

"I do not believe that is an option. The phone call we received while you were meditating was from Kama. The police visited your apartment looking for you. You are wanted for questioning in a case of industrial espionage involving the Suwa Corporation. They apparently received a complaint naming you from a prominent individual shortly after your interview with our enemy concluded. Kama did not reveal our location." Toshiro shrugged as if he was telling me I needed to pick up kitty litter on my way home.

I buried my head in my hands. I'd never been in trouble with the police before, I never got caught, and in the last two weeks I was sure they were sick of seeing my name. "My mother would call you two a bad influence."

"This is unfortunate," remarked Toshiro.

I looked up. "Not really. My mother's a lousy judge of character."

Toshiro chuckled while the whole thing went over Kunio's head.

"We still have no way to get into the building." I resumed pacing.

"I believe a direct approach. We should follow the chauffeur's vehicle. When he stops to make arrangements with a lady, we must pounce and force him to drive us into the underground parking." Kunio was really getting the hang of this planning thing.

"May as well blow a horn and say we're coming," I commented.

"Do you have a better idea?" demanded Kunio.

I quickly ran through the options in my mind and smirked with a mental image. "You could dress as a—"

"You may discard that notion!" Kunio scowled at me. "For one, I have limits. More importantly we don't know where our enemy's servant would stop for a pick up and cannot ensure he would choose one of us."

"I'd never pass." It's true; I'd make one ugly woman. "All right, I can't think of anything. If we're both going into the building I'll have to get Cathy to drive us. There's nowhere to park around there and we'll want to have a vehicle handy in case things change and we need to follow them someplace or make a quick getaway." I'm sure how thrilled I was to be putting Cathy in the line of fire was apparent in my voice.

Toshiro smiled at me and nodded, the expression saying more than his words. He was glad to have helped me face a character flaw. "This is a wise plan. Also if you have to follow our foe on the street he does not know the appearance of Cathy's car, so it may grant you the element of surprise."

"Works for me." I nodded back at Toshiro; I can take instruction if you hit me over the head with it repeatedly, really I can, if I have to. "I also have an idea for dealing with our foe in a way that will prevent us spending the next twenty years in prison."

Kunio and Toshiro stared at me then each other.

"I do suppose one such as Suwa would be missed, and it must be made to look accidental if we attack his physical form. Go on, my young friend," suggested Toshiro.

It took only a few moments to explain my plan, but hours to bring it into effect.

First, I had to call Cathy. She was happy to drive us; I never said I liked them sane. I also had her reference a load of facts and details in our respective libraries. What I needed to do crossed over and integrated three separate mystical traditions.

Before the last hundred years I suspect that no one would have had access to all the knowledge necessary. Even now, with books readily available and the internet, it was a stretch.

While Cathy did the research, Kunio helped me clear a section of the motel room's floor and I set up for ritual. We were against the clock, but this had to be done right.

Cathy called back while I was meditating and Toshiro returned from shopping for acupuncture needles, model paint, copper wire, vodka and a variety of herbs. By the time I started the ritual Kunio had ground the herbs and set them to soak in the cheap vodka. Toshiro had wrapped the thin, copper wire around the acupuncture needles, joining them in pairs, and painted them either, orange, pink, green, yellow, light blue, dark blue, purple or white; one colour for each major chakra and white for the spirit.

The ritual to enchant the needles was straight forward, dedicating each coloured set to the energy I needed them to carry and soaking them in the herbal tincture to make them permeable to that energy. When I was done Toshiro picked up one of the pairs of needles.

"It is impressive. If these can carry the healthy *ki* that the beast's tattoos interrupt, long enough for the natural energy flow to heal under the skin, it should restore its humanity and mortality."

"That's the plan." I looked down at my handy work. It was delicate. My spells tend to be a bit more of the sledgehammer variety. I really hoped I hadn't screwed it up.

"Master, you should come with us to place the needles." Kunio's voice didn't add to my confidence.

"No, my son. For me those days are past." I watched Toshiro let himself go. I'd not realized how much of his apparent vitality was an act. In seconds it was like he aged years. I noticed scars on almost every piece of exposed skin that I hadn't before. A limp that was almost unnoticeable became pronounced as the old man stopped forcing himself to seem vital. His aura pulled in tight around him, and, the thing that sent a spear through my guts, there were small flecks of black in it. Black denotes a terminal illness. Small flecks were the early stages, but it only appears when the damage is too great for the body to heal. Toshiro had between six months and five years depending on what was causing the flecks and how quickly it progressed.

"Toshiro." My voice broke.

"I know, Ray. I am old. I choose not to embrace it as some do. It pleases me that my long study of *ki* allows me to conceal it, even from one such as you, but the eve of battle is not the time for deceptions and half truths."

"Master?" Kunio's voice filled with anguish. I don't think he could see the black, but to see the man who was in all but blood his father bereft of the illusion of health must have hurt. Toshiro's body reflected the life he'd lived. It was battered. I suspected that he usually pushed himself, trading against the duration of his life for the ability to live instead of exist. It was a choice I could respect and prayed I'd have the body control to make myself when the time came.

"Kunio." Toshiro pulled himself up. It wasn't illusion, more a wilful manipulation of the life force. He consciously made it flow to compensate for his body's shortcomings. I realized why he needed so many naps and meditation sessions. They allowed him to martial his resources. The years and decrepitude fell away, his aura blazed back to vital life. The black flecks remained, but they were so tiny that I could forgive myself missing them before.

Toshiro smiled. "My son, I still have time enough to complete your training. However, I will not put myself into the fight if I can avoid it. My strength might fail when you or Ray are relying on me. I could not live with that."

Kunio bowed very low to the old man. I went into the bathroom. We were pressed for time, but there are things between a father and son.

Minutes later Kunio knocked on the door and I rejoined them.

"Very good. Now that all is in readiness, I will teach you the acupuncture points that will be most effective for use in bridging the gaps in our foe's energy systems." Toshiro unrolled a poster that depicted some actor with his shirt off. Lines of red symbols were drawn around the picture's neck and wrists. "You must begin by isolating the meridians."

I held up my hand. "Um, can we assume that all I know about acupuncture is that it involves sticking pins in people at specific points to affect their energy flows?"

Toshiro looked at me with a tolerant expression. "I will try to speak slowly."

"Thanks." I didn't try to sound genuine.

Toshiro grinned at me then continued. "We must make much of little time to re-establish the energy flows. Furthermore, we must pair proper types of energy through the bridge. Thus you should place the red needles at these points." He pointed to spots on the poster.

Over the next hour I learnt the spots by rote while Kunio discussed several of them and made suggestions. I never said I knew everything. Kama called to tell us that the police had returned to my place with a search warrant. After pawing my library and statues, while making improper jokes, they tried to arrest Kama for possession of marijuana, but the stuff in my cupboard was oregano. Fortunately, I had my ritual tools with me, so the cops hadn't been able to maul or confiscate them. I made a mental note to complain about police harassment. That was, of course, if I was still alive after dealing with the Nukekubi.

Cathy arrived to pick up Kunio and me as the last glow of the day descended into the west. She drove and had her ritual tools in a bag on the seat beside her. If everything went south, if we could get to her car, she might be able to pull us out of it. I didn't feel right bringing her into the fight but we needed a car close and with the way parking is in down town Toronto she was our only bet. We stationed ourselves outside the Suwa building's garage and waited.

– Chapter 20 –

BA++LE R⊕YAL

Shortly after midnight a red Mustang pulled up to the underground parking's entrance and stopped. Because we were positioned to watch the exit, the vehicle was behind us and only its lights in the mirror alerted us to its presence.

"I think that's him," said Cathy from the driver's seat.

Glancing over my shoulder, I saw a wrist in a white-plaster cast and a dark profile.

"Shit! Kunio!" I grabbed my sword and tried to leap from the car. Kunio's hand grasped my shoulder stopping me.

"Wait. Our foe does not know Cathy's vehicle. Let us remain invisible a little longer."

The metallic role-down door of the underground parking started to rise.

"Be ready." Kunio's hand left my arm. A second that seemed an hour passed.

"Soon." Kunio watched in the mirror as the Mustang started its turn into the parking lot.

"Now!" Kunio leapt from Cathy's car and sprinted to our target. I followed a half second later but fell further behind because of my comrade's speed.

The Mustang was halfway past the parking lot's door when

Kunio caught up to it. A woman screamed then there was a crash. I reached the entrance to find the front of the Mustang wrapped around a concrete pillar and the Nukekubi's chauffeur unconscious in the driver's seat. Kunio stood beside the driver's door, breathing hard. His hand slipped from the car's steering wheel as I ran up. Racing to the passenger door, I wrenched it open and pulled the girl sitting there to her feet. She was bone thin with track marks on both arms. Her terror filled eyes were surrounded by dark circles.

"*Run, damn it! Get the hell out of here!*" I yelled.

She didn't need to be told twice. She bolted out of the parking lot and disappeared into the night.

"Kunio, close the garage-door and wait for me. I'll knock three times then let me in." I ran back to Cathy's car.

"Is—" began Cathy.

"We're okay. The driver's down for the count. Pop the trunk so I can get our gear and the vodka." I moved to the back of the car.

"Vodka?" Cathy popped the trunk for me.

"To take care of the driver. D.U.I.s are being taken pretty seriously now a days." I clipped on my fanny pack, picked up Kunio's and my weapons, and grabbed the bottle.

I moved to Cathy's side before heading into the parking garage. "We'll meet you at the fire exit after sunrise."

Cathy pulled me into a kiss. "Go, and be careful. You're still the only cute guy I know my mum will let me bring to Sunday dinner."

I cupped her cheek and looked at my major reason for living before running to the garage-door. I knocked three times and waited. The door opened slowly and I ducked in before it was fully up.

"Close it down again." I unscrewed the cap on the Vodka as I walked to the car.

"What are you doing?" Kunio followed me.

"Getting rid of a problem." I tilted back the chauffeur's head and started pouring. He gagged and a large amount of the alcohol spilled onto his shirt, but eventually he started swallowing. I drained about three-quarters of the magnum into him. Wiping my prints from the bottle with my shirt, I laid it on the seat beside him and closed his fingers around its neck.

"If he doesn't die of alcohol poisoning he'll still be well above the limit by morning. The cops can take care of him."

Kunio smiled. "Very good."

We headed for the stairs and climbed to the third floor. Suwa's offices were locked when we reached them. I couldn't feel him so we continued up the stairs. Every one of my senses was honed to a razor's edge. Even the occasional twinges of pain from my legs served only to heighten my awareness.

I sensed our foe on the eighth floor and we left the stairwell to search for it. This floor was only half-finished; a few of the internal walls were up, but for the most part only the metal framing stood. Wires ran over the floor in all directions.

"Phillip, is that you?" demanded Suwa.

"Phillip?" the voice repeated after a second.

We moved around a section of internal wall and there was Suwa, dressed in a T-shirt and track pants, lying on a sheepskin rug with a cocktail in his hand.

"You!" he gasped, as we came into view.

"Now it ends, beast," snarled Kunio.

"Fools!" Suwa bolted across the unfinished floor.

"Go that way." Kunio indicated the way we had just come.

Sword in hand I ran down the passage and took up a station at the stairs' door. Seconds later Suwa appeared from the direction opposite to the one I had taken. I readied my sword and tried to strike. With a move from the glory days of the Samurai, Suwa dodged my blow, caught my arm and sent me crashing into a wall. I turned, but Suwa had already disappeared down the stairwell.

"Damn!" I swore as Kunio leapt after our foe.

I followed as quickly as I could. Two flights of stairs later I heard the sound of combat below me. Two more flights and I spotted Kunio and Suwa locked in battle. It was a sight. Whatever Kunio did, Suwa countered. Neither one could make a telling strike against the other. I moved closer and began projecting doubt and confusion at Suwa. While he maintained his human guise my powers over him were limited, but if I could get him to make a mistake that Kunio could capitalize on the fight would be over. The battle raged, then with a series of lightning feints Suwa forced Kunio back and bolted down the stairs. We chased him onto the third level where the trail ended at his locked office door.

"This will not stop me." Kunio stepped back to kick the door in. Before he could strike the buzzer lock sounded, unlocking the door.

I turned the knob and the door opened. "I don't like this."

We entered the first of the three offices. It was pitch black within.

Kunio produced a small flashlight and turned it on. "What is it the boy scouts say? Always be prepared."

I breathed heavily. We moved like cats towards the door to the first inner office. This one was unlocked and opened once more onto utter blackness. A brush of air moved against me and I hit the floor. A gunshot shattered the silence and Kunio cried out in pain.

"Do not move," ordered a cold, heartless voice, with an Oxford accent.

I froze; there was nothing I could do.

"Release your sword," commanded the voice.

I complied.

"Good," said Suwa, turning on the fluorescent ceiling lights. "Now the game ends." Suwa stood at the doorway to his office, wearing a pair of green-lensed sunglasses; a revolver firmly in his right hand. "It's a pity really. I was rather enjoying it, but in the end the wolf always wins. I did warn you, Ray. I do regret this. If it were within my ability, I would bring you into the fold. Unfortunately, this isn't a bad vampire movie."

"What are you going to do, Aritoshy, shoot us? That will look really good for the papers." I was stalling, hoping that the underlying loneliness I'd recognized in Aritoshy could buy us some time for Kunio to recover. From what I could see the bullet had only grazed the skin on his left arm. Pain and shock were a greater danger than the wound itself, although it was bleeding rather badly.

"The papers would be no problem at all. A pair of young ruffians broke in and tried to kidnap me. I, being a diligent businessman, was putting in another late night. We struggled and I seized their gun. They continued the attack and I was forced to shoot them. With my lawyers, it is doubtful it would even come to trial. That is beside the point though. I have other plans for you and your friend. Please, help him up and come this way." Suwa removed the glasses and gestured towards his office with the gun.

"What are those for? Wasn't it dark enough for you?" I helped Kunio to his feet.

Suwa smiled. He actually enjoyed my interest. "They are a toy one of my researchers gave me. They shift vision to the infrared. Now, if you would please." Again he gestured towards his office.

Kunio leaned against me, slipping a throwing star into my hand. What I was supposed to do with it, except cut myself, which I promptly did, I had no idea, but I pushed it up my sleeve anyway.

Aritoshy brought us into his office and produced some rope from a desk drawer.

"I did suspect that it might come to this, so I prepared. I thought of using handcuffs, but, to be honest, I find that a high level of a ferrous based metal on my food makes the fear less palatable." Suwa spoke as if we were at a tea party. The damage done to his spirit all those centuries ago made it so he couldn't even conceptualize the horror he'd become.

"It's the Mars influence. Iron is the metal of Mars, God of courage and the warrior spirit. It would naturally try and counter the fear. It works similarly to a coloured lens shifting the frequency of light. Energy hits it and is shifted in vibration to match it." I stalled as I waited for an opening.

"Interesting, I will miss the opportunity to discuss metaphysics with you, Ray. Phillip's skill tends to be in following instructions not comprehending the essence of what he does.

Now, please place all your weapons and other equipment on my desk. I will expect you to do the same for your associate.

Unclipping my fanny pack I tossed it on the desk with a few other items, like my utility knife. I put the obvious part of Kunio's arsenal beside it. It's amazing how many knives a person who knows what they're doing can hide on themselves.

Aritoshy smiled coldly as he stood back and glanced at the small pile on his desk. "Very good, now tie up your friend and please make the knots tight. I will check them. Keep in mind, there are many gradients of how unpleasant dying can be. I suggest you consider that fact if you've not denuded both of yourselves of weapons. This will be your last chance to make things easier on yourself."

Through all of this I was staring down a gun. What could I do? I tied up Kunio. Aritoshy checked my knots then secured me, chatting casually all the while.

With Kunio and I trussed up like pigs for slaughter Aritoshy moved to his office chair and sat. "I have a gift for you. You are about to witness something few mortals have ever seen. This should be of particular interest to you, Ray."

Kunio and I were lying on the floor, bound hand and foot about to be spiritually raped and eaten, and he actually thought it was the time for intellectual curiosity. It brought home to me that I wasn't just trying to save Aritoshy's victims. If my plan could be executed I might save the spirit of the man he once was. What he'd become was too twisted to be human.

"Aritoshy, one thing. For the sake of my parents, please use a cover story that doesn't dishonour them." I needed time to get the throwing star Kunio had slipped me out of my sleeve and cut my bonds. Since Suwa had left us Kunio had lain very still. I had taken it for shock. Now I saw a metallic glint moving against the ropes binding his wrists.

"As you have been an honourable foe, and it is an honourable request, I will see to it. Now if you will excuse me, it's time to dine." Suwa closed his eyes and took a deep breath.

Over the next thirty seconds, all the blood drained from Suwa's face. I grit my teeth in pain as putrid, mystic energy ripped through the room. The energy was blacker than a demon's heart, more foul than the most rotted recesses of Seth's soul. Being exposed to it sickened me.

The Nukekubi head and hands slipped free of the body. I was no stranger to astral projection, but this was a sick parody of that worthy art. Fear energy filled the room.

I was paralysed. I'd hoped to banish the beast, giving Kunio more time to free himself, but the energy blasts of our enemy's separation left me unable to focus.

"Yes, too late you see. I was always a foe too great!" The hideous abomination moved slowly towards us projecting fear energy as it came trying to drive us into a panic.

"*KIYAA!*" Kunio snapped the ropes about his wrists then sent a throwing star through the Nukekubi's forehead.

The beast howled and fell back as if burnt by the blessed metal, giving Kunio time to snatch a knife from his boot and cut his legs free.

Once Kunio was on his feet, he let fly the knife. This time the Nukekubi was not caught by surprise. It avoided the blade, which embedded itself into the wall.

The Nukekubi flew at Kunio, who dodged so the beast's back was to me. By this point, I'd used the throwing star to weaken the bonds on my wrists. With a heave I snapped the rope then freed my ankles.

Standing, I dove at Suwa's desk and grabbed my fanny pack.

"My turn." Pulling out a vial of salt I threw its contents at our foe.

"Gnomes of earth, citizens of Hapi, I summon thee to this time and place. By forest green and desert golden, by crystal halls, come earth's firm holding. Drain my foe of might and power. Ground his evil on this hour." As I spoke, I envisioned a cable of green reaching up from the floor, latching onto the Nukekubi and draining off its corrupt power.

The beast howled as it felt its energy drain away. It screeched in outrage and tried to attack me, but Kunio leapt onto the desk and snatching up a pair of long knives held it off. Each time the beast got close to me those blades would flash and what looked like a path of fire would cut across the Nukekubi's head or hand. With an agonizing scream the beast flew through the doorway.

I focussed on the spell for as long as I could but soon the Nukekubi was beyond its range.

"It's still out there," I panted to Kunio, who stood beside me. He'd put his gear back on and retrieved my sword for me.

"Do what must be done, I will track it." Kunio strode to the door.

"Keep your distance. Give me a chance to finish here and rejoin you," I cautioned as I started putting my equipment back into place.

"We will share the kill!" Kunio called from the outer office then he was gone.

"Just don't get yourself killed!" I yelled after him.

Steeling myself I drew the consecrated needles from my fanny-pack and laid them out on the desk in front of Aritoshy's body. The body appeared dead as I checked the pulse and respiration. I found them to be twenty and three respectively. I wish I'd had a BP cuff, with Suwa gone the physical form was barely ticking over. Folding out a set of diagrams that I'd drawn to spur my memory, I started placing the coloured needles so the wires interconnecting them bridged Suwa's tattoos at neck and wrists. It was slow, exacting work.

Finished, I stepped back and focussed my will. It was then I noticed a place on one side of his neck where the tattoos were a little smeared with scar tissue. It was as if someone had tried to scrub them away. I remembered Aritoshy's daughter, whom he'd murdered. She'd tried to save him, but she lacked the skill. I was back to finish a job undone.

I let my life energies flow, forcing channels through the needles and wires, for a moment, acting like a life support system to establish the energy paths. I could feel the hunger in Suwa's flesh. The physical head and hands practically clawed at my heart energy. I focussed my will into the body's chakra and tied them to the energy flow. Suwa took a deep breath and jerked. I leapt back. Now he looked asleep. The deathly pallor was gone from his skin. Checking his pulse and respiration they were sixty and ten. It was a good sign, but the proof would be in the pudding.

Finished with Aritoshy's body, I pulled Kunio's throwing knifes from the wall and pocketed them. The plan was to leave few if any tracks. So I tidied up the office. I was looking for a trash can under Suwa's desk when I noticed that the back panel in the leg section was lopsided. Grabbing a corner I pulled and a secret compartment was relieved. There was a sketch of a pretty, little Japanese girl's face, a briefcase, the hand guard off a Japanese sword, a diploma in business from Cambridge dated 1857 for Andrew Suwa and some other bric-a-brac spanning the last few centuries. I guess even monsters have treasures that are precious to them alone.

I pulled out the briefcase and shoved the other items back in and closed the hatch. The case had a combination lock on the front and an auxiliary clip to either side of the central combo. I pried the lock open with Kunio's knife. Why? I'm not sure; knowledge is power. If we got in another tight spot knowing what was so important to the Nukekubi that it kept it hidden might buy us another chance like when I'd used its name to stall it in the woods.

Opening the case, I gasped. It was filled with bills. My guess is it was the Nukekubi's cut and run money, in case things went completely wrong. Closing the case, I finished tidying up the room.

I was facing a long night and it had been hours since it started. I picked up my sword and moved to Suwa's private washroom. The entrance was behind the bar. The bathroom was beautiful. Everything was marble from the massage tub to the double sink and shower stall. The toilet alone probably cost what I earned in a week. I leaned my sword against the wall beside me as I used said appliance.

The Nukekubi energy was everywhere, which is why I think it was able to sneak up on me. It blended into the background. I had just zipped when I felt a spiking of the Nukekubi energy.

Dropping to the floor, I rolled, pushing my will into my personal shields. The Nukekubi slammed into my shield. It stopped but didn't back away. I felt the sickly energy of terror wearing against my defences.

"Now you die, Ray. I will eat you. I have not hungered like this in millennia. Your draining spell was most effective. In your death you can comfort yourself with the knowledge that I will now feed and feed and feed until I am fully restored to my proper nature."

"You will die," I growled from between teeth clenched in my efforts to reinforce my shields from within. If it reached my body proper it could enter me, and I had doubts about my ability to expel it.

"You will grant me life. I saw what you did to my flesh. It is no matter. I will be restored so long as I possess sufficient energy and your life will give me that," hissed my enemy as it pushed closer to me.

I screamed, sending a burst of power straight into its face, blasting it back. I rolled trying to grab my sword. Pain blossomed at the back of my neck as the Nukekubi's hands dropped a heavy bottle of cologne down onto me. I heard the thunk then I found myself sprawled on the bathroom floor fighting to stay conscious. I couldn't focus my will. I was vaguely aware of seeing blood and broken glass on the tiles.

The hideous Nukekubi face drew level with mine. The beast blasted me with waves of fear and in my daze there was nothing I could do to stop it. Panic took me and I tried to push it away. I could barely move. The beast drew nearer and nearer. It screamed. The fear it drove into me was so intense it was a good thing I'd just emptied my bladder.

I was helpless and then I saw a foot.

"Not tonight beast!" Kunio's voice was the most beautiful thing I'd ever heard. I rolled in time to see him drive his sword through the Nukekubi. The creature howled in agony then swept over Kunio and out the door.

Kunio came to my side. "Is it done?" He helped me to the sink and inspected the wound on the back of my scalp.

"Yeah, but if Suwa feeds before he reconnects, it might blast the spell to hell."

"Then, my friend, we must hound it until the dawn comes, but we must first bandage you."

"I... Kunio, you have to make sure Suwa doesn't reach the security guard at the lobby desk. He's the easiest prey around."

"You—"

"Go. I'll be okay."

Kunio ran. I pulled a dressing and triangle bandage from my fanny pack, which was looking rather empty, and patched myself up before sloshing water on the floor to hide the worst of the blood. I stank of expensive cologne, but it would have to do.

I joined Kunio on the landing of the emergency stairs.

"The guard is unhurt and he did not see me when I checked on him." Kunio watched the stairs above us as he spoke.

"Right. We'd better avoid the lower floors if we can. Suwa doesn't seem to be able to bring himself to pass through walls, so if we can keep him away from everyone until dawn—"

"Yes, he is obviously above." Kunio began to ascend.

"We could just wait it out," I suggested.

"No, you yourself said that if the beast has enough energy your spell might not work. We must hound it. Force it to exhaust its reserves. Only that way can we be assured of victory." Kunio looked grim. This was the final showdown. I could see it in his eyes. Tonight it was victory or death.

"Wait here one minute." Ducking onto the floor, I returned seconds later with the briefcase.

"What is that?" Kunio sounded suspicious.

"Something of lesser importance. We'll grab it on the way out if we can." I started up the stairs, my head throbbing with each step.

Suwa wasn't making it easy. I didn't feel his presence until we reached the top floor, by which time my knee was hurting worse than my head. This floor consisted of a single large room with occasional support pillars. Beyond the glass outer walls there was a backyard-sized observation platform, reached by a door, which was obviously kept locked.

The Nukekubi was trying to open the door and having little success. Muttering a spell, I concentrated on the air in the room. My spirit reached past the mix of oxygen and nitrogen that I was breathing to the mystical nature of air. Turning with a hiss Suwa soared towards us.

"Winds I have summoned, strike now I call, Sylphs heed me brothers, bring evil's fall," I commanded in a loud voice. So I'm not a poet, the words helped me focus my intent.

A mystic wind caught the Nukekubi, slamming it into the ground.

The beast rose, only to be slammed into the wall. There was no reason the Nukekubi shouldn't have flown through the solid matter except that some vestige of Aritoshy remained and didn't believe it could. In magic we are often what we believe we are. Our opponent was unsteady in the air when it drew near. It moved sluggishly and its face was battered. Red lines crisscrossed its mustard-yellow energy and sparks fell from it sinking into the ground like drops of blood. It looked beaten.

"You will die!" With a burst of speed the Nukekubi flew at Kunio. It had been dogging it to put us off our guard. It tried to slam into Kunio, but he sidestepped it like a matador facing an angry bull. One of Suwa's floating hands slammed into Kunio's aura at his back. There was a flash of energy and the hand bounced away from him.

Kunio flinched for a second as the contact sent a brief wave of fear through him then he smiled.

"*It is depleted!*" Kunio yelled with savage joy. Using his *ninjato* like a bat he proceeded to slice through the Nukekubi's face. The beast flew away trying to dodge and Kunio chased it hitting it time and time again.

I took a moment to breathe. I'd been throwing a lot of magic around and the tank was running dry. I saw the Nukekubi hands picking up a piece of two-by-four left by the construction crews.

"*Kunio, look out!*"

Kunio glanced my way in time to see the two-by-four speeding towards his head with every bit of power those disembodied hands could give it. He ducked, avoiding the blow but lost the Nukekubi's head as he did so.

Suwa's head raced for the stairs and I moved to block it. The head came closer. I readied my sword, then I repeated Kunio's mistake. Unlike the head and hands the two-by-four was physical substance; my personal shields didn't even slow it down as it slammed into my groin. I buckled over clutching my hopes for children as my foe flew over me into the stairwell.

"Ray, are you alright?" Kunio ran to my side.

"Shit, that throbs! When am I going to start remembering that thing has hands?" I straightened and jumped, landing hard on my heels.

"It seems that our foe is not as depleted as we may have hoped." There was a note of compassion in Kunio's voice. Any guy who does sports knows the one I mean.

"I'm okay. Go. Make sure he doesn't reach the guard."

With a quick nod Kunio vanished down the stairs. I took another minute to relearn how to breathe then followed him. For once I regretted not wearing a watch. With Kunio protecting the security guard my job would be to flush out our foe and force it to drain its resources still further.

I was on the fifth floor when I sensed the beast. I called to Kunio and entered the floor. Here the walls were almost complete, just some painting and minor work remained to be done. This created a labyrinth in which the Nukekubi could hide. Its emissions were weaker and it was harder to track.

While I was crossing an unfinished doorway the beast flew at me from the shadows and slammed into my shields. As the head attacked the beast's hands smashed a mop handle into the wrist of my sword arm and I dropped my blade. There was a flash of mystic energy as it tried to force its way past my shields and into me. The sickly sense of fear struck me, but it was less intense than before. The Nukekubi was giving it his all, but he didn't have much left. This let me play my ace.

Reaching into my fanny pack I pulled out the citrine Cathy

had given me, and fighting back panic, called up its stored enchantment.

"By Ra I call the sun's light here stored."

The Nukekubi screamed as I spoke the incantation, and it was all I could do to not run like a frightened child. I fought to keep my will focussed on the citrine blocking out everything else. Nothing appeared to happen physically, but the Nukekubi screeched and mustard-yellow energy began to curl out from it and dissipate like smoke.

"*Iye!*" screamed the incorporeal beast as it huddled away calling its hands to it to try and shelter its face from the mystic light. The hands seemed to burn and peel. Cathy had outdone herself. To my foe the stone was like having the morning sun come down upon it.

"*Kunio, over here.*" I yelled.

Kunio ran to my side and watched as the beast cowered and burnt in a light only those with the Sight could see. Kunio revelled in the Nukekubi's pain, avenging his parents once again. The energy stored in the stone waned before it snuffed out. I stepped back, pocketing the citrine and picked up my sword in my left hand. My wrist wasn't broken, but it hurt pretty bad.

Kunio watched the Nukekubi, now a tired, humbled creature, hovering just above the dirt that covered the concrete floor.

"I can make you both wealthy beyond your dreams," tempted the exhausted abomination.

"We are not like you," spat Kunio. His hatred for the Nukekubi excluded all pity.

"Goodbye Aritoshy. I pray that you reincarnate to be the man you were meant to be." I could feel compassion. I think I would have liked the man from whom the Nukekubi had been made. Perhaps, long ago, I loved him as a father. He wasn't the first to make bad choices because of a pretty face. "What time is it, Kunio?"

Kunio glanced at his watch and replied, "Six oh five."

"NO!" Our foe rallied a last burst of effort and flew by us.

Kunio and I smiled wearily at each other and turned to follow.

We hobbled to the third floor, favouring a host of injuries. We reached Suwa's office to find him back in his body and standing by his leather chair with a second gun in his hand. Where he kept them hidden I don't know.

He laughed as he took aim at us. "You miscalculated. Whatever minor harm you have done to my body was insufficient to slay me. I will feed and regain my strength, but now you will die. Good-bye Ray. You chose the wrong side."

I looked at him. His face was bathed with sweat and tears were streaming from his eyes. He'd pulled the needles from around his neck and wrists, but the tattoo was broken. Where all those centuries ago a loving daughter had tried to save her father from being a monster the band of red had separated. He pointed his gun at us and hesitated.

"I... Chou, Hana, I am sorry. I..." He looked at me. "What have you done to me?" He began to weep and his gun wavered in his hand.

"We healed you. You are now as you were meant to be, war chief of the down-stream village, a human being." I kept an eye on him. Aritoshy was no longer Nukekubi, but a man with a gun can kill you just as dead.

"I killed them, I killed so many. I..." Aritoshy looked at the gun in his hand and tried to raise it to his temple. His hand shook so much he dropped it.

"What have I done? Chou, where are you Chou? Hana, daughter, please forgive me." He fell to his knees, blood poured from his nose and he seemed to age years in seconds. His outward body didn't change but inside he was thousands of years old and now that he was mortal it was taking its toll.

"Forgive me," he whispered before collapsing to the floor.

"Hana does. She never stopped loving her father." Stepping over to him, I took his pulse. It fluttered under my fingers then went still.

"Goodbye Aritoshy, may you fair better in your lives to come." I turned to see Kunio scowling at the body. I picked up the gun, checked that the safety was on, and shoved it in my pants, then scooping up the needles and wires I led Kunio from the room. We descended to the garage in silence, picking up the briefcase on the way. The wrecked Mustang, with its unconscious occupant, was still there. We slipped out of the building and met Cathy on the corner.

"It's done," were my words of greeting.

She popped the trunk without saying a word. One of the things I love about her, she knows when to shut up, sometimes. We dumped our gear into the car and I, after popping the clip and making sure the chamber was empty, hid the gun at the bottom of the pile. I know just enough about guns to respect them.

I took the front passenger seat. Kunio took the back seat. Cathy looked at me.

"A park, please. Anyplace green and alive," I asked.

Cathy nodded then pulled away. Toshiro could wait. So could Cathy and Kama. This morning was for Kunio and I. Kunio must have understood. He kept silent as Cathy pulled into a parking spot beside a city park. She didn't say a word as we got out and limped to the top of a grassy knoll.

My knee throbbed, my head hurt and my wrist was swollen to twice its normal size, but I wouldn't have missed the glory of seeing the sun crest the building tops for anything.

Kunio and I didn't speak. There'd be time for tales later. Victory was ours and it was sweet.

EPIL⊕GUE

I spent the next two days in bed where I read a newspaper that said Aritoshy Suwa had died of a stroke while working late. I lit a candle for the war chief that had been. I also read that the cops had picked up some teenager who was slipping a party mix into the drinks of unsuspecting women. This mix was labelled Terror, ignoring the fact that it didn't show up on most of the tox screens.

I went back to work as soon as I could move well enough to do my job. Malcolm got on me about taking so much time off, so I told him straight, "If you're going to cut my hours, leaving me with only the shit shifts that no one else wants, then I have to explore other options. I don't like being pushed! I got people to cover for me, so you have no right to gripe."

His face went crimson and I thought he was going to can me. I guess he didn't want to lose me because he just shut his mouth and walked out of the guard office. An hour later I got a phone call from him restoring my hours. He's left me pretty much alone since. Better for me.

I was brought in for questioning regarding industrial espionage against the Suwa Corporation. It was unpleasant, but they had nothing on me, and the driving force behind the case was dead, so they dropped it.

For the rest of the two weeks following our victory we all did the tourist thing. Kunio and Kama were practically glued at the hip. Cathy stuck pretty close to me, I wasn't going to complain.

Toshiro and I divided the money, seven-hundred-thousand each. I'd have to be careful with my part. If I started throwing it around the police might start asking questions again, but it was a safety cushion. I have plans for laundering it, slowly. I arranged to take over the apartment below Cathy's at the end of the month. Kama, who was staying with Cathy, would sublet my place the day I moved. She'd apply for student welfare as soon as she had an address. We spent a bit of the spoils of war getting her clothes and the like.

The day came that we found ourselves sitting in a café with the bland decor of *Pearson International Airport Terminal Three's* adding to our dower mood. I hate goodbyes. Kunio and Kama were standing a little apart from us enjoying their privacy for the last few minutes while Cathy, Toshiro and I sat at a table and sipped overpriced juices.

"You all must visit us in Japan." Toshiro leaned back in his seat and stroked his moustache.

"Depends on how quick I can clear the ticket price." Having seen the flecks of black in his aura I couldn't ignore them. I hoped I'd see him again in this life, but it would have to be soon.

Toshiro nodded understanding my concern. "I will inhabit this body for a while yet, my young friend. Kunio still needs me, and my Sumi will wait a little longer."

"OH Shit!" Cathy's face reflected shocked dismay.

"What?" I turned to look at what she saw and my mouth dropped open. "Crap, it's a disaster!"

Kunio knelt on the dirty floor holding a jewellery box out to Kama.

I heard Toshiro sigh and caught him shaking his head out of the corner of my eye. "They are not ready."

Kama shifted from foot to foot, kissed Kunio then closed

the jewellery box, without taking the ring it contained, and left it in his hand. Kunio looked disappointed as he stood.

She hugged and kissed him until he blushed, smiled and nodded.

"Thank the Gods one of them has sense." I commented as I heard Cathy release a held breath.

"That was close. It's hard enough to make a marriage work when you're older. They're hardly more than kids." Cathy sounded relieved.

"Right grandma." I teased.

"It is often true that love is like fruit, picked too early it is bitter when tasted." Toshiro turned to Cathy. "However, one must not forget, fruit picked too late can spoil on the tree."

Cathy rolled her eyes. "Two against one is not fair."

Toshiro and I grinned at her.

"Fine, I'll think about it." Cathy took my hand and smiled at me. Somehow the airport terminal didn't seem so bad anymore. Kunio and Kama joined us at the table and all eyes focussed on them.

"She says maybe when she has finished school," Kunio answered the unspoken question.

Toshiro nodded. "Most wise, but now we must go. Ray, please think about what I said regarding the usefulness of your western skills."

"I will, but it's like I told Kunio. Nukekubi aren't the only thing that can wake you screaming in the night. I think the guys upstairs will guide me into doing what they think needs doing. Whether I like it or not."

"Such is often the way." Toshiro looked sardonic.

Cathy gabbed my hand and squeezed it. "Just my luck, I have to fall for the hero type. Just be careful, Sir. Lancelot."

Toshiro chuckled and I saw a twinkle in his eye. "I expect to be invited to the wedding."

"Fucking right! I wanna be a bridesmaid," added Kama.

"Dream on, and you, don't get any white picket fence ideas." Cathy glared at me, but her smile broke through and ruined the effect.

Kunio and Toshiro picked up their carry-on bags and we moved to the departures' gate.

Kunio hugged me and I hugged him back then we separated and bowed to each other. We'd been through a lot together.

"I never had a brother before," said Kunio.

"Love you too man. I'll see you again." I thumped his back.

The goodbyes were all said and Kunio and Toshiro passed through security.

Kama started crying and Cathy comforted her. I glanced at a table where a Toronto Sun newspaper was spread out. The headline read 'ACCUSED RAPIST COMMITS SUICIDE.' It stuck in my mind for a reason I didn't know then. For that moment things were looking up. I had a financial cushion and didn't have to live like a troll anymore, a great evil was gone from the world, and a tortured soul was freed of the curse that bound it against nature. Cathy was even thinking of monogamy, maybe. I could get use to this.

I just wish I could get used to other things. Things like flying silhouettes in the darkness and hissing whispers. These still make me start and sweat. Maybe that is for the best though. The Gods, it seems, have decreed I shall deal with these little jobs. Just my bloody luck,

I didn't negotiate for benefits. Then again, I look at Kama who is still alive and Cathy who is so much of my life, and I can't help but think maybe I did.

However you perceive the divine, may it walk with you and keep you safe from the dangers of the night.

ABOUT THE AUTHOR

Stephen B. Pearl is the author of several novels, including "Nukekubi," "Tinker's Plague," "Slaves of Love," and "The Hollow Curse." He lives in Hamilton, Ontario with his cats and his wife, whom he is quite happy to know she doesn't pole dance.

For more information about Stephen and his books:

www.stephenpearl.com